MISSING

Sheppard & Sons Investigations, Book 3

Eveline Rose

Sword & Rose

Dedication

This book is dedicated to all the women who are stronger than they think are, and the men who love them.

Also by

WebPage

E veline Rose

EvelineRose.author@gmail.com
MISSING
Sheppard & Sons Investigations, Book 3
by Eveline Rose

Chapter 1

Beth

"Mommy, will I ever have another daddy?" Chase's big blue eyes stared into mine.

Where did that come from? A few seconds ago, he'd been quietly coloring on the living room floor, his favorite dinosaur movie playing in the background.

He'd never asked me about having a new dad before. *I suspect it has something to do with the dads he sees at tee ball.* He'd asked about his father, my late husband, Phil, because he'd seen the pictures. But this was a first, and I wasn't sure how to answer him.

Do I want Chase to have a father? Of course I did, even if it meant changing the special bond we had, but I hadn't found the right guy yet. I'd recently started dating, after Mary and Meg convinced me to give it a try. After I confided in them following one too many glasses of wine. When I confessed, "I miss having a man in my life." They reminded me Phil would want me to be happy, to move on with my life. But that wasn't the reason.

I was afraid Chase would get hurt. If I was being completely honest, I was worried about a man inserting himself into our lives and assuming it was okay to discipline Chase without my consent. Dating was hard, but dating as an older widow with a young son was harder.

Plus, I always felt weird leaving him with a sitter when I went on dates. Even if that sitter was someone Chase adored and loved spending time with, like Nina, Meg, or Mary and John. It wasn't exactly guilt, though there was some. It felt dishonest to have a person in my life who wasn't in Chase's, like I was keeping a secret.

They reminded me I didn't have to introduce Chase to any guy I dated, until I was ready. I said I'd think about it, just to put an end to the conversation. In the end, I thought about it, and decided to wade back into the dating pool. I had control over who I dated, and who I let into Chase's life, and I'd be okay as long as I didn't forget that.

It wasn't easy dating as a single mom over forty, especially with a five-year-old child. I was upfront with everyone I dated, but they still seemed surprised when I'd mention Chase's age.

Not that I went out much, and never with the same guy more than twice. And no one had met Chase. It wasn't that they weren't good men; I'm sure they were, but there was nothing there. No spark. No desire to get to know them better. Ne need to get Chase's hopes up.

There are very few men who'll be able to fill Phil's shoes. He was a great husband and would've been an amazing dad. But he'd died while on duty during one of those rare occasions it snowed in Texas. He'd stopped to help a stranded motorist, like the good cop and man he was. Another driver lost control of their car and struck him. The impact hadn't killed him but hitting his temple when he fell had. I was seven months pregnant with Chase when it happened.

It still breaks my heart he'll never meet his son, and his son will never meet him.

I would've named Chase after his father, but Phil had wanted to name him after his best friend, a firefighter who'd died when the burning warehouse he was in collapsed, killing him and his shift-buddy. *How could I not honor his wish?* When Chase was born, I named our son after both of them, Chase Phillip Wyatt; honoring two men who'd sacrificed their lives serving their community.

Chase was staring at me with his father's beautiful blue eyes, his green crayon poised over the coloring page.

Honesty is the best policy. "I don't know, baby. Why do you ask?"

Deflection worked too. *Sometimes.*

"I want a daddy to help me practice tee ball like the other boys have." Chase answered matter-of-factly. He didn't sound nearly as sad as I felt, but then he'd never known Phil.

I will not cry. Damn you Phil, why'd you have to leave us? I could tell him I'd help him practice, but knew it wouldn't be the same. "Why don't you ask your Uncle John if he'll help you?" I suggested the next best thing.

Chase's face lit up as he jumped up and ran over to me. "Can we go ask him now?"

My five-year-old son loved visiting the Sheppard & Sons Investigations office. Not only was the company owned by his Uncle John and his two oldest sons, who Chase adored, but his favorite babysitter, Auntie Meg, worked there too.

I didn't answer fast enough, so he begged, "please," with his hands in the prayer position. I couldn't help but laugh.

"I'll call and ask if he can schedule a visit today," I reached over and grabbed my phone, "but you have to be patient."

Completely ignoring the last half of what I'd said, he jumped up and down, clapping his hands. "Will Auntie Meg be there too? She's been gone forever."

"I think so." His positive energy brought a smile to my lips.

He adored Meg. Who, along with her new husband, Jack Sheppard, had returned from their two-week Hawaiian honeymoon two days ago and were supposed to return to work today, but I wouldn't promise Chase without verifying.

Meg answered and after exchanging a few pleasantries, including scheduling a girl's night so I could hear all about her honeymoon, she put me through to John.

John couldn't see Chase today, but agreed to meet with him the following afternoon. He said he'd have Meg add Chase to his schedule, knowing Chase always got a thrill out of seeing his name on John's calendar.

Chase might not have a dad, but he had John and his sons. It wasn't quite the same, but at least he had strong male role models.

Chapter 2

Doug

I clicked save and just like that—I'd made my last alimony payment to my ex-wife.

The judge back home in Chicago had granted my ex five years of payments, one for every year we'd been married, citing the economic hardship of moving back home to Colorado and starting over. Jane made sure her attorney added how emotionally difficult it was for her to support an airman who was "married to the military" and never around to meet her needs.

I'd wanted to call bullshit, but my attorney advised against it.

Jane had loved being an Air Force wife, at least in the beginning, but her tune changed when we learned I was sterile after months of failing to conceive. She couldn't tell the judge she wanted to leave me because I couldn't have kids;

that would make her sound insensitive and wouldn't get her the sympathy, or alimony check, she wanted.

I need a coffee. I got up from my desk at Sheppard & Sons Investigations and went to the lobby to ask Meg if she wanted anything from Grannie's. Poor kid was elbow deep in paperwork after being gone for two weeks.

Meg didn't just work at SSI, the company her husband had started with his father and brother, she was now officially a Sheppard.

The Sheppards started SSI after a family tragedy left Jamie, the oldest, a widower. John was lucky to be working with his sons, even if their reason was heartbreaking.

I was supposed to join my family's business.

My father had wanted me to go to law school and join his firm, but I didn't want to be an attorney. My older sister had, and she was their favorite child because of it. Not only had she joined the family business, she'd given them the grandkids I couldn't.

I was supposed to be his heir and provide him with a grandson to carry on the family legacy.

But I discovered my love of computers and gaming in middle school and it didn't take long for me to realize I wanted to make a career out of it. Finding out I couldn't pass on the family name, made our already strained relationship worse. He'd expected me to follow in his footsteps, like he had his father's, and to someday hand the reins to my son. But I'd disappointed him on both accounts.

I'll never forget the day I told him I wanted to change careers. I was in junior high and had a meeting with my guidance counselor. When she'd asked what I wanted to do, my answer was: I have to go to law school. She was a good counselor and questioned my use of the words, "have to". She eventually got me to admit I didn't want to go to law school and encouraged me to take classes and join after school clubs that would help me find my calling.

My father was furious. He'd screamed at me as he stomped around his home office. His final threat was to tell me he wouldn't pay for college unless I went to law school.

I'd found the courage to stand up to him and claim my future, creating a rift that still existed between us.

I hadn't wanted to disappoint him, but I didn't want to be a lawyer and couldn't imagine living every day hating my career.

I didn't regret my choice to join the Air Force (USAF), and despite leaving active duty earlier than I'd intended because Jane gave me an ultimatum, I didn't regret getting out. I'd earned a debt-free bachelor's degree in computer science while serving and put it to good use working with law enforcement in Chicago, before moving to Texas and joining SSI.

I've come a long way since high school.

I was a shy, awkward, tech geek in high school, and unlike my friends, I couldn't put my head down and hide. I'd reached my full height by my sophomore year and being a gangly six-foot-four red-head meant I couldn't hide anywhere.

My life changed when I met an Air Force recruiter at a college fair. It sounded like a perfect fit, and I enlisted the day

I turned eighteen. I started basic training three weeks after graduation and never looked back.

The AF had paid me well to use my tech skills, travel the world, and get in shape. Turns out, I liked going to the gym—just not with cruel teenagers. Before long I added martial arts to my training routine. In three years, I went from being a tall skinny geek all the girls teased to being a tall, muscled, highly trained, badass geek in a uniform that no one made fun of.

I walked out of the office I shared with Andrew Janerek, Jack's best friend, laughing as I thought about it. Never in a million years would I have imagined being a private investigator in Texas. *But here I am.*

And happy about it too. Despite being a bit of the odd man out here at SSI (I was the only person who hadn't known the Sheppards prior to getting hired) I felt right at home. Texas, and SSI, was the new start I'd needed to break me out of my post-divorce funk.

I was halfway across the large, open lobby when I was almost run over by Chase, an energetic five-year-old who, at three-seven, was a smidge over half my size.

Chapter 3

Beth

Chase ran in as soon as I opened the front door to the SSI office and made a beeline for Meg at the front desk. He was so focused on Meg he didn't see Doug, which was insane because he was a six-foot-four wall of solid muscle. The top of Chase's head barely reached Doug's belt buckle.

"Hey Little Man." Doug steadied Chase before getting down on one knee to talk to him. "Where's the fire?" Doug held out his large fist and waited for Chase to bump it with his smaller one.

Chase giggled. "There's no fire, Mr. Doug." He looked over at Meg, who was holding back a laugh. "I want to give Auntie Meg a hug and talk to Uncle John."

Doug assumed a serious tone. "Do you have an appointment with Mr. Sheppard?"

I loved watching everyone at SSI interact with Chase, no one ever treated him like a nuisance. Though he could be with his endless energy and non-stop questions.

"I do," Chase put his hands on his hips. "I'm in his calendar and everything."

"Well then, I won't keep you." Doug held out his hand to shake, but Chase had already turned towards Meg.

Doug looked at me with a soft smile and humor in his steel-blue eyes. "Hi Beth."

Doug was more reserved than most of the guys at SSI and was usually content to sit back and observe, but with Chase he was different. He showed a fun, outgoing, almost playful side. He'd get down on one knee, or lift Chase onto a chair, so they could talk eye-to-eye. Doug was the one who started calling Chase "Little Man", which Chase loved.

Seeing how naturally Doug interacted with him always made my heart do a little somersault. I'd be lucky to find a man like him. *It doesn't hurt that he's easy on the eyes.* Light from the window danced on the copper highlights in his short red hair.

I felt heat creep up my neck as realized I was staring at Doug, who was now walking towards me with a concerned look on his face.

"Beth, are you okay?"

Oh God, please tell me I'm not blushing. "Hi Doug. I'm good, thanks." I almost choked on my words as I tried to sound normal. "How are you?" I resisted the urge to fan myself with my hand.

Luckily, John saved me from further embarrassment when he came out of his office and scanned the reception room, intentionally looking over Chase's head. "Meg, is my next appointment here?" He tried to be serious but gave himself away when he caught my eye and grinned.

I smiled as Chase waved his arms over his head and yelled, "It's me, Uncle John, I'm right here!"

At five-ten, John Sheppard wasn't nearly as tall as Doug, but he kneeled to address Chase anyway. He laughed as he gently corrected Chase, "What voice do we use when we're inside?"

"Inside voice." Chase had the good sense to look apologetic.

"That's right." John ruffled Chase's hair. "Would you like to meet in my office, or–"

"Next to Auntie Meg." Chase pointed at Meg's desk.

John picked Chase up and sat him down on Meg's desk. She never seemed to mind, which was good because it was his favorite spot in the office. You'd think it'd be John's office, but no, he wanted to sit near Meg every time.

"Your mom said you have a question for me." John got down to business.

"Will you help me practice for tee ball? I don't have a dad like all the other boys and mom can't help because she's a girl," Chase said, ignoring the fact that there were two girls on his tee ball team.

John coughed to cover his laugh. "I'd be happy to help you, but don't count your mom out. I bet she'll be a great helper on the days I can't make it." He looked at me and gave me his trademark wink.

"But she can't help me with everything." Chase pouted.

When John asked him why, he answered, "Because I have to wear a cup to protect my peen and she doesn't have one." Chase didn't know how to whisper, so naturally everyone heard him.

Kill me now. In that moment, I'd never regretted anything more than I regretted telling Chase the difference between boys and girls.

Meg's hand flew to her mouth to stop herself from spitting out her coffee. I could see John holding back a laugh, so were Doug and Jack, who'd come out of his office.

John composed himself before answering, "I'm sure I can help you with that. Why don't we step into my office?"

After John closed the door, I made eye contact with Meg, and we burst out laughing. What else could we do? With Chase occupied, I had time to welcome Meg and Jack back with hugs.

It wasn't long before John and Chase came back out. Chase was smiling and bouncing as he closed the distance to Meg's desk. I'd talk to John later and find out what I needed to know about buying a cup. I'm sure it was assumed parents would know, but Chase wasn't wrong, I knew nothing about cups or jockstraps or how to find the best one for a growing boy.

My heart filled with gratitude for John. And his wife Mary, who happened to be my boss and best friend. I didn't know what I would've done without them these last five years. I thanked God every day John was assigned as Phil's field training officer when he'd joined the Parker County Sheriff's Department. They'd both served in the Marines, making them instant friends, despite the decade between their ages. The same thing happened between Mary and I when I started working at Grannie's part-time.

After Phil died, I needed a full-time job and tried to give Mary my notice, but she wouldn't accept it. She said it was about time she hired an assistant manager and couldn't imagine anyone better for the position. Of course, I accepted. She immediately transitioned me to full-time, which included benefits.

Chase and I are blessed to have them in our lives.

Chapter 4

Doug

I hadn't meant to stare at Beth as she watched John and Meg interact with Chase, but I couldn't help it. Her sunglasses were pushed back on her head, holding her curly brown hair off her face and she practically glowed with her love for them.

She and Meg hadn't known each other long, only about a year, but were close, despite the age gap. I wasn't sure how old Beth was, but I guessed she was in her mid-to-late thirties, while Meg was twenty-four.

Have I only been at SSI a year? When I started Meg was new to Weatherford and had just started working at Grannie's, the coffee shop Mary Sheppard owned. Jack and Meg had just started dating when I accepted the position and agreed to start a week earlier than originally planned because Meg was in some sort of danger.

I learned later she'd been a victim of trafficking and had testified against the Boston mob boss who'd trafficked her. After getting paroled, he'd come to Weatherford and kidnapped Meg so he could exact his revenge. We'd tracked him down and put a bullet in his head.

Hell of a way to start a new job.

Not exactly what I expected when I became a PI in a small town, but I loved it.

Beth's hand on my arm brought me back to the present. "Doug?"

From the look in her eyes, she'd probably called my name at least once before. "I'm going to Grannie's to grab coffee. Want one?"

"I was just headed there myself. Want me to come with you and help?" I hadn't intended to invite myself but couldn't take it back now.

"Sure, thanks." She smiled before asking Meg if Chase could stay with her. Chase clapped his hands and answered yes, and luckily for him, Meg agreed.

This would be the first time I'd be alone with Beth, and I was a little nervous. I'd noticed her the first time I'd walked into Grannie's. Her quiet beauty and kind, caramel colored eyes had captured my attention, and I always looked forward to seeing her on my daily trips to Grannie's.

I wasn't a buy coffee every day person, but 'new guy buys the coffee' was the SSI version of hazing. I didn't mind; it meant I got to see Beth, and the coffee was good too. I didn't get to see her as often now that we brewed Grannie's Blend here at the office. It made perfect sense, given the quantities we drank, but that didn't mean I had to be happy about it.

"Want me to drive?" I asked as I held the door open for her.

"Mommy!"

Beth turned around and asked, "What, Baby?"

"Can you bring me a cookie?" I choked back a laugh when I saw Beth look from Chase to the plate of cookies on the counter then back to Chase.

"There are cookies here." She pointed to the counter.

Chase scrunched up his nose. "Aunt Mary has gooder cookies."

He wasn't wrong. The cookies in the SSI office were from the grocery store deli and weren't nearly as good as the giant fresh-baked cookies sold at Grannie's.

"Better," Meg gently corrected him, "she has better cookies." Meg turned to Beth and said, "Actually, can you make that two? I want one too," Meg smiled down at Chase and said, "because they're better."

"I'll take a peanut butter, if she has any left," Jack added to the order.

"I'll grab a dozen," I said, knowing if we didn't bring back enough for everyone, there'd be chaos. I smiled at Beth. "I guess it's a good thing I'm coming along." I tilted my head towards the parking lot. "Now let's get out of here before they add to the list."

I trusted she'd know I was kidding, since I didn't care how much they added. If they wanted me to lug the entire store back, I would, though John might balk when I handed in my expense report at the end of the week.

"Thanks for offering to help. I don't know what came over me, offering to pick up coffee for the office." She rolled her eyes and laughed as she asked, "How'd you do it every day?"

"I have big hands." I wiggled my fingers in front of me to drive home my point before opening my passenger door and helping her up.

At first, awkward silence filled the truck. Beth and I usually shared pleasantries at the counter, so this was new, and we didn't really know what to say to each other. *Being shy sucks.*

"I bet you're happy you don't have to do this every day now that Meg brews Grannie's in the office." Beth broke the silence.

"Not really, I miss my daily trips to Grannie's." I didn't add, *because I miss seeing you every day.* "As far as frat boy hazing goes, it was pretty enjoyable."

Her laugh was soft and musical. I think I missed that the most. *I'll have to find an excuse to go to Grannie's more often.*

"AJ didn't seem to mind either, for all he pretended to complain about it."

Had they put Jack through the hazing? Probably not. It didn't seem like something John or Jamie would do. Not wanting to own my ignorance about the tradition, I asked Beth if Jack had complained.

"He never had to do it. According to AJ, it was Jack's idea to haze the new guy."

"Why aren't I surprised?"

.Hazing and teasing were a part of any military friendship, so it made sense Jack suggested doing it the new guy. Who just happened to be one of his best friends, having bonded while serving in the Army.

Once the ice was broken, we settled into comfortable conversation, making the rest of the drive go by in a flash. I half wished it'd taken longer so we could keep talking.

As we approached Grannie's door, I saw the colorful Wyatt Foundation Halloween Dance fundraiser flyers in the window. The Sheppards held the initial fundraiser for Beth after she lost her husband. The event was such a huge success, they started a foundation and named it after him. The money they raised went to the families of fallen officers, police and fire, in the local community.

This year would be the third event, and the second I'd attend.

I got to meet a lot of the local police officers and other first responders, and quite a few political players at the fundraiser the year before. It'd been a whirlwind night as John introduced me to everyone. *Most of whom I've forgotten.*

As I held the door open for Beth, the rich smell of freshly brewed coffee filled my nose, making my mouth water. Mary and Amber, the full-time barista who replaced Meg when John poached her, were helping a group of customers in suits and ties.

Beth compulsively organized the cream and sugar counter as we waited.

"Beth. Doug. It's so good to see you." Mary rushed around the counter and hugged Beth. You'd think they hadn't seen each other in months. "What brings you in during your vacation?"

"I made the mistake of offering to make a coffee run while Chase was talking to John." Mary looked at me as Beth answered.

"How many do you need that you brought backup?" Mary asked with a laugh.

"I was heading here when Beth came in, so I offered to help." Mary patted my arm, I could almost hear her thinking, "good boy", before she asked how many.

"Eight, plus a hot chocolate with marshmallows, and whatever Beth wants. Oh, and we need a dozen cookies."

She raised her eyebrows. "Eight, must be a full house today."

"Yes, ma'am." It was rare for all six full-timers to be in the office at the same time, and rarer still for a few part-timers to be there as well. Most of us worked outside the office, providing protection duty, on stake outs, serving papers, or investigating. It was one of the things I liked most about the job—it was never boring.

"John mentioned he had an appointment with Chase. Is everything okay?" Concern laced Mary's voice as she headed back behind the counter. She was the Mama Bear of Sheppard & Sons, and Grannie's, and it showed in her actions and her words.

"Oh, he's fine. I thought he didn't want me helping him practice tee, ball but it turns out he wants help with his cup." Beth tried not to laugh as she explained the situation. "And John to practice with him."

Mary's laugh filled the space. "John'll love that."

Jealousy reared it's ugly head as I saw a future I'd never have.

Mary sent Amber out back to grab a box, then packed our coffees and cookies into it. Mary added a pumpkin muffin, saying, "On the house, for my new daughter-in-law. I know how much she loves them." If her smile was any bigger, the top of her head would have fallen off.

When Beth and I both reached for the box our fingers brushed and our eyes locked. It was the briefest of touches, but I felt it zing like a shock straight to my core. It wasn't the first time it had happened, but it was the first time I considered acting on it. *But not here.*

During the ride back to the office, Beth stared out the window. She had the box of coffees balanced on her lap with the bag of baked treats balanced on top. She was tapping her fingers on the box in a steady rhythm, though I don't think she realized it. I didn't know her well enough to know if it was a nervous habit or not, but erred on the side of experience and assumed it meant something was up. *It never hurts to ask.*

"Everything okay?" I asked, not expecting her to open up or spill her guts to me. *We're acquaintances, not friends.* If I had my way, that'd change sooner rather than later.

Chapter 5

Beth

When Doug's fingers brushed mine, I felt it to my toes. Something I hadn't felt since losing Phil.

It caught me off guard. Before I could process what it meant, my thoughts turned to Phil and how much I missed him. I stared out the window, my mind racing between memories of Phil and my reaction to Doug's touch, as we drove back to the office.

Of course, Doug noticed. But I couldn't tell him I was thinking about Phil. I couldn't tell him what his touch had done to me. And I definitely couldn't tell him how much I wanted to find a man who'd be a good husband to me and a loving father to Chase.

I wasn't ready to open that can of worms with anyone, let alone Doug. *Hell, I need an extra glass of wine to admit it to Mary and Meg.*

When we got back to the office, Doug told me to wait, then came around and opened my door before grabbing the box off my lap. He balanced it carefully on one arm and helped me out with the other.

Such a gentleman. His old school manners made me wonder how old he was. I made a mental note to ask Meg. Doug looked to be in his mid-to-late-thirties but had the demeanor of someone a few years older.

My hand felt small in his as he helped down. When I tried to open the door for him, since he was carrying the box, he beat me to it. "Ladies first."

"Mommy, Mommy, Mommy." Chase ran across the reception area as soon as he saw us. "Look what Auntie Meg and Uncle Jack got me." He held up a couple of plastic toys that looked like different types of sharks.

"That was nice of them. What are they?"

"Water dinosaurs." He said as he lifted them higher, so I could see them better, before running to Doug who was handing out coffees. "Did you bring me a cookie?"

"Chase, manners." I gently corrected him.

"Did you bring me a cookie, please?" He emphasized the end of the word please.

Stifled laughter filled the room. I had to tell Chase to say please and thank you so enough he assumed that's what I meant any time I corrected his manners.

Knowing one of the cookies was for Chase, Doug made eye contact with me over Chase's head, silently asking permission. I nodded.

He opened the bag as he kneeled. "Okay, we have acorn chip, peanut butter and dirt, and frosted tree-bark cookies. Which kind would you like?"

My eyes rounded and my jaw fell slack as I watched—I'd never heard Doug crack a joke or act silly. *Not that I spend much time with him.* But from what I'd heard, Doug was the strong, silent type. I glanced at Meg; her raised eyebrows confirmed my suspicion; this was unusual behavior for him.

Chase's face fell as Doug listed the cookies he could choose from. I worried he might start crying, but should have known better. Doug opened the bag and said, "Oops, I must have grabbed the wrong bag because this one smells like chocolate chip cookies." He grabbed one and handed it to my now smiling son.

He's going to make a great dad someday. Then he turned his smile on me. *And probably a great husband.*

Chase said, "Thank you Mr. Doug," a half second before shoving the cookie in his mouth and taking a too big-for-his-mouth bite.

"You're welcome. Can you bring this bag to your Auntie Meg, it's a special treat for her."

"Ooh, what did Mary give me?" Meg's eyes lit up. She loved her baked goods as much as I did and was lucky she could eat them without feeling like she gained ten pounds with every bite.

After a few more minutes, I asked Chase to gather up his things and say his goodbyes. He didn't want to leave, but SSI had work to do and we'd distracted them long enough.

Chapter 6

Doug

The day after helping Beth with the coffee run, I left for an assignment in Houston. It was a security gig for a twenty-one-year-old model but it felt more like a babysitting job. She was spoiled, entitled, and she spent more time drinking than working. After three long ass days, I couldn't wait to say goodbye.

On my way back to Weatherford, I stopped to have a beer and celebrate because, despite her best efforts to start trouble, nothing had gone wrong.

During the long drive back, I thought about how close I'd come to asking Beth if she wanted to go out for a coffee but hadn't because I thought it sounded lame. Then I'd thought about asking her if she wanted to meet for drinks instead but that sounded too much like I was hitting on her. *Which I was.* Or would've been if I hadn't over-thought myself into inaction.

Now I regret chickening out.

I kept thinking about how I'd joked with Chase about the cookies. I hadn't planned it, but it felt natural despite being in complete opposition to my normal behavior. I didn't have a lot of experience with kids and was usually a little stiff around them.

I'm never nervous around Chase.

Just because I couldn't have kids, didn't mean I didn't want them. I did, and I hoped whoever I found to spend my life with would be open to adoption. First I'd have to find someone willing to spend their life with a broken man.

I hadn't shared my secret with anyone I'd dated, and wouldn't unless I thought we had a chance at a future. There was no logical reason to face the ridicule and embarrassment unless I was falling in love. And that hadn't happened yet.

How will Beth react?

Why was I thinking about telling Beth? I hadn't even asked her out yet.

She's under my skin.

I wasn't arrogant, but I was usually more confident when it came to asking women out. So why was I so nervous about asking Beth out?

Because she's different.

I'd been watching her for a year, slowly getting to know her one pleasantry at a time. The way her eyes lit up when she smiled at someone she loves. How she glowed when she talked about Chase. The way she looked down and blushed when someone complimented her. You could learn a lot about a person by watching them interact with others, and after a year of watching Beth, I wanted to learn more.

It was late when I got back to my apartment, but I wasn't ready to call it a night. I started a load of laundry, then turned on the tv and my gaming console. Blowing up aliens sounded like the perfect way to relax after the last few days. Luckily for me, it was Friday night, and I didn't have any assignments on Saturday so I didn't have to worry about staying up late. I pressed pause and poured myself a glass of single malt Scotch. The strong smoky notes hit my nose after the initial waft of alcohol wore off. *Just what I need.*

This wasn't the life I'd imagined for myself; thirty-two, divorced, living in a furnished studio apartment above a small real estate office. But it was better than living with someone who'd come to hate me because I'd robbed her of her dreams. Her words, not mine.

I hadn't chosen to be sterile, but she blamed me anyway. When I suggested adoption, thinking we could give a child, some children, a loving home, she'd shut me down. She wanted to carry and raise her own babies, not take care of someone else's brats. Her words, not mine.

I wondered for the thousandth time—why hadn't I seen that side of her?

My mom and dad saw it. They'd advised me to take my time before marrying her, get to know her better. I thought they were just being their judgmental selves. Turns out they were right. I should have waited. I also should've asked for a prenup like my father suggested, but I'd refused. I was in love and didn't think I'd need one. After all, enlisted men weren't exactly rolling in the dough, so it wasn't like she was marrying me for my money.

They'd welcomed her into the family with polite indifference after we said I do. When she left me and filed for divorce, they were less than sympathetic as they peppered me with, "I told you so". They pointed out all the times they'd noticed her selfish, narcissistic behaviors. Listening to their stories, I'd realized just how often I'd made excuses for her behavior—to myself and to them.

The buzzer from the washing machine interrupted my thoughts. I transferred my clothes to the dryer, poured another glass of scotch, and sat down to destroy an army of alien invaders.

It's not the life I expected, but it's not so bad.

Chapter 7

Beth

When I dropped Chase off at daycare Monday morning, he was excited to see his friends again but sad he couldn't stay home with me. I felt the same way. While I was happy to go back to work after seven days of trying to keep up with Chase, I felt sad I wouldn't be with him all day.

I shook my head. *The bittersweet paradox of parenthood.*

I was lucky Chase's daycare served a lot of police and firefighter families, so they opened earlier and closed later than most others, since I started at Grannie's at six am. Two sisters, Shawna and Angela, whose parents had been police officers, and whose husbands were still active duty in the military, ran the daycare. When I interviewed them, they said it was a win-win situation; they served the community while earning extra money.

I had to agree. Plus, it was a bonus for me that Chase liked them, and they never had more than six kids at a time, so each kid felt special.

"I'll be back around three to pick you up, okay?" I kissed the top of his head as I hugged him goodbye.

"Then I get to practice tee ball with Uncle John, right?"

"Yup, after dinner."

"Yay." He clapped his hands while he hopped up and down in place. "Love you, Mommy."

"Love you too."

It felt good to be back at work, which I was sure was mostly due to spending the day with Mary and seeing my regular customers again, many of whom I called friends. Most people might not consider working in a coffee shop a rewarding career choice, but it was perfect for me; I had flexible hours, good pay and benefits, a community of friendly regulars, plus my boss was my best friend. If you'd asked me in high school what I wanted to do, I wouldn't have said manage a coffee shop. I wouldn't have predicted leaving Louisiana either.

But life happens, and here I am. I smiled, knowing I wouldn't change a thing.

Which wasn't entirely true, there was one thing I'd change—Phil would be alive and well, helping me raise Chase.

The bell above the door chimed, disrupting my thoughts. I greeted two WPD officers as they strolled in and waved. We chatted while I poured their coffees. Two minutes after the door closed behind them, Mary held out the phone and said, "It's Angela."

Angela? Chase's daycare Angela? *Why didn't she call my cell?*

My breath caught in my throat. The only reason she'd call was if something had happened to Chase. *Oh God.* I willed my legs to move and watched as my trembling hand reached for the receiver. I held me breath as I brought it to my ear.

"Is Chase okay?" I asked, sounding as panicked as I felt.

"He is. He fell and bumped his head and wants to talk to you."

Thank God. "How bad is it?" I asked, taking the first full breath since hearing Mary say the call was for me.

"Not bad, he didn't break the skin. The fall scared him more than it hurt him, but he won't stop asking for you." She paused. "Hang on."

"Mommy?"

The fear in his voice crushed my heart. "I'm here, what happened?"

"I fell and hit my head."

"Miss Angela said you didn't bleed, and you were brave while she checked." I wanted to distract him from the pain and fear.

"I was," he said. "I have a big bump on my head."

He must have touched it because I heard him yelp in pain. "Chase, don't touch your bump. Okay?"

"Are you coming to get me?"

Trusting Angela and Shawna were more than capable of taking care of Chase and his bump, I told him I couldn't but would be there right after work. He whined he wanted to go home, but got over it when I reminded him he had tee ball practice with his Uncle John.

After talking to Angela, and being reassured Chase was okay, I hung up. Mary told me to take my lunch break early so I could pull myself back together. In the break room I saw the reason Angela called me on the work line—I'd left my phone on the table.

After the lunch rush, Doug stopped in for a coffee. I couldn't help but notice a bruise forming under his left eye. "Are you okay? What happened?" I asked, sounding like a worried mom as I reached out to touch his face. I yanked my hand back. *You can't just touch him.*

His grin told me he hadn't missed the gesture. "I'm okay, dude sucker punched me when I served his papers." Serving legal papers was one of the many jobs the private investigators at SSI performed.

"Sorry." I didn't know what else to say since it wasn't my place to worry about him. I asked, "Your usual?"

"Please. And an acorn chip cookie." His grin made my stomach do little loop da loops.

My laugh, as I turned to pour his coffee, sounded nervous.

Is Doug flirting with me? Why else would he bring up the joke he'd played on Chase. And be grinning at me with that look in his eyes? Doug had never cracked a joke before. He'd always been nice, polite, friendly but not overly so, but he'd never flirted.

It felt like something had changed between us. *I'm not complaining.*

"One large black coffee, and an acorn chip cookie coming right up." It couldn't hurt to flirt back a little even if I had butterflies in my belly, right? Right.

I might be over forty, but I'm not dead. A strong, sexy, polite male could still turn me on.

Doug scanned the coffee shop when I handed him his coffee. There was no one else here, not even Mary or Amber. At least not at the moment, though one or both would be back soon.

Doug looked me in the eyes and held my gaze, the air between us thick with tension. His Adam's apple bobbed as he swallowed. "Beth, would you consider letting me take you to lunch?"

Did he just ask me out? The butterflies in my stomach did a happy dance. It wouldn't be a date-date, but a lunch date still counted as a date.

"I'd like that." His grin changed into a full-blown smile causing the lines around his eyes to wrinkle.

He put his steaming cup of coffee down and reached into his pocket. "Here's my card." His strong fingers brushed against mine as I reached for it. "Text me your number. I'll call you later so we can set a date."

"Okay." Suddenly I felt shy, which was silly. I'd known him for a year, and while we weren't friends, we weren't strangers either.

That was about to change.

Which made me giddy because I'd been crushing on Doug from afar for a while now. I wasn't usually attracted to redheads, but something about his quiet demeanor and steel blue eyes pulled me in. Maybe suddenly feeling shy wasn't so silly.

It's been a long time since I've felt this excited about a date.

"Beth?" Doug's soft voice cut through my inner ramblings.

"Right, sorry." Heat flooded my face as I blushed.

"No need to apologize, just wanted to know what time I should call."

I rushed to answer. "Oh, right, of course, after seven-thirty is good. Thanks." Chase would be asleep by then. *At least he should be.*

He grinned. "I have to run, there's a stack of paperwork calling my name. I'll call you around eight."

"Have fun with that." *Really?* I chuckled at my stupidity and waved. "I'll talk to you later."

The bell above the door hadn't finished jingling when I heard Mary clear her throat. "Did Doug just ask you on a date?"

I couldn't hide my girlish grin. "He did."

"Good for you." She came over and gave me a quick hug.

"You're not going to ask if I said yes?" It was a silly question since she'd heard our conversation.

"Have you seen your face?" Mary laughed. "Even if I hadn't overheard you, I'd be able to tell by the ear-to-ear smile, the beautiful blush in your cheeks, and the sparkle in your eyes."

It was a little awkward when John stopped by to play tee ball with Chase. I'd just agreed to a date with one of his employees, and wasn't sure what he'd think about it. So I did what any mature woman would do, and didn't mention it.

I wasn't trying to hide it from him, at least that's what I told myself. Not that it'd matter; Mary would probably tell him later. I didn't want to make a big deal out of it. In all likelihood, we'd have a date or two and he'd decide dating a single mom wasn't his cup of tea. Or coffee. Or his glass of beer. *Whatever suits him.*

Before they started practice, I told John about Chase's fall earlier so he'd know to be careful.

While John occupied Chase, I took advantage of the free time and read. It was a thick book and taking me forever to read; but I was enjoying the story so far. It was a time travel romance, recommended by Meg and Emily, Jamie's girlfriend. Apparently, they thought the redheaded Scottish hero was swoon-worthy.

That'd make two swoon-worthy redheads in my life. *Is Doug Scottish?* He could be, with his pale complexion and red hair.

"Mommy, Uncle John said I'm good at tee ball." Chase announced as soon as he opened the sliding glass patio door.

I slipped my bookmark in place and set my book aside. "I bet. I can't wait to watch you play."

John stood back and listened, a calm expression on his smiling face, as Chase told me all about their practice. John had raised four athletic children and was used to the energy. If I didn't know better, I'd think he missed it. Or maybe he was already thinking about what it'd be like to be a grandpa.

When it was time for John to leave, I thanked him as I hugged him goodbye. Then I herded my little ball of energy into the bathtub. It was never an easy task, getting a boy to take a bath, but tonight was extra hard because he was super-charged after an hour of playing with one of his favorite people.

I tucked Chase into bed and read him his favorite bedtime story. Then, after cleaning up the mess in the bathroom, I checked to see how I looked in the mirror. Which was silly because I'd be talking to Doug on the phone. I shrugged; *it's for me, not for him.* Looking good helped me feel good about myself so I brushed out my hair and put on some lip gloss.

My phone rang promptly at eight. I shouldn't have expected anything less from someone who served in the military and worked for John Sheppard. John ran a tight ship; tardiness was not acceptable without a good excuse, like death or dismemberment. I was sure there were probably a few other excuses he'd deem acceptable, but I didn't think anyone had ever tested the theory.

Answer your phone.

"Hello." *Did my voice just squeak?*

"Hi Beth, it's Doug. Is it a bad time?"

"No, Chase is asleep, so I'm free."

"Good. Did he have fun with John?"

It was sweet of him to ask about Chase first. "He did. He was a bundle of raw energy afterwards, but John must've worn him out because he fell asleep two pages into his favorite bedtime story." I laughed and so did Doug, causing my heart to do a little leap in my chest.

We talked for a few minutes, sharing pleasantries, before setting our date for Saturday. I had to work the morning shift, so I'd already arranged for Chase to be at daycare and would call tomorrow to ask them if he could stay for a few extra hours. They were usually flexible, if they didn't have plans.

"I should probably warn you; Mary overheard you ask me out."

"So, John knows by now." He finished for me. He didn't sound upset, but then I'd never heard him sound upset so I didn't have a point of reference.

"Yeah, they don't keep secrets from each other. But it's not a bad thing. Mary approves." I didn't see a reason to tell him she was giddy we were finally going on a date. Mary was the only person who knew about my crush on Doug. Though Meg and Emily suspected. *Which means Jack and Jamie do too.*

"Should I expect the dad-talk from John?" I could hear the humor in his voice. Thank God he wasn't worried. John could be intimidating when he wanted to be, and I didn't want Doug worrying about his job.

"You might get a variation of it, but don't worry, it's not like he'll be waiting on the porch with a shotgun if you bring me home late."

"Well, I wasn't worried before. Now I'm wondering if I should wear my vest."

His deep laugh did weird things to my body, stirring up a physical reaction I hadn't had in years. *Since Phil.* I felt a brief flash of guilt before reminding myself it was okay. Phil would want me to find someone who made me happy.

We talked for a few more minutes before he asked, "Do you have a favorite lunch place? Or do you want me to pick?" Usually I'd want the man to take the lead on a first date, but this was lunch and finding a good lunch place was harder than finding a quality restaurant for dinner.

"I don't have a favorite place, but I know of a great little café that serves breakfast all day. If you don't mind breakfast for lunch." It might sound weird, but the restaurant only opened for breakfast and lunch, and their menu was mostly breakfast items. "The weekly specials are different dishes from around the world." They offered a limited selection of deli sandwiches for the lunch crowd, but most people order breakfast.

"Breakfast is good any time of day. What's the name?"

"The Breakfast Joint." I deadpanned. Doug laughed. I couldn't blame him, the name was simple and on point, but didn't do it justice.

"If I pick you up at one, does that give you enough time to get ready?"

"It does." It gave me more than enough time, since I got off work at twelve. I didn't usually work Saturdays but had offered to fill in for our part-time shift leader who needed the morning off.

"Great. I'll pick you up at one. Good night, Beth."

"Good night, Doug." I hesitated before hanging up, then giggled like a schoolgirl because what forty-one-year-old woman does that?

One who has been lonely for far too long.

Chapter 8

Doug

Sure enough, John called me into his office the next morning. I closed my laptop, topped off my coffee in the lobby while saying hello to Meg, and then knocked on his door. Taking a deep breath, I reminded myself I hadn't done anything wrong, and anything John said to me would be out of love for Beth and Chase.

"Come in."

"Morning John." I raised my mug in a salute. "You wanted to see me?"

"I do, close the door." He leaned back and pointed at the chairs in front of his desk. "Have a seat."

This isn't how he acts when he hands out assignments. I sat on the edge of the chair, adjusting myself so I wasn't so far forward I looked nervous, and not so relaxed that I looked disrespectful. For the first time since starting at SSI, I felt nervous.

I forced myself to sit still while I waited for him to break the uncomfortable silence.

"It's come to my attention you're taking Beth on a date." John grinned.

A good sign.

"Yes, sir."

"I've learned my lesson, so I won't ask you not to." He laughed and leaned forward, resting his forearms on his desk. "With my luck, I'd ask you to keep your distance and the two of you would run off and elope."

He didn't have to remind me that Jack and Jamie had both dated clients—two women who were once off-limits but were now family.

Well, Meg was, and Emily would be as soon as Jamie got up the nerve to propose. He and Emily had only been dating a few months, but they were so obviously in love it was almost painful to watch.

Taking a risk, I answered with a touch of humor. "I don't know, sir, Beth's not a client."

"Technically, neither was Meg." He grinned before turning serious again. "Beth's a good woman, and Mary and I consider her family. She deserves nothing but the best." He leaned back and crossed his arms across his chest. "All I'm asking is you treat her with the respect she deserves, and if things don't work out, be honest with her." I wiped my palms on my pants as John's stare bore into me. "And be careful with Chase, that little boy wants a dad so desperately I can almost taste it."

"Yes, sir." I'd heard how hard it could be to navigate a new relationship when a young child was involved, both from friends who were single parents and the people who'd dated them. The child was a part of the relationship, but you couldn't risk leaving them feeling deserted if things didn't work out. The general rule of thumb, according to my friends, was to not involve the child right away. Some wouldn't even introduce their kids until things got serious.

I'll have to be careful with Chase. We already knew each other, so not introducing us wasn't an option. I made a mental note to talk to Beth about how to handle if, should he start asking questions. I wanted to honor her wishes, and not overstep my bounds.

"Good." He picked up a manila folder. "I have a new assignment for you. It's a one-day security job, escorting a witness to and from the courthouse. It's a closed testimony, so only the judge, witness, and attorneys will be in the room. You'll have to wait outside for however long it takes."

"Yes, sir." I grabbed the file. "Anything special I should be aware of?"

"It's a high-profile case, so expect crowds and the press. Take the sedan with the tinted windows. And Sharpe, wear your vest." I nodded as I stood up, eager to get back to my office so I could read the file.

"Expecting trouble, sir?" The sedan didn't just have tinted windows, it was also bullet proof.

"Always. Stay sharp, Sharpe." Then he snickered.

Out of respect I held back the impulse to roll my eyes while I faked a laugh. "Good one." It was funny the first time. *How do you tell a man his dad joke is getting old?* There was only one answer if that man was your boss: you didn't.

The file had the basics about the client, a woman in her mid-twenties who was the key witness in an abduction case. From her office window, she'd witnessed two men grab a young girl on the street. She'd snapped a bunch of pictures and called 9-1-1. Most of the photos were blurry but they were good enough for the cops to read the plate and put out a BOLO (be on the lookout).

Because of her quick thinking, they'd found the van and arrested two guys. Unfortunately, the girl was gone, and they claimed they never had her. The forensic evidence from the van proved otherwise. It was enough to keep them in jail until their trial, despite their pleas of innocence. No one believed they were the masterminds behind the crime, but they refused to speak or turn on the person who'd hired them.

Shortly after their arrest, someone called 9-1-1 to report seeing the girl from the Amber Alert outside a gas station. The local police located her and brought her home. She was physically unharmed, but terrified.

Unfortunately for our client, someone threatened her for doing the right thing.

I hope they catch the bastard, I thought as I emailed the client. I introduced myself and asked if I could call, so we could discuss logistics.

Whoever was behind the crime was the type of person who wouldn't think twice about hiring a hitman to carry out his threat. It wouldn't be hard for a professional to take her out from a distance. With or without security.

I called the head of security at the courthouse and asked for permission to use the back entrance. The press, and hopefully anyone looking to stop her from testifying, would be at the front of the building, while we used a service door in the back.

Around six, a knock on my door frame brought me back to the present. "Hey Jack, what's up?"

"Just dropping off the keys to the sedan, she's gassed up and ready." He walked over and dropped them on my desk.

"Thanks man."

"You okay? You look… disorganized." His eyes scanned my desk.

It was cluttered with the spread-out case files covered in post-it notes. "Yeah, just doing some research."

"Well, I suggest you call it a day, you're the muscle on this mission, not the brains." Jack laughed at his own joke. Like father, like son.

"I just want to know what might be coming my way. The guy behind this sounds like the type to call in a cleaner."

He nodded. "I've got a meeting in the morning, but it shouldn't last long. Call me if you want backup."

"Thanks. Appreciate it." One of the many things I loved about working at SSI was the people. I could always count on anyone here to have my back, and I'd always have theirs.

I packed up my notes and shut down my laptop. I'd done all I could do from here and I needed to get some rest.

"Meg and Emily are having a girl's night with Ma and Beth on Friday, so the guys hanging out at our place, video games, pizza, beer. You in?"

"Yeah, thanks." The Friday night gaming sessions were relatively new, and a great way for us to bond. It was also better than gaming alone. *He mentioned Beth, but not our date.*

Did he know? If he didn't, it was only a matter of time. If Meg didn't hear about it from Beth she'd definitely hear about it from Mary. I sighed as I realized I wouldn't have an ounce of privacy if I started dating Beth.

I shrugged internally. *There are worse problems to have.*

The next morning, I escorted the client in, unseen, through a service entrance in the back, waited outside the door while she gave her testimony, then escorted her back out the way we'd come in.

A few clever reporters had migrated to the back, and got in her face.

"Get back!" I yelled as I stepped between them. I used my left hand to guide her as I moved, so I wouldn't lose her.

The reporter shouted something about the public having the right to know as she tried to push her way around me, microphone held high.

I should have called Jack. I couldn't scan the area for threats while keeping the reporters at bay.

To protect her privacy, I took my jacket off and used it to cover her head. I strong-armed my way through rowdy crowd, forcing them to keep their distance while shouting, "No comment."

Once we were back in the car, I checked on her. She was pale and shaking from fear, but otherwise okay. I didn't like leaving her alone when I dropped her off, but my job was to get her to the courthouse, then home again. Which meant the job was done.

Hopefully, she wouldn't be in danger now that she'd testified. After seeing my client safely inside her apartment, I went back to the office to return the sedan and file my report.

The rest of the week was less exciting, I served a few papers, flirted a little with Beth on my self-appointed coffee runs, and covered an overnight security shift on Thursday for Eric, one of our part time security guys so he could cover a shift at his PD.

No one, other than John, had said anything to me about my date with Beth. Though judging from their glances, and on more than one occasion Meg's wide-eyed, ear-to-ear, all-knowing smile, I figured they all knew. *Why hasn't she said anything?* I could only guess the amount of effort it was taking her to keep quiet.

I decided to let the cat out of the bag Friday morning.

"Hey Meg, got a sec?"

"Of course, what do you need?" she answered, a wicked gleam in her eyes.

"I'm sure you've heard I'm taking Beth out on a lunch date." Her smile split her face in half as she nodded a little too vigorously. "I'd like to bring her flowers. Do you know her favorite flowers or colors?"

"She loves orchids, but that's not a good first date flower. I know she likes daisies and sunflowers. Want me to order some?"

I had a feeling this was a test. "Nah, I got it. Thanks."

Her smile told me I'd passed. Meg was more than a receptionist—she was the heart of SSI. She kept us all organized, and made our clients feel comfortable and at ease. Not an easy task considering people didn't come to see us unless they needed help or protection. She even kept our coffee fresh, and the water and snack counter stocked, though it wasn't part of her job.

"Good boy," she said with a smirk.

"How long have you known?" I asked. "And have you told Jack?" I shouldn't have felt nervous, but I did. Meg's opinion of me mattered. I hadn't known her long, but I had mad respect for her. She was one of those people who'd gone through hell and come out stronger for it. The abuse she'd suffered didn't break her, and now she used her experience to help others.

She blushed before answering, "I talked to Beth and Mary on Tuesday, but Beth made me promise not to say anything. And yes, I told Jack, but I made him promise not to say anything."

I laughed, surprised she'd been able to keep quiet for so long. "Thanks, I appreciate it."

Meg had the expression she always got when she was dying to say something but holding back. "Go on, say it," I said with a smile.

"I'm happy for you guys," she paused and looked back at Jack's door, "can I tell Jack the cat's out of the bag?"

"Yeah, that's fine. I'm sure everyone knows by now, so no point pretending otherwise." I found that despite having a few nerves about the whole situation, I didn't actually mind everyone knowing; *not that it would matter if I did.*

Meg clapped her hands together, and said, "This is so exciting." He fingers flew over the keyboard. My suspicion, that she was messaging Jack, was confirmed a few seconds later when Jack walked out of his office. AJ was half a second behind.

"What's up?" Jack asked as he walked to her desk.

"It's not a secret anymore." Meg didn't bother hiding her excitement. *I shouldn't complain. They could be against us dating.*

"Congrats, man," Jack shook my hand as he asked, "Where are you taking her?" At the same time AJ said, "Congrats, don't do anything I wouldn't do."

From what I knew about AJ, that was a very short list. Though I had a feeling he was mostly all talk. He had a lot more respect for women than he let on. *Someone must have fucked him over.* I didn't have a chance to answer their questions because Jamie came out of his office and joined our huddle. He didn't have time to ask what was going on before Meg told him about my date. He smiled at Meg and shook his head before shaking my hand.

"You knew, huh?" I asked.

"Yeah, sorry man, it's impossible to keep something like that a secret around here." He looked at Meg.

She quickly defended herself. "Hey, your mom told your dad. It's not all on me."

"It's no big deal. Thanks for letting me be the one to bring it up." I looked at Jack. "Has she been driving you crazy all week?"

"You have no idea," Jack said with feigned exasperation.

"Hey, I'm right here." Meg punched him in the arm.

"Anyway, I'm happy for you two." Jamie said before asking, "You still coming over tonight?"

"Yeah, anything I should bring, besides beer?"

"Your gaming controller," Jack answered. He and Meg were still living with Jamie, but only until the renovations were done on their house. Since Jamie wasn't in a hurry to get rid of them, they were taking their time and saving money by doing as much of the work as they could on their own. With our help, of course.

Chapter 9

Beth

Between work, Chase's tee ball, and running errands the week flew by. Doug stopped by Grannie's a few times during the week, flirting a little each time. Nothing too open or wild, just the occasional wink or brush of the hand.

And a lot of grins and smiles. From both of us.

I always felt ten years younger after he left.

We texted a few nights, after Chase was in bed. There was nothing overly flirty or sexual about our conversations, but I went to bed with a head full of romantic fantasies anyway. It'd been a long time since I'd felt the thrill of anticipating a first date. And five years since I'd had the pleasure of a man in my bed.

On Friday, Doug messaged me mid-afternoon to warn me that everyone at SSI knew about our date. I wasn't surprised. I'd told Meg, and fully expected her to tell Jack. Mary had told John, who'd already talked to Doug about it. So really, the only people who might not have known were Jamie and AJ, and I doubted they were left in the dark.

SSI was one big family, and Grannie's was an extension of that family. It was nearly impossible to keep secrets.

I texted back, saying I was surprised it'd taken this long for it to come out and reassured him I didn't mind. I didn't ask him for the details, knowing I'd hear all about it from Meg tonight when we got together, along with Emily and her mother Anne, at Mary's house for Craft and Booze Night.

Mary, Meg, and I had been doing our monthly girl's night for a while now, but tonight was the first time Emily and Anne would join us.

Our first get together was supposed to be a book club, and we'd all read the book, but as the wine flowed our discussion quickly devolved into which actor we thought should be cast as the love interest.

The second time none of us had finished the book, so we decided it'd be fun to do crafts instead. We'll see how long it lasts. Usually, Mary and Meg came over after Chase went to bed, but tonight John had volunteered to watch Chase so we could meet at Mary's and not have to worry about keeping our volume down.

It'd never been a problem before, but there'd be five of us tonight, and I had to admit, it was nice not having to worry about it.

I was looking forward to getting to know Emily and Anne better. Emily and Jamie had been dating for a couple of months, and it was the happiest I'd seen him since Isabelle died four and a half years ago. Things had started a little rough for them; she'd just left an abusive boyfriend, and her older brother, Chris, Jamie's best friend, was hesitant to give his blessing. That was all in the past, now Jamie was head-over-heels in love with Emily, and she was just as in love with him

When John knocked on my door at five-twenty, Chase practically tripped himself in his excitement to let him in. As he reached for the door handle, I reminded him to ask, "Who is it?"

Which he did, loud enough for the neighbors to hear. Even through the closed door, John's laughter was evident as he answered. I unlocked the deadbolt, and let Chase open the door to greet his Uncle John.

"Chase," I waited for him to look at me, "be good for your Uncle John, okay?"

"Yes, Mommy." He nodded his head up and down fast enough to make my neck hurt. "Did you tell him I can stay up late tonight?"

"Not yet. Go get in your pajamas while I tell him."

"Okay." Chase ran upstairs to his room.

"Thanks for sitting tonight. I appreciate it."

"Not a problem. Mama Bears need a night away from their cubs, no matter how much they love them."

"As you heard, I told him he can stay up late, he'll probably be asleep by seven-thirty but if not, I told him he could stay up until eight if he brushes his teeth by seven. He knows he's not allowed to have snacks after brushing, but I'll let you decide if you want to bend the rules when he asks."

John nodded. Chase called him Uncle John, but given their ages, John fell more into the grandpa role. *Which makes sense, his kids are all old enough to have kids Chase's age.* If John wanted to play Grandpa and spoil Chase, who was I to take that from him?

"He may argue when it's time for bed," I looked at John, "or maybe not, given it's you." I chuckled when he grinned. Chase respected John as an authority figure and was less likely to argue with him than he was with anyone else, including me.

Especially me.

"Got it. Teeth at seven, no snacks, bedtime at eight. Will he want a bedtime story?"

"He will. He'll tell you which one he wants to hear, then-"

John cut me off with a laugh and finished for me. "He'll fall asleep three pages in." Being a cop meant crazy shift work, so he wasn't always there to help Mary put their kids to bed, but she'd told me he'd taken advantage of the opportunity any night he was home, so he knew the drill.

"Exactly."

Chase came running down the stairs in his pajamas, with two handfuls of plastic dinosaurs. "Can we play dinosaurs?"

"Sure, but why don't you say goodbye to your mom first." John held out his hands for the toys.

"Bye." He waved without moving.

"Oh no you don't! I want a hug and a kiss before I go."

After saying goodbye, I thanked John again, grabbed my wine and snacks, and told John I wouldn't be home too late.

He looked up at me from the floor, where he was already making roaring sounds, much to Chase's delight, and said, "Stay as long as you'd like."

Fifteen minutes later I was the first to arrive at Mary's, which gave us a few minutes to talk. Wanting to avoid talking about my upcoming date with Doug for as long as possible I asked about Madi and Jaden, the two Sheppard children still serving in the military. Madeleine, Jamie's older twin, was a Navy Corpsman, and Jaden, the youngest Sheppard, was a Marine Raider.

Mary was counting the days until they'd all be home for good. She figured she'd have all her kids in the same state by the end of the next year. "They're both doing great. Jaden is finally finishing his college classes now that he's stateside."

"John must be thrilled."

"He is, though he'll be okay if Jaden decides not to become a PI. SSI is growing so fast; they'll need guys dedicated to the personal protection side of things."

"Has he said when he's moving home?" I asked. His enlistment was up at the end of January, but he planned on taking six months off to travel with friends before coming home. At least that was what he told his parents a few months ago.

"No, but he's coming home for two weeks at Christmas. He said it'd be a shame not to use his accrued leave time." She chuckled.

"Do you think Madi will come home?"

"She's not sure she can, but wouldn't it be great? Having all my kids home, at the same time, twice in one year?" I could hear the longing in her voice. Madi would be home the following summer and was hoping to find work in the Ft. Worth/Dallas area, which shouldn't be hard—hospitals always needed nurses.

Jack's wedding was one of three times Mary had all her kids together in the same place at the same time since Jack joined the Army. She was in seventh heaven for days. They celebrated holidays and birthdays over zoom, and even then, it wasn't always on the exact day, and they were rarely all present.

"We'll have to invite Madi to our craft nights." I suggested knowing Meg would agree; she loved Madi and couldn't wait to spend more time with her sister-in-law.

"I already have. She said she's looking forward to it."

Before long, Meg and Emily arrived. They'd driven together since they were coming from the same place. It was good to see the two of them developing a deep friendship. They were both great women who'd suffered through more than their fair share of trauma. Having a girlfriend to talk to was helping them both on their healing journeys. *And they'll be sisters-in-law soon.*

Anne arrived as we were setting up our snack buffet, which included Meg's now famous bacon mac and cheese, sliced meats and cheeses, veggies, homemade baked treats, and lots of wine.

Mary set the table with beads of different shapes, colors, and sizes, along with fishing wire and elastic, as well as other tools we might need to create necklaces or bracelets. Last month we tried knitting, but decided it was too hard to learn while chatting and drinking. We kept losing our stitch counts and after starting over a couple of times we gave up. We didn't care. We'd talked and laughed late into the night and our friendships were stronger because of it.

After we poured our wine and filled our plates, we settled in at the table. The conversation flowed like we were all old friends who'd been meeting like this for years, not a couple of months.

"When do you expect to move into your house Meg?" Anne asked.

"Early December, if there aren't any more delays and we can get it furnished." Meg radiated happiness. She'd had a rough go of it early in life, having been abused and trafficked, but was embracing the new love-filled life she had with Jack and his family. "I can't wait to host my first craft and booze night!"

"It'll be weird when you move out of Jamie's house," Emily said.

Emily technically lived at her parent's house, though she was rarely there. When she first moved back to Weatherford, after leaving her abusive boyfriend, it was all she could afford. Her original plan had been to find her own apartment after things settled down, but her mom convinced her it'd be silly to waste her money since she was rarely ever home.

I had a feeling Emily would move in with Jamie after Jack and Meg moved out. Though Meg had made it clear she and Jack had zero objections to her moving in before then.

"I'm sure you two will appreciate the privacy." Meg looked at Emily and then turned to me. "But enough about us. Are you excited for your date tomorrow?"

I looked down at the bright blue and green beads in front of me as my cheeks turned pink. "I am. Doug's taking me to The Breakfast Joint for lunch."

"Oh, I love that place," Anne said. Her head tilted, her eyes focused on something far away, like she was trying to remember something. "Is this the same Doug who works at SSI?"

Mary, Meg, and I all said it was.

"He's a tall drink of water," Anne said.

"Mom!" Emily looked embarrassed.

Anne didn't. "What? I'm married, not dead."

We all laughed. I had to agree with her, Doug was a damn fine-looking man.

Mary asked if anyone else wanted dessert when she got up to get her own. Most of us said yes, but Meg declined saying she was trying to be good after eating so much junk on her honeymoon.

"Meg, what are you talking about, you look amazing," Emily said.

I had to agree. She looked healthier now. Meg had been too thin when she first moved to Weatherford, a byproduct of her nervous energy.

"I agree," Mary said, putting the plate of baked goods in the middle of the table. "So enjoy yourself. You can always work it off tomorrow."

"You can come running with me before we go to the range," Emily teased her. Everyone knew Meg hated running.

"No thank you. I'll let you and the boys run for me."

"Are you shooting for fun tomorrow, or training with the guys?" Anne asked.

"Training. I'm not confident enough to carry every day, so Jamie's helping me."

"And I'll be there for moral support, and to practice," Meg added.

Anne asked, "Did I tell you Jamie offered to help your Dad and me get better? We both had our License to Carry back in the day, but let them expire." She shook her head. "I can't even remember the last time I shot a gun."

"He told me. When are you taking him up on it?" Emily's question sounded more like an order.

"Soon," Anne answered.

All this talk of guns got me thinking, when was the last time I'd shot my gun? Before Phil died. I could use some help, too.

The conversation ebbed and flowed as time ticked on. The night was filled with lots of laughter, plenty of wine, and a little bit of crafting.

"At least we finished this time," I said as we showed each other our masterpieces and joked about how long it took us.

Around ten, we started packing up and saying our goodbyes. When Meg hugged me goodbye, she told me she wanted to hear all about my date before the end of the weekend.

Chapter 10

Doug

I took a deep breath and shored up my resolve as I got out of my truck, and another as I grabbed my backpack, which had a six-pack of beer, my gaming controller, and headset. The guys had been mostly quiet about my date with Beth while we were in the office, but I knew that'd change tonight. And while I didn't mind a little friendly ribbing, I tended to keep my personal life, well, personal.

The only reason anyone at SSI knew I had a date this weekend was because Beth was a part of the extended Sheppard family. I took another deep breath and knocked.

Jack opened the door, a huge shit-eating grin on his face. "Come on in."

"Thanks," I answered as I walked to the kitchen and put my beer in the fridge. "Anyone need a beer?" I asked as I twisted the cap off mine.

A chorus of, "nah, I'm good," rang out.

We quickly decided what to order for dinner, with Jamie making a joke about how much easier it was with just us guys—the girls always hemmed and hawed about what they wanted. After ordering two large supreme pizzas and chicken wings, we set up the game system for some friendly team competition. I partnered with Jamie, and AJ with Jack. AJ and Jack joked about our team having an unfair advantage—I'd been trained by the Air Force to use gaming systems to operate drones and test special operations strategies and tactics. One of my favorite things about the job.

Jamie was quick to remind them, "I don't game half as much as either of you, so Doug will have to pick up the slack." He slapped me on the shoulder. "You don't mind, do you?"

"I got your back, bro." I laughed. *Dare I hope they won't bring up my date?*

"Before we start," AJ said, a sly grin on his face, "let's hear about Doug's lunch date."

No such luck. All eyes focused on me. *Damn it.* I hated being the center of attention, preferring to linger on the edges and observe.

"It's no big deal." It was, but none of them knew I'd been harboring feelings for Beth for months, "I'm taking Beth out for lunch tomorrow." I shrugged, trying to play it down.

It didn't start out that way, but my attraction to her grew every time I saw, which was almost daily when I picked up our coffees. I'd thought about asking her out a few times before, but chickened out, worried things would be awkward if she wasn't interested.

"Where are you taking her?" Jamie asked.

"She suggested The Breakfast Joint."

"You guys will like it. It was Isabelle's favorite restaurant." Isabelle was Jamie's late wife. She'd been murdered by a stalker just over four years ago—Jamie was the first cop on scene. I could only imagine what that was like. Her death was the catalyst for creation of Sheppard & Sons Investigations. John and Jamie both retired from their police departments, and together with Jack, started SSI. Jack was a silent partner while he finished his enlistment in the Army and put in his time to get his PI license. He'd become fully vested at the beginning of the year.

When I first started at SSI, Jamie barely mentioned Isabelle, and when he did, his grief was still palpable. Emily had changed that, helping him heal one day at a time with her love. Now, when he talked about his late wife if was with love and sadness, not grief.

"Meg's dying to go," Jack said. "She loves breakfast food and wants to try their French crepes. But she wants us to double date with Jamie and Emily, so she's trying to be patient."

Jamie laughed, "Meg's patience won't last long, so we should probably set a date." He made fun of Jack for always giving Meg what she wanted, but Jamie adored his new sister-in-law and rarely said no to her.

"Done." Jack turned to me and asked, "did dad give you the 'dad talk' yet?"

"Dude, I wouldn't want to be in your shoes for that conversation." AJ said, shaking his head in mock terror. He was a big guy, compared to most people, and he had extensive weapons training in the military. He was also a black belt in Brazilian Ju Jitsu. AJ wasn't intimidated by many people, but John Sheppard had made it to the top of the list.

"Sort of. He said he expected me to be respectful and honest, especially if it didn't work out."

"Or?" AJ asked. Jamie and Jack looked as eager as AJ to hear what threat John had given me.

"Or nothing. No threats. Though I'm sure I'll hear about it if I fuck up." I had no intention of doing anything to hurt Beth. If I did, I'd hear about it from John. And Meg—her opinion mattered as much to me as John's.

I wondered if Beth was getting interrogated, too.

"Well, I know Meg will be pissed if you do anything stupid." Jack took a swig of his beer then pointed at me with it. "So don't do anything stupid." Jamie seconded the order.

"Yes, sir." What else could I say? It wasn't like I didn't know how risky it was to ask out Beth. John and Meg weren't the only ones I had to consider. Jack and Jamie would be upset too. And Mary. God only knew how Chase would react, and that would piss everyone off even more.

What was I thinking? If this went south, I'd probably have to quit my job and leave town. Unless she was the one to dump me; then I'd just have to avoid Grannie's until the dust settled.

Saved by the doorbell, signaling the arrival of our food, I handed Jack a twenty then went to the kitchen to grab another round of beer for everyone. We talked while we ate, but, thankfully not about my love life. I preferred sports and gaming strategies; they were familiar territory.

"My plan is to let Doug do all the heavy lifting while I cover his six," Jamie joked.

"So, the same as last time?" Jack asked. "You know, big brother, you could play more and get better, so Doug doesn't have to carry your sorry ass every time we play."

"I could, but I have better things to do with my time," Jamie answered.

We all knew he'd rather spend his time with Emily than gaming. For him, tonight was about the company, not the competition. The rest of us were out for blood.

"I plan on kicking your asses with or without Jamie's help," I bragged. Jamie might not be a good partner in the game, but in real life, when it mattered, he was someone you could count on to always have your back. In real life he had the skills to do it.

"Care to put your money where your mouth is?" AJ asked.

Jamie groaned, despite the fact I won more often than I lost.

"How much?" I asked.

"How much do you want to lose?" AJ was feeling extra confident tonight.

"Hey, I'm still paying to renovate my house and I have a wife to support. So don't go too crazy." Jack was all bark, no bite. SSI was turning a good profit, and Meg could support herself.

"Don't let Meg hear you say that," Jamie interjected.

"She won't if you keep your mouth shut," Jack said.

"So how much, Sharpe?" AJ asked.

"A hundred."

"A hundred it is. Ante up." AJ said as he pulled out his wallet.

The game lasted late into the night with only the occasional pauses to refresh our beers, hit the head, or eat the brownies Meg had left for us. I wasn't the only one who appreciated the tasty baked goods she always left for us on game nights; we usually killed the pan.

Jamie and I won, but it wasn't easy. "Thanks, boys." I said to AJ and Jack, as Jamie split up our winnings.

"Double or nothing next time." AJ said knowing we never went over a hundred. We were competitive, not high rollers.

"Maybe we're paying him too much," Jamie said to Jack.

"No, sir. But I'm a single man who just got a pay raise, so I can afford it." AJ flashed a grin before draining his beer.

AJ had recently earned his degree and finished the other requirements needed to become a licensed private investigator in Texas. Going from a bodyguard to PI came with a nice pay raise, and a lot more responsibility.

Meg came home as we were leaving and didn't waste any time telling me to behave myself on my date with Beth before hugging me goodbye. Jack and Jamie echoed her sentiment, shaking my hand and clapping me on the back.

Chapter 11

Beth

I ran home after my shift on Saturday to get ready for my date. I showered and shaved faster than normal. Not that I expected anything to happen, but having smooth legs was a luxury I rarely bothered with but I it was a special occasion. I even put on matching bra and panties. He wouldn't see them, but they were for me not him so it didn't matter. It was empowering to wear something lacy and silky instead of my normal cotton mom-undies.

I pulled my wavy brown hair off my face in a cute hair clip and brushed on some neutral brown eyeshadow before applying mascara. I had long thick lashes, *thanks mom,* and liked to highlight them, knowing it made my caramel eyes stand out. The warm Texas sun had given my cheeks a natural sun-kissed color, so I skipped the foundation and finished with a red tinted lip gloss.

The yellow amber pendant and matching earrings I wore were a gift from Phil and matched my outfit.

Before turning off the light, I checked the mirror to make sure everything was as good as it would get, then went to the kitchen to wait.

A glance at the clock on the microwave let me know I only had twelve to fifteen minutes to wait, depending on how early Doug was. I knew he'd be at least a few minutes early; it was a man-in-uniform thing—they were often early. Never late. I couldn't sit still so I picked up my book. After reading the same sentence three times, I put it down.

Sure enough, the doorbell rang at three minutes before one. I filled my lungs and slowly let the air out. *Why am I so nervous?* I hadn't been nervous about any of my other dates. *Because I hadn't cared that much.* But I'd been crushing on Doug for the last year, and I wanted this date to go well. The thin curtain covering the window in the door wasn't enough to prevent me from identifying Doug, so I opened the door without asking who it was.

The first thing I noticed was his smile. The second was the bouquet of gorgeous bright yellow and orange sunflowers in his hand.

"Hi." His eyes looked me up and down as his smile widened. "You look beautiful."

I wasn't prone to blushing, but I hadn't been called beautiful in years, so of course I did. "Thank you." I held the door open and stepped back. "Come in."

"Thanks." He handed me the flowers after I closed the door.

"They're lovely, thank you. Do I have time to put them in water?" I asked as I held them to my face, letting their scent fill my nose. *How'd he know they're my favorite?*

"Of course."

I motioned for him to follow me into the kitchen, grateful I'd cleaned up Chase's mess before leaving this morning. My house wasn't dirty, but with an energetic five-year-old it frequently looked like a hurricane had blown through.

Doug waited patiently as I quickly found a vase, filled it with water, and arranged the flowers. After taking one last sniff, I turned to Doug. "Ready."

Damn he looks good. Now that the flowers were taken care of, I had time to take a nice long look. His black slacks hugged his muscular thighs, thighs I'd dreamed about on more than one occasion, and a pale green button-down shirt that complemented his red hair and fair skin. It fit snug, showing off his strong upper body, and the top button was undone. *Someone taught this man how to dress.* My brown slacks, and pink knit sleeveless shirt with matching cardigan felt like the perfect matching level of casual, erasing my earlier concern about being over or underdressed.

I grabbed my small purse, happy I didn't have to lug the gigantic bag I always carried when Chase was with me, and keys off the table. Doug opened my door and held it for me, then closed it behind me. He waited as I locked the deadbolt.

"Here you go." Doug opened the passenger door to his truck and helped me climb in. I wasn't at all surprised his personal vehicle was a large, black, dual cab truck. *It fits him, size and personality.*

"Thanks." I looked around the interior as I waited for him to walk around and get in. It was clean and organized, no fast-food wrappers, empty water bottles, or unopened mail to be seen. He'd probably think I was a slob if he saw my car, no matter how hard I tried, I couldn't keep up with Chase's mess.

Doug got in and made sure I was buckled in as he clicked his seat belt in place. It was a sweet gesture; one I didn't think any of my previous dates would have done. *Not that I let them pick me up.* John had made me promise not to give my address to any of my dates when I joined the dating site, so I'd driven myself.

John was the big brother I'd never had, but always wanted. He was more than a tad over-protective, a trait he'd passed on to his two oldest sons, but I appreciated it.

I hadn't even considered telling Doug I'd meet him at the restaurant when he asked what time to pick me up. Not even John could fault me for that since he trusted Doug enough to hire him. *I'm surprised John didn't do background checks on my other dates.* I chuckled at the absurdity of it.

"What's so funny?" Doug asked as he started the car.

"Just thinking about how protective John can be."

He looked at me and laughed. "Yeah, I'm pretty sure he ran a background check on me before he agreed to let me take you out."

Did he read my mind? I couldn't help laughing at the idea of John running a background check on Doug.

"I was literally just thinking I'm surprised John didn't do that to my previous dates."

"What makes you think he didn't?" he asked.

His grin made my insides melt. "I was smart enough to not give him their names," I paused before adding, "or tell Mary anything except their first names."

"Can't say I blame you." He laughed.

Once the pleasantries were out of the way, Doug asked if Chase's cup situation had been resolved.

"It has." I chuckled. "I probably could have helped him but understand why he wanted John's help."

"Is this his first year playing?"

"It is. I'm lucky my schedule allows me to go to his practices and games. I'm not sure what I'd do otherwise." I hated the idea of someone else taking him, especially since Phil would never get to see his son play sports. Or graduate from school, or go on his first date, or give him fatherly advice when he needed it. He couldn't, but I could. And I would.

Not wanting to think about it anymore, I changed the subject. "Did you play sports as a kid?"

"I did, like Chase I started with tee ball. My dad wanted me to play hockey, he's a huge Blackhawks fan, but I hated it. I played little league for a while but gave it up after I discovered computers and gaming." He chuckled. "I was a total geek by the time I started high school."

He was a geek. Looking at him now, I never would have guessed he wasn't a jock. "Do you like sports?"

"I like watching them, especially baseball and football. How about you? Did you play sports?"

I hadn't. And as an adult I'd only watched them with Phil—so I could spend time with him. Now I'd have to become a fan of whatever sports Chase decided to play.

When we got to The Breakfast Joint, Doug parked and told me to wait a second before hopping out and running around to open my door. It had been a long time since someone had acted like such a gentleman on a date. I'd denied my dates the opportunity to open my car door, but they'd missed other opportunities to act gentlemanly.

The restaurant was cute, with flags and pictures of foods from all around the world hung on the walls and a bright colorful atmosphere. When the hostess showed us to our table, I let Doug have the seat with a line of sight to the front door, figuring he'd feel more comfortable sitting there. Phil said it was a cop thing. John told Mary the same thing, explaining he was never really off-duty.

"This place is really colorful," said Doug as he looked around.

"It is. I like it."

This week's specials were from Turkey and included: Menemen (a dish with eggs, tomatoes, green peppers, and spices such as ground black and red pepper cooked in olive oil), and Shakshouka (described as eggs poached in a sauce of tomatoes, olive oil, peppers, onion, and garlic, spiced with cumin, paprika and cayenne pepper).

The Menemen sounded intriguing, so I ordered it without so much as a glance at the rest of the menu. Doug ordered the other special. We both ordered Turkish coffee.

"Do you come here a lot?" Doug asked after we placed our order.

"No, but now that Chase is a bit older, I'll probably come more often." It'd be a fun way to introduce him to different foods and hopefully expand his palate beyond hot dogs and macaroni and cheese. Though I didn't have high hopes he'd order more than pancakes for the first few years. *Maybe I can convince him to try my dishes.*

The conversation shifted to foods we'd tried, what we liked and what we didn't. Doug told me he'd developed a love for Italian food when he was stationed in Italy. Then he shared some of his European adventure stories. When I asked him why he chose the Air Force over the other branches, he said a recruiter at a college fair sold him.

"It wasn't a hard sell. I loved their high-tech gadgets and ended up signing my intent to enlist that day." His pensive look didn't match his words.

"Did you like it as much as you thought you would?"

"I loved it."

Something in his voice told me there was more to the story, but I didn't want to pry so I changed the subject.

When our server brought us our meals, we inhaled deeply. The heavy scent of rich spices promised us a culinary delight, and they didn't disappoint. We ate in relative silence, only speaking to praise the food or offer each other samples.

While we ate, it occurred to me, based on his timelines, Doug was probably younger than I'd thought. Not that I had a hard number in mind, but I'd assumed he was only a couple of years younger than me. Now I second-guessed my assumption.

Will it be a problem for him if I'm a lot older?

I was about to ask him, but he asked me about the Wyatt Foundation before I could.

This year would be the third annual fundraiser. Mary loved Halloween, so she'd scheduled the first fundraiser as a Halloween bash and went all out with decorations, costumes, dancing, and raffles. Now it was an annual party.

"It's great how much Mary and John do for the community," Doug said.

"It is. They've lived here their whole lives, so they have deep roots."

"Have you always lived here?" he asked.

"No, I grew up in Louisiana and moved here after getting engaged to Phil." We'd met while he was stationed at the local Marine base.

"Is your family still in Louisiana?"

"No, my mom moved here after my Dad died. She said it was because she wanted to see her grandkids, but I think she didn't want to be alone." I sipped my water. "It was a blessing having her here to help with Chase after Phil died."

"Does she still help out?"

"No, she recently got sick and never fully recovered. Sadly her health has been declining ever since." I paused while the sadness washed over me. "She doesn't have the energy to handle him anymore. But we visit her as often as we can." She was his last grandparent and I wanted them to have as much time together as possible.

He nodded in understanding. "Do you have any brothers or sisters?"

"No, I'm an only child." I ate my last bite of egg and closed my eyes in appreciation. When I opened my eyes, I felt heat rush to my cheeks when I saw the look Doug was giving me. I wiped my mouth with my napkin and tried to hide my flushed cheeks.

"How about you? Where are you from?"

"Chicago. Both my parents still live there. So does my older sister."

"Are you close?" I had a feeling they weren't.

"No." He didn't elaborate.

He seemed sad when he talked about his family. I couldn't help but wonder what had happened. Before I could ask anything else, our server brought the bill and started clearing our table.

I would have liked to sit and talk more, but people were waiting so we didn't linger. Doug paid the bill and held the door open for me as we walked out.

"This place is great, thanks for suggesting it." He patted his stomach as he spoke.

"I'm glad you liked it."

We talked more about our families on the ride home. I told him about growing up in a small town in the south, and he told me about growing up in a big city in the north. I joked about how I didn't think I could handle northern winters and he joked that he couldn't handle hurricanes and sweltering summers.

"Wait, aren't summers in Chicago hot and humid?"

He laughed as he answered, "Uh huh."

"And you live in Texas? Where we get hurricanes."

"I do."

I rolled my eyes and shook my head. "You'd be fine in Louisiana."

When he asked about my Dad, I told him he'd died from cancer the year before Phil's accident. His death hit us hard but it wasn't a surprise. He'd been suffering for so long; we almost considered it a blessing that he was finally at peace.

When I asked about his parents, his voice took on a cool edge as he shared what little he did. It wasn't much better when he talked about his sister, who'd joined the family law firm. The almost robotic quality to his voice made it clear this was a sore spot in his history.

"Did your family expect you to join the firm too?"

"They did." His answer was stiff.

I debated changing the subject but had one more question. "Are they disappointed you didn't?" *I have a feeling I know the answer.*

"They are."

"Would you rather talk about something else?"

"I would." Doug released a deep breath and uncurled his fingers, loosening the white-knuckle grip he had on the steering wheel. "Thank you."

After a few seconds of silence Doug apologized for being rude.

"Forgiven. Family can be a touchy subject." I appreciated his apology, but was curious why he had such a negative reaction to talking about his family. I could understand them being disappointed he'd joined the military instead of going to law school, but this felt bigger than that.

"They can be." His chest rose as he inhaled deeply then fell as he slowly released it.

When Doug parked, I wasn't ready for the date to end so before he could say anything, I said, "I have about thirty minutes before I need to leave to pick up Chase. Would you like to come in for a coffee, or I have a pitcher of sweet tea if you'd prefer that?"

"I'd like that," Doug answered with a smile as he shut off the engine.

Chapter 12

Doug

No way in hell was I declining her offer and missing out on the opportunity to extend our date. There'd been a few tense moments when she asked about my family, and I needed to redeem myself for behaving like an ogre. This would give me a chance to show her that wasn't the real me. Unfortunately, my mother had bad timing and I was still on edge after getting her phone call reminding me that my nephew was turning six in a few weeks and asking if I'd be home for his party.

I wouldn't, which irritated her. *Nothing new there.*

None of that was Beth's fault.

When Beth asked me if I wanted coffee or sweet tea as we walked towards the kitchen, I confessed that as a northern guy sweet tea wasn't a normal choice for me, but I'd grown to like it since moving south. Which had surprised me; the only iced tea or sweet tea I'd had back home was from the store and it was always too sweet for my taste. Homemade sweet tea in the south was so much better.

Beth handed me a tall glass filled with ice cubes, amber liquid, and a slice of lemon. "Sometimes I add fruit, but this batch is just plain black tea."

"Thanks." She watched as I took my first sip. It could have been the worst tea I'd ever had, but I wouldn't have told her. Lucky for me, it wasn't. "It's delicious. Way better than the stuff I buy at the store."

"Thank you." Her cheeks turned the cutest shade of pink.

"Beth," I waited for her to look at me, "I'm sorry about earlier. I'm not close with my family, and we recently had a," I searched for the right word, "disagreement and it's still pretty fresh."

"It's okay."

"It's never okay to be rude," I said. "I'll do better next time."

"Thank you for explaining. And Doug, if you ever don't want to talk about something, it's okay to say so."

"Noted." I held my glass up and she tapped hers to mine. "Thank you for understanding."

We talked for a few more minutes. When I saw her look at the clock on her microwave, I asked, "Time to go?"

"It is."

I hid my disappointment while I finished the last of my tea and rinsed out my glass.

"I had a great time today. I'd like to take you out for dinner."

When she lifted her caramel eyes to mine, I held my breath, resisting the urge to brush a wayward curl off her face while I waited for her to answer.

I'd been building up the courage to ask her out for the last three months, and now that we'd had our first date, there was no point pretending I wasn't hooked.

"I'd like that."

I smiled as I released my breath. I'd been worried she'd hesitate after my attitude earlier. Other than that, I thought the date had gone well, and believed she felt the same. I considered myself to be good at reading people, a necessary skill in my line of work, and a helpful one in everyday life. Usually I trusted my ability, but, because of my nerves, today was different.

"Good." I couldn't stop smiling. "Can I call you later to schedule?"

"Sure, Chase is in bed by seven-thirty," she said as she walked me to the door, "so any time after that is good."

I wanted to kiss her, feel her soft lips on mine, but it felt wrong to ask for one after a lunch date. Instead, I lifted her hand and pressed my lips to the back of it. "Thank you for a wonderful afternoon."

Her soft smile and pink cheeks made my heart do a jig. "Thank you, Doug."

It was still early, so I decided to go to the range and get in some trigger time. I went at least once a month, sometimes more if my schedule allowed. *I'll be happy when the SSI range is done.*

The builders were making great time on the training building, having already laid the concrete foundation and put up the walls. A second set of contractors recently broke ground on the outdoor range, but it was a long, drawn-out process to build a hundred-yard range.

The indoor range would be a two-story, twenty-yard open range, allowing for everything from introduction classes to multiple level room clearing. The ranges were ambitious and would take another six to eight months to finish because SSI wasn't taking out loans to pay for it. They didn't have to. The Parker County and Weatherford police departments invested heavily in the training center, allowing them full use for their officers. SSI was footing the rest of the bill.

I stopped home to grab my range bag, rifle, and training log.

After fifteen minutes of shooting, I assessed my targets. *Not my best day.* Most people would look at them and be happy, but I was capable of better. I'd let my mind wander. Never a good idea with a lethal weapon in your hands.

I took a few deep breaths and cleared my mind of all thoughts of Beth.

For the next half hour, I shot with the speed and precision I expected from myself.

The first thing I did when I got home was clean my guns. Afterwards, I jumped in the shower. My mind drifted to Beth as I lathered up— she looked beautiful in her sleeveless top, and slacks that accentuated her curvy hips.

An image of Beth wearing jean shorts and a loose-fitting American flag decorated tank at the Fourth of July BBQ flashed through my mind. My blood rushed south, making me hard.

I laughed at the memory—I'd come 'this' close to asking Jamie who the beautiful woman standing next to his mom was. Though I would have left out the word beautiful because I wasn't the type to broadcast my attraction.

Then I heard John yell. We were being rowdy while playing corn hole and aiming the bags at each other instead of the holes in the boards. It wasn't until I saw Chase that I realized the beautiful woman was Beth. She looked different with sunglasses covering her eyes and her curly brown hair framing her face.

That was the first time I'd seen her curls, and I'd been dreaming about running my hands through them ever since. I took care of myself in the shower, imagining my hands clutching her curls while she was on her knees in front of me.

After throwing on shorts and a t-shirt, I tossed the clothes I'd been wearing in the washer.

I grilled a burger and made myself a Right Side Old Fashioned, a recipe I'd duplicated from my favorite bar in Chicago. Savoring the sweetness of the drink, I reflected on my date with Beth.

The conversation had flowed, and we'd been comfortable enough to feed each other bites of our meals. I wouldn't normally do something so intimate on a first date, but it'd felt natural with Beth.

When should I tell her I'm sterile? The fact that I was already thinking about it was eye opening. I'd dated since my divorce but hadn't considered confessing since I couldn't imagine a future with them.

One lunch date with Beth and I'm already thinking about it.

Which was good in the sense that I liked her enough to be thinking about a possible future.

And bad, because it'd hurt like hell if she dumped me because I can't have kids. I didn't know if she wanted more, or if she'd be open to adoption.

Not exactly first date questions.

But they lingered in my mind. I needed to tell her sooner rather than later; it wasn't fair to either of us to wait until we were invested in the relationship. I didn't want a repeat of what happened with Jane.

The memory of my ex-wife's high-pitched voice as she hurled insults at me still stung. According to her, I'd destroyed her dreams, wasted years of her life, and no woman would ever want me because I was half a man.

I can't believe how fucking blind I was. How many red flags I'd missed, excuses I'd made.

Was I doing the same thing with Beth? Was I ignoring red flag behavior because I wanted to believe she was different?

No way.

I made myself a second Right Side and drank it down quicker than normal. The burn in my throat brought me back to the present. I made another, picked up the Clancy thriller I'd started the week before, and sipped my drink while I read.

The distraction was exactly what I'd needed.

After I finished the novel, I went right back to thinking about Beth. But this time without my ex's voice bouncing around in my head.

I'd learned a lot in the last five years. Like how to read people and how to spot red flags. I felt like I had a good read on Beth and had to trust the Sheppards wouldn't love her as much as they did if she was a bad person. So, while I couldn't predict how she might react when I told her, I took comfort in trusting her not to verbally attack me.

I was about to turn on a movie when my phone buzzed.

Beth.

Thank God no one can see me smiling like a teenage geek who just got a compliment from the head cheerleader.

Chapter 13

Beth

Later that night, after Chase was in bed, I texted Doug and thanked him again for a great date. He asked if Chase was asleep. A few seconds after I texted back, yes with a smile emoji, my phone rang.

Doug. I smiled as I answered, appreciating him wanting to talk rather than text. It felt more personal.

"I thought it'd be easier to talk," he said instead of hello.

I agreed, plus I got to hear his deep, sexy voice.

"I had a great time, too. Are you still interested in a second date?" He sounded unsure of himself.

"I am." I hoped he could hear me smiling, even if he couldn't see it.

"Good, because I'd love to take you to dinner." I blushed at the tone in his voice.

"As long as I can find a babysitter, most nights are open for me. Though finding a babysitter who can stay a little later is easier on weekends."

There was silence from his end. *Was I too forward, assuming I might need a late babysitter? Did he think I wanted to spend the night with him?* I didn't. Well, I did, but I didn't want to rush things.

"I, I just meant–" I stuttered as I rushed to explain.

A soft laugh came over the line. "Is this weekend too soon?"

More than a few butterflies did somersaults in my belly. "Let me make some calls. Is Friday or Saturday better for you?"

I couldn't believe how easy this was. Doug's schedule was chaotic, and I had to work around finding a babysitter, so I'd expected it to be harder to find a day that worked for both of us.

It won't always be this easy. I didn't even know if it'd be this easy this weekend, I still had to find a babysitter.

"My weekend is open, so either one works for me."

Immediately after hanging up, I texted my favorite sitter, Nina, and asked if she was available either Friday or Saturday night.

I was giddy when Nina said she was available Friday. I wasted no time telling Doug.

I saw him every day during the week when he picked up coffee. Some days he ordered for the office, some he didn't.

He's coming in to see me. Which made me smile. A lot. Which didn't go unnoticed.

I had a goofy grin on my face all day Friday. At least, that's what Mary told me, and I had no reason to doubt her. I was like a giddy schoolgirl and couldn't stop thinking about my date. When I'd asked Doug where we were going, he said it was a surprise and told me I should dress up, "but not formal," he'd added. Fancy but not formal, I could do that. I tried to guess where it might be, but soon gave up. He probably wasn't taking me anywhere in Weatherford, and I didn't know Fort Worth or Dallas well enough to figure it out.

Mary shooed me out the door as soon as I clocked out, calling out as I reached the door, "Have fun tonight, and call me in the morning."

After showering and putting on a green long sleeve dress that showed off my assets, and played down my muffin top, I did my hair and makeup. I rarely fussed with my hair, usually opting for a bun since it had to be up for work, and I liked it out of my face when I was chasing Chase around. In the end, I left it down. I did my eyes a little darker than normal, which meant adding mascara to the liner I usually wore and brushing some glittery shadow on my lids. I finished the look with red lipstick, hoping it didn't scream, "I'm desperate."

Nina arrived a few minutes before five, and a cheerful Chase immediately dragged her to the backyard. He wanted to show off his new water dinosaurs (sharks). The warm fall day was perfect for letting him play outside in his kiddie pool.

"Chase, I'll be home after you're in bed, so can I get my goodnight kiss now?"

"Okay." He got up, wiped his hands on his wet shorts, and then wrapped his arms around me. For a half a second I thought about telling him not to hug me, but kids grew up so fast and before long he wouldn't want to hug his mom goodbye. *I'm not missing out on a single hug.* Dirty hands and wet shorts be damned.

"Be good for Miss Nina, okay?"

"I promise."

I squeezed him, and sent him back to play. I asked Nina if I had Chase sized handprints on my back, grateful when she said no. Out of habit, I reminded her of the house rules. Not that I had many; no boys or friends over, no drinking or drugs, and keep the doors locked. Then I went back inside to wait for Doug.

Doug handed me a bouquet of yellow roses and white daisies when he picked me up.

"Is it okay if I take them with us instead of putting them in water?"

"Of course, but we have plenty of time."

"It's not that, I'm afraid Chase won't want to let us leave if he sees you." Guild washed over me as I explained. Doug and I dating wasn't a secret from the adults in my life, but I hadn't told Chase yet. And the last thing I wanted to do was explain it to him in front of Doug. I couldn't risk him getting attached.

"Ah, that makes sense." Doug nodded as he scanned the room. "We should go then." He stepped back and held out his arm.

"Thanks for understanding." I locked the door before putting my free hand in the crook of his offered elbow.

When I asked him where he was taking me, he smiled and said, "Dallas."

Which hardly answered my question. I didn't want to be a pain, but now my interest was piqued. I asked again, but made a joke of it.

"Is it some kind of top-secret location that you can't tell me? Or you could, but then you'd have to kill me?"

He laughed. "I can tell you without having to kill you." He looked over and flashed me a dazzling smile. "It's this great little family-owned Italian place I discovered while on a job in Dallas. It looks like a hole in the wall from the outside, but the inside is nice, and the food is fabulous."

"Sounds delicious." I loved pasta. "What's your favorite dish?"

"Shrimp Scampi. It sounds simple, but it's the best I've ever had."

He told me about a few other dishes he'd tried from their authentic Italian menu. Just hearing him talk about it had my mouth watering. *Please don't let my stomach growl.* I'd been so excited for tonight I'd forgotten to eat lunch.

Doug was once again the perfect gentleman, opening my door and helping me out of his truck. Putting his hand on my lower back protectively, possessively, as we walked across the parking lot. It lingered there as we approached the hostess.

Apparently, he came here often enough that the hostess recognized him. She greeted him with a huge smile, which quickly faded as she realized he was on a date.

Doug's description was spot on, the outside wasn't much to look at, but the inside was clean and decorated in an old-world Italian motif. At least, I thought it was. I'd never been to Italy so I could have been wrong. It didn't matter; I liked it.

After we sat, I asked Doug how often he came here.

"I come about twice a month, more if I'm in Dallas for work," He paused and reached across the table for my hand, "I've never brought a date here."

His confession—I was the first—made me feel special. *That's why the hostess looked disappointed.*

"I think the hostess likes you." I wasn't planning on saying anything, but the way he was rubbing the back of my hand with his thumb had me a little scatter-brained and I blurted it out.

"Really? I've never noticed." He turned to look at her.

I found that hard to believe, given the sad puppy-dog look she kept sending his way. Maybe she'd been too subtle for him to realize she was flirting. I wasn't worried about it. he only had eyes for me.

Everything on the menu looked so good it was hard to decide. After much deliberation, I ordered the special, sea scallop Alfredo, earning me a "good choice," from Doug. Doug ordered the shrimp scampi, saying he couldn't resist, and suggested the fried ravioli with their homemade marinara sauce as an appetizer.

When our server asked if we wanted anything to drink, I asked him to suggest a wine that paired well with my meal. Doug did the same.

The entire meal was to die for. I was tempted to lick the bowl after we finished the ravioli; the marinara was that good. When our meals came, I tried his scampi, and he tried my Alfredo. Both were mouth-wateringly delicious, though I liked mine better. His scampi had a bit more zing than I liked.

Our server asked if we wanted to see the dessert menu as he cleared our dishes.

"I'm so stuffed I couldn't possibly eat another bite." I leaned back. "I may regret it later, but I'm going to pass. Thank you."

"Would you like another glass of wine?" Doug asked.

"No, thank you."

Doug settled our bill, left a generous cash tip for our server, and walked me back to his truck.

"What time do you need to be home?"

"I told Nina I'd be home by midnight."

We looked at the clock on his dashboard. It was just past eight-thirty; the drive home was about ninety minutes.

"Any objections to taking a walk?"

Object? I'd be thrilled. "None at all."

Chapter 14

Doug

After dinner, we talked as I drove to the canal walk, a place known for its scenery and romantic setting. During the day, the area was packed with families and tourists, but by nightfall, the crowd usually thinned out.

Without thinking, I raised Beth's hand to my lips and placed a soft kiss there after I helped her out of my truck. Because I never took my gaze off her face, I saw the slight blush on her cheeks. If I could make her blush by kissing the back of her hand, I wondered what would happen if I slowly kissed up her arm to her neck.

Fuck. Who cares what it'll do to her. I'm making myself hard just thinking about it. When I stepped back to close her door, I used it as cover so I could quickly adjust myself without her seeing me.

"Have you ever been here before?" I asked.

"No, but I've been to places like it. My friends and I used to love going to the boardwalk when I was in high school."

I reached for Beth's hand and smiled when she didn't hesitate to lace her fingers with mine. Holding Beth's small, soft hand felt like the most natural thing in the world.

It was a beautiful evening, and I considered myself lucky to be here with Beth. The sky was clear enough that we could see the crescent moon, and the light breeze coming off the canal was the perfect complement to the warm evening weather. Every few yards, a fresh smell would fill our noses as we passed by different restaurants. If we hadn't just filled ourselves, the aromas might have been enticing.

I was taking my normal long strides as we walked, not thinking about Beth being in heels. Or walking at a relaxed pace instead of marching along like she was on a mission. Not wanting to drag her behind me like a caveman, I adjusted my steps to match hers.

After a few minutes, Beth stopped and turned towards the water. Lights from the restaurants and shops surrounding the canal reflected on the dark waves in rippling colors, giving the water a hypnotic quality.

"It's pretty," Beth said softly beside me.

"It is." I wasn't usually one to stop and smell the roses, or watch lights reflect on the water, but it was nice. *Better than nice because I'm doing it with Beth.* The colorful lights reflected in her eyes, as she watched a tour boat sailing by, giving them a magical quality. It took all my strength to break the spell, so I didn't lean down and kiss her then and there.

Chapter 15

Beth

Strolling along a canal walk with Doug was a much different experience than going to the beach boardwalks as a teen in Louisiana. Back then, it'd been all about hanging out and hooking up, so we'd barely noticed the beauty. But tonight, I noticed everything. The way the lights reflected on the water, the couples strolling hand in hand, the feeling of Doug's large, strong hand holding mine, and the sounds and smells drifting from the different restaurants.

"You want to stop for a second?" Doug asked.

"We don't need to, I was just watching some geese play, but I think they're done now."

He nodded. "There's a chocolate shop a few doors down and I hear their ice cream is fantastic. Want to grab some and sit near the water?"

The little girl in me jumped for joy. I loved ice cream, especially the soft, creamy, extra rich kind they served at The

Chocolatier. I usually bought whatever ice cream was on sale when I went grocery shopping so this would be a real treat. Doug's pupils dilated when I licked my lips in anticipation.

"Their ice cream is decadent." I tried to sound calm, cool, and collected, but the sparkle in Doug's eyes, and the grin he didn't hide fast enough, told me I'd failed. *It's not like it's a bad thing I'm excited about getting ice cream.*

"Come on, let's go." He pulled my hand playfully, leading the way.

When we got to the door, Doug let go of my hand so he could open it for me. A lot of modern women complained about men doing the little things like opening doors for them, but I liked it. I didn't feel any less capable, nor did I feel insulted by it. Sure, I could open my own door, but I appreciated his old school manners.

It was something Phil had done for me. Something John did for Mary, and their boys did for Meg and Emily. *It's something I'll teach Chase.* After I taught him to say please and thank you—he often got so excited he'd forgot to use them.

The blast of cool air from the shop wasn't the only reason a shiver ran down my spine; Doug had run his large, warm palm down my spine, settling it on my lower back as I walked by.

The Chocolatier wasn't just an ice cream shop. They also had homemade fudge, assorted truffles, and a variety of chocolates delicious enough to make anyone lose control. I almost drooled as the thick, rich smell of chocolate reached my nose. I'd never been to the one on the canal, but they had a few shops near us, and I'd been to the one in Dallas a few times.

I wasn't the only one reacting to the displays and aromas of the shop. Doug inhaled deeply as he looked around. "It smells good in here."

"It does. I miss the days when I could order the largest ice cream with extra whip cream, but I can't afford that luxury anymore." Doug didn't see me pat my belly.

"Well, it's on me so you can order as much ice cream and as many chocolates as you want." We stepped forward as the line ahead of us moved.

I laughed. "Thank you, but that's not what I meant. I meant my waistline can't afford it anymore. I'm not as young or as active as I used to be."

Doug took a second and looked me up and down before saying, "You look great. Beautiful." He tucked a wayward curl behind my ear, sending another round of shivers down my spine. "And we all deserve a guilt-free treat once in a while."

Easy for him to say. It was obvious to anyone with eyes he worked out. All the time. He didn't have to worry about every spoon of ice cream, every bite of cookie, or every sip of wine sticking to his hips and thighs.

"Thanks." I looked up and saw our reflection in the wall mirror. The bright lights in the shop made the displays look enticing, but they didn't do much for me. They made the gray in my hair and the lines around my mouth and eyes stand out. I self-consciously tucked the offending hairs behind my ear, wishing I'd thought to dye it.

How old is Doug? I'd meant to ask him, but it'd never felt like the right time. I'd assumed he was only a few years younger than me, but now, seeing us side by side in the mirror, I wasn't so sure.

"You're welcome." His smile didn't quite reach his wrinkle-free eyes, his expression curious.

It was probably because I wasn't good at hiding my thoughts and feelings, and as a PI Doug was more observant than most people. He'd likely picked up on my uncertainty.

Luckily, it was almost our turn and we had to focus on what flavor we wanted. The Chocolatier always offered eight flavors, four never changed and four rotated daily. I scanned the flavor of the day selection, and quickly made my decision.

"What are you getting?" Doug asked without taking his eyes off the display.

"The chocolate with sea salt caramel swirl." I pointed to the half empty bucket. "Have you decided?"

"Hmmm… I'm debating between mint chocolate chip and chocolate."

"You can order half and half." I suggested.

"Problem solved." He rubbed his hands together in anticipation.

"What can I get you?" the woman behind the counter asked as we stepped up.

When Doug nodded to me, I placed my order for a small bowl with no extras. Then Doug ordered his, a large bowl with two flavors.

"You want anything else? Maybe some chocolates?" Doug turned towards the chocolate display I'd been doing my best to ignore.

It was filled with assorted chocolates, including my favorites: dark chocolate sea salt caramels and cashew turtles. Everything looked so good, but after eating all of my too-delicious-to-stop-eating-even-after-I-was-full dinner, I barely had room for the ice cream we'd just ordered.

"I'm good. Thanks."

After getting our ice creams, we walked to a bench that faced the canal and sat down. We ate our first few bites in silence, savoring the creamy goodness.

"How is it?" I asked.

"Delicious. I'm glad I got both." He smiled as he brought his spoon to his mouth. "How's yours?"

"Heavenly." I was eating it slowly, enjoying every bite. "Want to try it?"

He looked at me like he couldn't believe what he'd just heard. And to be fair, I wasn't sure I believed it either. It was really good, and I had half as much as he did.

He must have read my mind, because he countered with, "Tell you what, I'll trade you bites."

I could do that. I liked mint chocolate chip, especially when it wasn't green. Something about the fake green color in ice cream always turned me off, even if it didn't affect the taste.

"Deal." We swapped bites and commented on how good the other person's choices were.

"Growing up, I thought mint ice cream had to be green," Doug said as he scooped a bite with a little of both flavors.

I laughed and thought about telling him I'd just had the same thought, but his comment provided the perfect segue to ask his age. Though I wasn't sure I wanted to find out. What if he was a lot younger than me? Would it bother me? Would it bother him? *Does he have any idea how old I am?* I doubted it, because I didn't think he would've asked me out if he did.

I lowered my bowl and turned on the bench, so I was facing him. "Doug, can I ask you a question?"

"Of course."

Great, now that I'd started the conversation, I wasn't sure how to actually ask without sounding rude. *Best to just do it.*

"How old are you?" I blurted out before I lost my nerve.

When he turned to look at me, he didn't just turn his head, he shifted his body, so he was giving me his undivided attention.

"Thirty-two," he stated matter-of-factly.

I cringed. *He's nine years younger.* It might not be a big issue if I wasn't past child-bearing years, and he was at the age most people started a family.

"Is that a problem?" Doug didn't blink as he waited for me to answer.

"No, but I'm quite a bit older."

If he was surprised, he hid it well. Maybe he already knew. After all, he was a private investigator and it'd be easy enough to find out. Hell, all he had to do was ask someone at the office.

"You can't be that much older." He sounded incredulous.

I felt my cheeks flush at the compliment, even if he didn't realize how much of one it was. I looked at my ice cream to avoid meeting his gaze as I answered, "I'm forty-two."

"Really?" His surprise lingered between us. "You look great for your age."

If I hadn't already been blushing, I would have then. Guys had told me I looked good for my age before, but it always sounded like lip service. The way Doug said it, the strength of conviction in his voice, made me believe it.

He was definitely earning his brownie points tonight.

"Thanks," I said shyly.

"Beth?" He waited for me to look at him. "Is the age difference a problem for you?"

I took a second to think about it. *Is it?* I didn't think it was. But I already had kids, a kid, and he might want his own someday. Which meant it might be a problem for him down the road.

But no, it wasn't a problem for me. I liked Doug for who he was—a responsible well-mannered man—his age didn't change that.

"It's not. Is it a problem for you?" I trusted him to tell me if it was.

"Nope." He grinned, putting me at ease.

The sudden, deep sound of a boat horn interrupted us, putting an end to our conversation as we both turned towards the water.

Doug glanced at his watch. "We should probably get on the road." He held out his hand for my empty cup.

After tossing them in a nearby trash can, he reached for my hand again. As we walked, I replayed our brief conversation and searched for clues. Doug hadn't hesitated when he said our age gap wasn't a problem. He hadn't even spared a single second to think about it. I over-thought myself to the brink of doubt. Did he say it so I'd feel better? Would I have to worry about it in the future?

Or maybe he doesn't want kids.

That'd be a problem; I was a package deal.

His response hadn't convinced me the difference in our ages wouldn't be a problem in the future, but, at least for tonight, I could pretend it wasn't.

Chapter 16

Doug

Late Tuesday morning I knocked on the doorframe of John's office before walking in. He held up his hand, causing me to pause. His lips curled into a soft smile as he said, "I won't forget." Pause. "Yes, dear." Pause. "Love you too."

I rarely thought about it, but, John and Jack looked a lot alike. They had the same piercing amber eyes and thick wavy brown hair. *John has more gray.* They looked more like brothers than Jack and Jamie, who took after his mom with his thin dark hair and kind hazel eyes.

He looked up and waved me in after putting his phone face down on his desk. "What can I do for you, Doug?"

"I got a hit on Will. A traffic cam picked him up near an established homeless camp." Will's parents had hired SSI to find him after he went missing two days ago. They'd reported it to the Fort Worth police as well, but the

FWPD was short-staffed and overworked so looking for an eighteen-year-old drug addict with a history of running away wasn't a top priority for them. "I'm heading there now to search the area."

He nodded as he asked, "Want someone to go with you?"

"Nah, I got it. I'll keep Meg updated via text."

"Sounds good. Be careful out there. A random needle poke or bite can do a lot of damage."

"No, sir." In addition to my soft body armor, I planned on wearing my thick leather jacket and gloves, despite the warm fall weather, for protection. They'd prevent most incidental sticks from puncturing my skin. I wasn't willing to risk getting stuck and being exposed to drugs, or worse, an infectious disease that could mean a death sentence if not diagnosed and treated fast enough.

On my way out, I let Meg know where I was going. When she reminded me to check in regularly, I grinned and said, "Yes, ma'am." Meg was practicing her Mama Bear skills on the SSI team.

Half an hour later I parked a few blocks from the bridge and circled around to the far end. I held my gag reflex in check when the wind shifted, filling my nose with the scent of stale cigarettes, urine, and body odor. I steeled myself for the job at hand, knowing the smell would get stronger with every step I took towards the camp.

As I approached, I scanned the makeshift tents and cardboard box homes. If I was lucky, I'd spot him right away and convince him to leave without having to talk to anyone else. I had a pocket full of five and ten-dollar bills to loosen their tongues, just in case. I also had two photos of Will, one clean and sober, the other from a previous arrest when he'd been strung out.

Lady Luck wasn't on my side.

The homeless camp was about the length of two city blocks. *This could take a while.* Before talking to anyone, I sent a quick text to Meg to check in, then put my phone in my front pocket along with my wallet. I made sure my jacket covered my gun before taking out the photos of Will.

I steeled my resolve as the wind picked up. The smell filled my nose again, leaving a nasty taste in my mouth. As I entered the camp, people turned away or hung their heads to avoid making eye contact.

The hair on the back of my neck stood up as I walked on. Knowing they were watching me, I glanced back every few steps to make sure no one followed me.

Only one person didn't avoid looking at me. If fact, he'd openly watched me as I walked down the street. When I got close, I lifted my chin in greeting and asked, "Can you help me?"

"Who are you?" He crossed his arms in front of his chest and tilted his head back, attempting to look down at me. An intimidation technique that might have worked if I wasn't five inches taller, a good forty pounds heavier, and armed.

I rounded my shoulders, hoping he'd be cooperative if he thought he'd succeeded in intimidating me. *I can pretend for a few minutes if that's what it takes.*

"Name's Doug. I'm looking for someone." I held up the pictures. "Goes by Will, maybe you've seen him?"

"You a cop?" He asked as he looked at the pictures. Recognition flashed across his eyes.

"No. His parents hired my investigation company to find him and bring him home. They're worried about him." I appealed to what I hoped was his compassionate side.

"He's here." He tilted his head towards the far end of the encampment. "But I doubt he'll want to leave with you." He spat at the ground between us.

I nodded. Would he be a problem if I had to drag Will out? Just because I could handle him in a fight didn't mean I wanted to. I handed him a ten and thanked him for his help.

I turned and walked a few more yards, actively listening for footsteps matching my cadence behind me, before spotting Will coming out of a tattered, makeshift tent.

Slowing down my steps, I studied him as I approached. He looked more defeated than defiant, giving me hope he'd come willingly. Though I didn't like the look of the bigger, older guy he was talking to. Something about his eyes made me suspect he was cruel.

"Excuse me, Will?"

Will turned towards me and looked me up and down, his expression changing as he realized I might be a cop. Hope flashed across his bloodshot eyes a second before fear replaced it. He looked down at the ground. His eyes were puffy and covered in bruises in varying shades of green, blue, and purple. *Poor kid.*

All I had to do was convince him to leave with me. The flash of hope I saw in his eyes meant he probably wouldn't put up a fight. Especially if I offered him a warm meal and some cash.

But it wasn't Will who answered me, it was the mean looking guy standing near him. "Who the fuck are you?"

I kept my eyes focused on Will, but moved so my body was turned towards the other guy. I felt the energy around me shift as a small audience formed to watch. I did some quick math, knowing I could handle the mean guy if it came to a confrontation, and maybe one or two from the crowd, without having to draw my gun.

Maybe.

I didn't like the odds of getting out of here without firing a shot if the crowd turned into a violent mob. I took a few deep breaths, to gain control of my rapidly accelerating heart rate, and instantly regretted it, thanks to the stench.

I answered his question but directed my attention towards Will. "My name is Doug, and your parents hired me to bring you home. They're worried about you."

Will glanced over his shoulder just as Cruel Guy answered, "He ain't goin nowhere." Will flinched when the guy grabbed his shoulder.

Possessive grip. Noted. A quick glance told me the crowd was still keeping its distance. *For now.*

"Will, do you want to go home?" I kept my voice calm as I shifted my body weight, ready to step between them if I had to.

"I said, he ain't goin' nowhere. He owes me money."

Will tried to step forward, but the guy pulled him back.

I quickly scanned the small crowd around us, keeping the cruel guy in my peripheral vision at all times. The general body language of the crowd didn't give me confrontation vibes. *Hopefully they won't interfere.*

I took a step towards him, hands held out in front of me, palms up. I wanted him to think I was submissive, and to imply I was unarmed. "How much does he owe you?" I was sure whatever it was would be grossly inflated since we both knew I was asking with the intent of paying off Will's debt.

Not anticipating paying off someone's debt, and not wanting to risk the loss if shit went south, I hadn't brought a ton of cash.

"Five hundred," he paused, "plus interest." His smirk reminded me of a shady used car salesman. If he thought I'd leave without a fight because he'd thrown out an impossible number, he was sorely mistaken.

I didn't have five hundred, so I'd have to negotiate, or fight, our way out. I'd prefer not having to fight, but I would if I had to. I wasn't leaving without Will. He looked hurt and terrified, and I didn't think he'd survive long if I left him.

I pulled the cash from my jacket pocket, knowing the total was only about a quarter of what Will supposedly owed, not including the unspecified interest.

"I don't have that much." I counted the money slowly in front of him, knowing a hundred and thirty-five in cash was more than he'd likely seen in a long time.

He licked his lips as he looked from the cash to Will, calculating. "I'll tell you what. You give me that, and when you come back with the rest, you can take Willie here home with you." He reached for the money.

I pulled my hand back. "That's not going to happen. I'll get you the rest, but Will comes with me." I stepped forward, stretching to my full height as I squared my shoulders and straightened my knees, hoping to intimidate him.

"We both know if you leave with Will, you won't come back."

"And we both know if I leave without him, you'll raise the amount." I kept my voice even as I stepped closer still. I'd been watching Will slowly edge towards me as I negotiated. "Will, walk towards me." I held a hand out towards him.

Will started to move in my direction but his dealer moved fast, faster than I would've thought possible, and grabbed Will by the elbow. He yanked him back with so much force, Will tripped over his feet and fell to the ground. He let out a started cry when his head smacked the ground with a sickening thud. He clutched his head as he curled into the fetal position.

Fuck!

In a flash of inspiration, I threw the money behind me as I closed the distance between me and Will's dealer with two long strides.

He held his hands up to block me, but I was too big, too strong, and too pissed off for him to stop my advance.

After the longest thirty-second fight I'd ever been in, I got past his flailing arms and ended it. He crumpled to the ground, unconscious, after I connected with a solid punch to the left side of his head.

I scanned behind me to make sure the crowd was staying back. They'd collected the money and were watching me, wide-eyed. No one moved to interfere. *Thank God.*

Ignoring the scratches on my face, I crouched by Will and carefully lifted him so I could check his head. He had a nasty gash, but it'd heal.

Thankfully, no one challenged me as I escorted Will out of the camp.

I sucked in big gulps of air; grateful it was fresher with every step. Will kept pace with me but didn't speak. Once he was safely in my truck, I grabbed my trauma bag from my back seat. I cleaned and wrapped his head before cleaning the scratches on my face with an alcohol wipe.

"Thank you," Will mumbled as I started the engine.

"You're welcome."

I called Meg as soon as I was on the road.

"Hey Meg, I have Will. I'm stopping for food then bringing him to the office. Can you call his parents?"

"Of course."

Something in my voice must have sounded off because she asked, "Are you okay?"

"Yeah." Then because I figured she'd still worry, I added, "nothing but a few scratches, I promise."

"The kind of scratches that barely bleed, or the kind that need stitches?"

I couldn't blame Meg for not trusting any of us if we said we had a scratch. Early in her relationship with Jack, he'd told her a wound was only a scratch. It had required sixteen stitches. She'd been giving us all shit ever since.

"The barely bleed kind."

"Good. I'll call Will's parents. See you soon."

I looked at the clock on my dashboard. *Fuck.* It was almost five, and I was supposed to see Beth tonight after Chase went to bed. I had no idea what time I'd get home, or if I'd be good company.

"Doug?" Meg sounded worried.

"Yeah, sorry."

"Need me to do anything else?"

"No, I'm good. Just let me know once you've reached Will's parents."

"Will do. Drive safe."

"Thanks." I checked on Will, who was staring out the window, looking dazed.

I stopped at a fast-food joint. While Will ate, I texted Beth and asked to reschedule. I apologized and told her there was some trouble on my assignment.

Are you okay?

I am.

Good. Next time lead with that.

Noted. Sorry.

I owe Beth on hell of an apology when I get home. I'd call later and give her a proper explanation.

At the office, it felt good to seeing Will reunited with his parents. I prayed he'd get the help he needed and stay sober. As soon as they left; Meg, Jack, and I locked up.

I walked back to my truck on autopilot, wanting nothing more than to go home and take a long, hot shower to wash the day off my skin. And maybe have a Right Side to help take the edge off.

Chapter 17

Beth

The first text I got from Doug was a request to reschedule and an apology for the late notice. The second said he ran into some trouble with his assignment.

Trouble? What kind of trouble? *Is he hurt?*

My heart skipped a beat as a dozen scenarios flashed through my mind: none of them good.

Fear set in as I remembered how I felt the day I got *that* knock on the door.

The day the County Sherriff came to our home to tell me Phil was dead.

The day I lost the man I loved, the father of my unborn child.

The day my world turned upside down.

I took a few deep breaths to steady myself and wiped at the tears rolling down my cheek.

I didn't like how it felt to worry about Doug, or how quickly it had brought back the heartache of that day.

Can I go through that again?

It felt like a boulder had been lifted off my chest when Doug said he was fine but had to stay with his client.

Then, irrationally, I got mad. Anger was easier to deal with than fear.

He needs to start conversations, regardless of the format, with the fact that he was uninjured. His job was dangerous, so it was never a given.

A reality I understood all too well.

A little while later, Doug called sounding like he was in a wind tunnel.

"Where are you?" I shouted, thinking he probably wouldn't be able to hear me otherwise.

"Sorry, all my windows are down." There was a brief pause, while the noise lessened. "Better?"

"Yeah, thanks. How are you?"

"I'm good, but in desperate need of a shower."

"How's the client?" I knew he couldn't give me any details, but he should be able to tell me if the kid was okay.

"He's home with his parents."

"Are you on your way home?"

"I am." Pause. "I'm sorry, can I call you later? I need to roll my windows back down."

I could only imagine what had happened for his truck to smell so bad. "Of course. Drive safe."

I didn't have a chance to give him a piece of my mind for making me worry. *I'll tell him when he calls back.*

I looked over at Chase. He was engrossed in an animated dinosaur movie, some of his favorite plastic ones lined up beside him, completely oblivious to the fact his mom's emotions had gone haywire in the last few minutes. *Thank God for that.*

"Chase, time to pick up and get ready for bed."

"But my movie's not done."

"You can finish it tomorrow after dinner." Bedtime was never easy with Chase. "Come on, pick up your crayons."

"Okay, just let me finish this part."

I sighed and counted to three so I could find some patience. "You have two minutes."

Twenty minutes later Chase was asleep. He never wanted to go to bed, but almost always fell asleep before I finished reading his bedtime story.

I poured myself a glass of wine and turned on a rom-com. I didn't have the emotional capacity for anything else. The opening credits had barely ended before my phone rang.

Doug sounded much better. After apologizing again, he told me he'd taken a long, scalding hot shower, and scheduled a deep clean for his truck's interior.

"Thankfully, I can drop it off first thing in the morning." Then he explained why he and his truck were in such desperate need of cleaning.

I remembered the stories Phil and John would tell about people vomiting or relieving themselves in their squad cars, and how awful it would smell until it could be detailed. *Poor guy.* We talked for a little while longer then rescheduled our plans for the following night.

"I'm sorry again for having to reschedule."

"I totally understand." I was disappointed but understood. It came with the territory when dating someone whose job was unpredictable.

Not to mention dangerous.

Did I really want to get involved with a man who risked his life to save others? *Am I ready for the chaos that comes with his schedule, the risk that comes with his job? Would it be fair to Chase?* The rescheduled dates, the canceled plans, the missed holidays?

The freak storms that caused life-ending accidents?

Could I put Chase through that?

"Thanks for understanding, Beth. I'll see you tomorrow."

"You're welcome. Good night."

I finished my wine and poured myself another glass. I barely paid attention to the movie as my mind kept pondering the reality of dating Doug. Before long, my mind drifted to his client. Doug hadn't shared much, but he had mentioned the homeless camp, and the drug addiction. I couldn't help thinking about how I'd feel, what I'd do, if Chase ended up in a situation like that. I'd love him and support him, of course, but would I be able to provide the tough love required to help him? Could I force him into rehab and therapy? I'd like to think I could, if that was what he needed, but I didn't really know.

And I hope I never find out.

I finished my second glass of wine and debated pouring another. Drowning out the negative thoughts in a third glass didn't sound like a bad idea. But having a third glass in such a short period of time would leave me feeling like shit, so I decided against it. *I'm not as young as I used to be.*

After washing my glass, I re-corked the bottle and put it in the fridge. My mind wandered back to Doug's client as I got ready for bed. As I turned off my light, I prayed to God Chase would never want, or feel the need, to use drugs.

Chapter 18

Beth

The next night, Doug came over after Chase went to bed. It wasn't a date, per se; all we'd be doing was sitting on my couch watching TV or talking. I changed into a nice shirt and applied a little lip gloss anyway. *It never hurts to look good.*

The first thing I noticed when I opened the door was The Chocolatier bag in Doug's hands. The thrill of seeing the bag was quickly replaced with worry—Doug's face looked like he'd gone a round with an angry cat, and lost.

He said he didn't get hurt.

"What happened?" I shut the door behind him and turned the deadbolt. It was compulsive for me to lock my doors, both in my car and at home.

"A few scratches, that's all." He handed me the bag, and changed the subject, "I hope you don't mind that I brought ice cream as an apology instead of flowers."

"Not at all." Instead of taking the bag, I reached up and turned his head so I could look at his scratches more closely.

Doug endured my examination, a patient smile on his lips. "Is this the worst of it?" They didn't look deep enough to scar.

"Yes, and I washed them out with alcohol onsite and hydrogen peroxide after I got home."

I nodded as he talked, my eyes scanning the bare skin on his strong arms looking for evidence of other injuries.

"Beth, honestly," he lifted my chin with his free hand, "these scratches are my only injuries."

"Okay." Men like Doug tended to underplay their injuries, so my skepticism was warranted. I nodded as I mumbled, "Good. Good." My concern slowly subsided.

"Come here," he said as he set the bag on the counter and pulled me into his arms. "I'm okay, I promise," he whispered in my ear before kissing the top of my head. When he pulled away, he asked, "Are you ready for some ice cream?"

I wiped away a wayward tear, this one from relief, as I stepped back. "Always. What flavors did you get?"

"Brownie Delight and Pistachio. Please tell me you like at least one of them," Doug said as he took the containers out of the bag.

"I like both. Though I'm not a fan of generic pistachio, it always tastes fake to me."

"And it's green. What is it with companies making ice cream green?" He laughed. "Grab some bowls, we'll split them. Unless there's one you want all to yourself."

"I'm good with sharing." I handed him two bowls. "Do you want anything to drink? I have beer, wine, water, coffee–"

"I'm good for now. Thanks."

Doug split the two large servings of ice cream in half, which meant I was getting more than I would have given myself. I was thinking of ways I could work off the extra calories when Doug handed me a bowl.

"Apology ice cream is calorie free, so enjoy."

Damn it. I needed to get better at not broadcasting my thoughts all over my face.

We sat on the couch, almost close enough to touch, but didn't turn on the TV. He told me how he got his scratches and picking up his truck after the interior was cleaned.

"Did they get it all out?" I asked.

"It's hard to tell, right now the disinfectant is so strong I think it killed off my sense of smell. I've been airing it out since I picked it up."

I felt bad for him. "Hopefully all the smells will dissipate soon."

"Hopefully." He shook his head as he chuckled. "How was your day?"

He's even tempered. Not the kind of guy to throw a fit about things he couldn't change. Not once had he mentioned billing the clients for the cleaning. Though I was confident John would cover it, once he found out, because it had happened on the job. But it said something about Doug that he wasn't expecting or demanding it.

"A little stressful. Chase wandered off at the park today and gave Angela and Shawna a scare." I didn't tell him I'd panicked when they called; he didn't need to know I'd had a few heart palpitations as they recounted the story.

Luckily, he'd ran back as soon as he heard them calling his name and was standing safely at their sides when they called me.

"He chased a frog behind a bush so they couldn't see him. He came running, carrying said frog, when they called him. He was so excited, he tripped and fell."

"Is he okay?" I could hear the concern in his voice, and see it in his eyes.

"He is. He scraped his hands and knees a little when he fell, but he was more upset about losing the frog."

"Poor kid."

"He wasn't a happy camper when I picked him up, not only was he sad he'd lost his frog, he was worried he'd get in trouble for wandering off. He calmed down after I cleaned him up, put dino Band-Aids on his knees, and reassured him he wasn't in trouble."

He wasn't in trouble, but that didn't mean he didn't get a talking to about the dangers of walking away from Angela and Shawna. Chase didn't wander off intentionally, he was just a typical kid who was easily distracted, especially when animals were involved.

"Then I made him his favorite foods, dinosaur shaped mac and cheese and a hotdog."

"He's really into dinosaurs, isn't he?"

"They're his favorite things. He's been into them for over a year now, which means he'll probably change his mind soon."

Doug laughed.

I was only half done with my ice cream but couldn't eat anymore. "Will you be offended if I save the rest for later?"

"Of course not."

When I came back from putting our bowls away, I sat just a hair closer to Doug. We still weren't touching, but a slight shift by either of us and our legs would make contact.

We leaned back on the couch and relaxed while we talked. We starting talking about our favorite TV shows while deciding what to watch. I liked comedies and fantasy, while he liked crime shows, sci-fi, and documentaries. We never turned on the TV. Doug admitted to playing video games more often than watching TV. I could relate, I read more than I watched TV. Well, more than I watched what I wanted to. The TV was often on as background noise for Chase when he played.

"I was one of those awkward, skinny, gamer geeks in high school." He admitted with a self-deprecating laugh.

I still had a hard time imagining him as a geek. But I knew he was because I'd heard the SSI guys talk about his mad skills, their words not mine. It was one of the reasons they'd hired him. The rest of the team wasn't computer inept, but Doug was brilliant.

"It's hard to visualize you as a skinny geek." I bumped my knee into his as I laughed.

"Yup, I was a total computer and gaming geek." He didn't move his leg.

The heat of his large, muscular thigh against mine was distracting.

I forced myself to not think about his body touching mine and asked, "When did you stop being a gamer geek?"

"I'll let you know when it happens." He chuckled as he stretched one long, strong arm on the couch behind me, leaning a little closer as he did.

I could feel my heart beating faster in my ears.

"You're not awkward or skinny anymore." I held eye contact as he reached out and brushed my cheek with his knuckles.

"No." His grin did funny things to me.

My voice was barely above a whisper when I asked, "When did it change?"

Doug drifted closer.

I can feel his breath on my lips. I glanced down at his lips and licked mine.

"Does it matter?"

I shook my head. It did not, not one bit.

Doug lips gently brushed mine. An invitation.

I shouldn't, not here. What if Chase wakes up?

Doug's scruff tickled my chin as he waited.

Do I really need to worry about it?

Chase was a solid sleeper, and if he did happen to wake up he wouldn't come downstairs. He screamed my name until I went to his room.

There's no reason I shouldn't kiss Doug, right here, right now.

I parted my lips just enough to release a sigh as I leaned in to return the kiss. Doug cupped the back of my head, gently holding me in place. Not that I had any intention of moving.

The kiss started soft, gentle, slow.

It'd been a long time since I'd kissed any one, and my long-dormant desire came back to life as his kisses sent a wave of shivers all the way down to my toes. I clutched his head as he gently pulled my head back and trailed kisses down my neck.

I want more.

I moaned when his tongue flicked my earlobe. He covered my mouth with his, stealing my breath as his tongue danced with mine. I shivered as his warm hand caressed my side, the promise of more making my head spin with desire.

Oh my God! Chase is upstairs.

I pulled back, my chest heaving as I tried to catch my breath.

When Doug opened his eyes, they were dark with desire.

"We have to stop," I said, or more accurately panted, as I placed my hand on his chest—a wall of solid muscle over his rapidly beating heart—to create space.

He nodded, as he untangled his hand from my hair. The other he left on my leg, but slid it from my hip to my knee, leaving a trail of warmth along my thigh.

"Not that I want to," I added, worried I might have given him the wrong impression. "It's just, Chase is upstairs, and I'm afraid if we keep going, I won't be able to stop."

Being a single parent came with a lot of dating challenges, one of them was not being able to give into your sexual desires, no matter how hot they burned. Because a five-year-old might catch you in the act.

He grinned before saying, "We should schedule a date night at my place."

The deep, husky tone of his voice caused heat to rush to my face. It was sexy as fuck hearing the desire in his voice. I couldn't believe I turned someone on so much.

"We should." My hand felt the loss as I let it drop from his chest.

"Is it hard to find a late night," his eyes sparkled as he looked me up and down, "or overnight sitter?"

Damn, asking about finding a babysitter should not sound sexy. But it did.

"I'm not sure," I looked down to hide my embarrassment, "I've never had to ask."

There hadn't been anyone worth asking for. Doug and I had only been on two dates, but I already knew he was worth asking for.

Was I moving too fast, getting too attached, only to find out I couldn't handle living with the inevitable fear and sleepless nights? Or setting myself up for heartbreak when he decided he wanted kids of his own. Kids I couldn't give him.

It's too soon to worry about all that. I inhaled sharply, forcing myself back to the present. I could worry about the future later, right now I wanted to let go of fear and enjoy the moment.

"I have a three day protection assignment next weekend, but my schedule is open this weekend."

This weekend.

My mind filled with hesitation.

My body shivered with anticipation.

"I'll see if Nina is available Friday."

Chapter 19

Doug

Kissing Beth was everything I thought it'd be, and more. She was hesitant at first, which made me nervous I'd crossed the line, but then she relaxed and matched my passion.

Selfishly, I was disappointed when she said we had to stop, even though I understood. It'd be weird if Chase caught us kissing.

I half expected her to say no when I invited her to spend the night at my place. But to my shock, and immense pleasure, she agreed—pending her babysitter being available for the night.

Please God, let her be available.

I wanted to wake up next to her, and maybe get in a little morning sex before making her breakfast.

Where the hell did that come from?

I hadn't woken up next to a woman since I moved out of the house I'd shared with my ex-wife. I hadn't been celibate, but I hadn't even considered bringing someone back to my place, let alone asking them to spend the night.

Beth Wyatt had gotten under my skin. Every minute I spent with her left me craving more.

I need to tell her I can't have kids. Sooner rather than later. It might not be as big a deal as I'd originally thought, given her age. But that didn't mean she wouldn't think I was less of a man for shooting blanks.

My ex had, and she hadn't hesitated to tell me how much of a failure I was. I could still hear her cruel words, cutting me down and destroying my self-esteem.

Being sterile didn't mean I didn't want kids. I did. I always had.

I could be a good dad to Chase. And a good husband to Beth.

Whoa. Slow down. It was way too soon to be thinking like that, even if it was true.

First, I had to reveal my secret and hope she wouldn't walk away from me.

I poured myself a glass of whiskey, inhaling the smoky peaty scent as I brought the glass to my lips. The warm amber liquid burned as it coated my tongue and throat, bringing me back to the present.

I sat on the couch and turned on my gaming console—shooting a few bad guys would help derail the negative thought train my mind had boarded.

And maybe help keep my mind from visualizing what it'd be like to kiss Beth senseless and hear her breathlessly beg for more as I worshiped her body.

Chapter 20

Beth

At the end of my shift on Thursday, I joined Mary, Meg, and Emily in their booth. I sat down just in time to hear Meg tell Mary about a shooting group she'd heard about, the Women's Shooting Club.

"They meet once a month, there's an hour of classroom training and an hour of range time, with instructors. Emily and I are going next month."

Emily nodded. "I'm looking forward to it. Don't get me wrong, Jamie's great. But it'll be nice to practice without him hovering over me."

Jamie had insisted on teaching Emily how to shoot after what happened earlier in the summer, when her abusive ex-boyfriend took her and her parents hostage and almost killed them. He wanted her to get her license to carry, but she was still nervous about doing it.

"Do you know who the instructor is?" Mary asked.

"No, but each group is led by local female instructors, it'd be easy enough for me to find out," Meg answered.

"Sounds interesting." I asked Mary, "Are you going?"

Mary wasn't one to go shooting for fun, but she'd had her LTC forever and carried her gun every day. She just didn't talk about it.

"I am. It'll be a nice way for us girls to get some quality time together. You should join us," Mary answered.

"Why don't I know if you shoot?" Meg asked.

Because I never said anything. It wasn't a secret, and I wasn't sure why I'd never brought it up. *Maybe because shooting reminded me so much of Phil.*

He'd taught me to shoot early on in our relationship. Well, he took me shooting and tried to teach me, but was so impatient I had to stop going with him. To prevent us from fighting, I'd taken an intro course at the local range. It was easier for me to learn that way.

Phil was a great guy, and most of the time he was a patient man, but for some reason he was kind of a bully on the range. Eventually, after I'd learned how to ask him to back off, we were able to shoot together without fighting.

"I do, Phil taught me. Though it's been a while." *Since before Phil died.* "Maybe it'd be good for me to get in some practice." I sipped my chai tea, savoring the rich spicy flavor.

"So, you'll come with us?" Emily asked, hope filling her eyes.

"Maybe, if I can find a sitter." And if I can remember how to clean my guns. I hadn't cleaned them, hadn't even taken them out of the safe, in years. I had my own twenty-two and a nine-mil S&W and was a decent shot with both. *At least I used to be.* I also had a handful of pistols and rifles in the safe that had belonged to Phil. They'd be Chase's someday, if he wanted them.

I should ask John for help. I could watch videos to refresh my memory on how to clean them, but I'd never cleaned Phil's and wasn't willing to tackle the rifles without help.

Or maybe I could ask Doug. I smiled at the thought.

Meg interrupted my thoughts. "I hope you can, it'll be fun to have a girl's range day."

"What are you thinking about that's got you smiling like a kid with a new toy?" Mary asked.

"Nothing, just thinking I'll need some help cleaning my guns before I can shoot them."

She raised an eyebrow in disbelief, but didn't call me out on it. Instead she suggested, "You could always ask Doug."

Meg giggled at the hint of mischief in Mary's voice.

God, I love these women. Each of them was strong in their own way, and I was blessed to have them in my life. It was strange how, at this stage of life, the three-decade difference in our ages didn't matter. Mary was in her mid-fifties, Meg and Emily were in their mid-twenties, and I was in the middle.

We sipped our coffees and teas, chatting about random things for a few more minutes before Meg burst out, "I can't take it anymore, you have to tell us about your date with Doug!"

Mary already knew about it, so she didn't join in when Meg and Emily squealed as I told them about our evening. They wanted details about the goodbye kiss, but I wasn't willing to share that detail, so I said, "A lady doesn't kiss and tell."

To my surprise, they let it go.

I asked the group, "Did you know he's only thirty-two?"

Emily shook her head, as Meg said, "Really? I knew he was older than Jamie, but not by how much. I kind of assumed he was older than that."

"Is it an issue?" Mary asked.

"I don't think so, but I'm too old to have any more kids. What if he decides he wants his own?" I hadn't meant to voice my fear out loud, but it was too late to take it back. I trusted them, but things had a way of spreading in our group and I didn't want it getting back to Doug and causing issues. The last thing he needed was to hear my fears from someone else.

The girls offered generic platitudes, saying if it was meant to be, it wouldn't matter. Mary nodded thoughtfully but didn't say anything.

"It's really not a big deal, forget I said anything."

"Our lips are sealed." Meg slid her fingers across her lips like she was closing a zipper.

"Thanks." I looked at my watch. "Time to pick up Chase."

As we hugged and said our goodbyes Meg said, "Save us a seat at the game tonight."

Chase was thrilled to see Meg and Jack in the stands.

Later that night, after putting a tired but happy Chase to bed, I punched in the code to the gun safe in the garage. Grateful Phil had chosen our wedding date, backwards, for the code otherwise I might not have remembered it after so many years.

Talking to the girls today had lit a spark in my belly, and I'd fanned it into a full flame by the time I'd put Chase to bed.

As a single mom, I was not only responsible for my safety but Chase's too. Something I'd forgotten in my grief.

I'm sorry Phil, I won't forget again.

I pulled out the plastic case that held my S&W M&P, then closed and locked the safe before walking over to Phil's workbench. I appreciated how he had always cleaned his guns out here so he wouldn't make a smelly, oily mess in the house.

Tears filled my eyes as I stared at the layer of dust coating everything while clutching the hard case to my chest.

Why'd you leave me Phil?

Knowing it hadn't been his fault, or his choice, didn't lessen the pain. Most days I was okay, having gone through the five stages of grief many moons ago, but some days grief would well back up and grab hold of my heart.

Like today.

I wiped the tears off my cheeks. *I've put this off for far too long.* Phil would be disappointed to learn I'd let my license to carry a handgun expire.

Not disappointed, pissed. He'd always told me that being married to a cop didn't mean I didn't have to worry about protecting myself. He'd often remind me, "I can't be with you twenty-four-seven, so you need to be able to defend yourself."

Now he's gone and can't protect me at all. *Us, he can't protect us.*

Not bothering to dust, I placed the case on the bench and opened it, making sure the muzzle was pointed towards the brick wall. Just like Phil had taught me.

Then I carefully picked up the gun, keeping my finger off the trigger, and made sure the gun was empty. Just like Phil had taught me.

I pulled up the Smith & Wesson YouTube channel and found a video on cleaning the M&P. I watched it to refresh my memory, then hit replay, following along as I broke it down and cleaned it.

It took me longer than it should have because I was out of practice, but I eventually got it cleaned and put back together. After doing a function test, which my instructor, not Phil, had taught me, I put it back in the case and returned it to the safe.

It wouldn't do me any good in the safe, but I didn't have any way to lock it up in my room. I made a mental note to call John in the morning and get some advice on renewing my LTC, talking to Chase about gun safety, and getting a small safe.

I added one final thing to my list—find a babysitter for the first Wednesday of the month so I could go to the Women's Shooting Club meetings with the girls.

Chapter 21

Doug

When Beth's name popped up on my screen Thursday afternoon, I got up and closed the door. AJ was on assignment so I had the office to myself. Which was good, because the excitement in Beth's voice meant she'd found a sitter for Friday night.

I didn't need a mirror to know my smile was stupidly big. AJ would never let me hear the end of it, had he seen it.

"Nina has to be home by ten Saturday morning."

"That won't be a problem." My mind was already thinking of all the ways we could fill the morning hours before she had to head home. *Does she like to sleep in on her days off?*

I planned on cooking for Beth, hoping to impress her with my culinary skills.

"Do you have any food allergies, or is there anything you don't like?"

"No allergies and I'll try just about anything."

That made planning the menu easier. "Great. Want me to pick you up?" It was a date, after all.

"That's okay, I'll drive. Nina's available after six, so let's plan for six-thirty."

"Perfect. I'll text you my address."

"Sounds good. Can I bring anything?"

"Just yourself and whatever you need for the night."

"Alright…"

It sounded like she wanted to say more, so I waited. When she didn't, I said, "Beth, you know you can change your mind right?" I wouldn't be mad, disappointed for sure, but not mad. I'd respect her decision.

I reminded myself there was no guarantee we'd sleep together, even if she stayed the night. Hell, we could be naked in bed, me between her legs with only half an inch separating me from heaven, and she could still change her mind.

If she didn't want it to happen, it wouldn't. *But I hope it does.* I'd been thinking about getting Beth into my bed for longer than I cared to admit, and was ready to exchange the fantasy for reality.

"I know. It's not that. It's just… it's been a while, that's all."

The slight tremble to her voice gave away her nervousness.

"We can go as slow as you want or need. No pressure, I promise."

I could hear her tension subsiding as she said, "Thank you."

Beth relaxed more as we talked for a few more minutes.

After we hung up, I checked my email to make sure there were no new messages then started making a list of things I needed at the grocery store. I wanted to make chicken cacciatore, a dish I'd fallen in love with when I was stationed in Italy. I'd loved the food there so much that before returning stateside, I went shopping for a cookbook. I could have looked online, but I liked the idea of getting an Italian cookbook in Italy. I hit the jackpot when I found one filled with old world Italian recipes.

I'd made a few of the recipes, and liked them. This one was my favorite.

I hope she likes it. I'd made it for my ex once, but she'd complained about the carbs and always asked for something else whenever I suggested making it. At least Beth wasn't anti-pasta, though given the number of times she made mac and cheese she might want something different.

This isn't box mac and cheese. Stop worrying.

At least I kept my apartment clean, so I wouldn't have to scramble to clean it. But it needed some decorative touches. Right now, the only things decorating my living room walls were an American flag, and some shadow boxes with commendations from the Air Force over my desk.

It'd be easy enough to get a few pillows and a throw blanket for the couch, maybe a couple of fake plants, and some candles – women love candles. There really wasn't much else I wanted to add. I could probably get some wall art, but that felt like something I should put some effort into selecting, not just buy on a whim.

Lists in hand, I got up and went to the reception area to hand in my report for the Spencer job. I waited for Meg to hang up the phone before handing her the folder.

She looked up when she reached for it and a mischievous smile spread across her face, her emerald green eyes sparkling.

"What?" I asked.

"Nothing, I just don't think I've ever seen anyone so happy to turn in their paperwork." Amusement coated every word.

I didn't have time to think of a clever reply before I heard Jack.

"There has to be some other reason he's happy, because no one likes doing paperwork." He paused and looked at Jamie's door as it opened. "Except maybe Jamie, but he's weird that way."

"I'm weird in what way?" Jamie asked.

"You like doing paperwork," Jack answered, clapping him on the shoulder.

"No, I don't. I just don't whine about it like a baby," he shrugged off Jack's hand, "unlike some people."

Every day. It was like this every day. Well, some days it was worse, but AJ wasn't here to escalate the crazy. I loved it, though no one suspected as much because I rarely joined in.

"So why am I being singled out, inaccurately I might add, for liking paperwork?"

"Because, Meg said Doug looked happy to be handing in his," Jack answered.

Naturally, they all turned to look at me. Stupid me hadn't had the forethought to school my features while they teased one another and got caught with a very large smile on my face.

"You do look rather happy." Jamie asked, "Any particular reason?"

"No, just planning my weekend." Then before they could ask, I added, "And no, I won't tell you."

"Good for you," Meg said to me before turning to the brothers and shooing them away with a wave of her hand. "Now if you guys don't mind, I have work to do."

Thank you, Meg. I wasn't ready to be on the receiving end of a tag-team interrogation.

Chapter 22

Beth

Dating Doug felt effortless.

The hardest part was working around our schedules, but so far, we were making it work. It'd been less than three weeks, but I was already contemplating asking Doug to join Chase and I for dinner in the near future. A casual dinner with the three of us was the perfect chance to see how they'd get along.

Who am I kidding? Doug had been interacting with Chase for months, and Chase adored him.

I was still nervous. It would be the first time I introduced Chase to someone I was dating. No one before Doug had been 'Chase-worthy' as I'd started to think of it.

When I started dating, I swore to myself I wouldn't introduce Chase to anyone unless I serious. He desperately wanted a dad, and I wouldn't, couldn't, get his hopes up.

Am I seriously thinking of crossing the line with Doug after only a few dates? Yes, because it felt like we'd packed a lifetime into those dates. Not to mention the hours of conversations we'd had in-between.

After fantasizing what it'd be like to kiss him and feel his strong arms wrapped around me, I finally got to experience the real thing after our first dinner date. It was everything I'd imagined, and more.

I let myself relive the moment. His hand cupping my face as he stared deep into my eyes before asking if he could kiss me. His deep husky voice would have removed any resistance, if I'd had any. Me nodding because my ability to speak had fled—Doug stepping closer and closing the distance between us one painful inch at a time.

Our eyes stayed locked until we were close enough for our lips to touch if one of us puckered them. Then he closed his eyes.

When our lips met, it was electric. It robbed me of my breath as electricity shot through my body.

It started off sweet, just his lips gently pressed to mine. Wanting more, I parted my lips in invitation. Not needing to be asked twice, Doug deepened the kiss.

I'd been so absorbed in his kiss, I lost all track of time as we stood there, lip locked.

He broke the kiss and leaned his forehead against mine.

"Beth." His voice was a throaty whisper as his hand massaged the back of my neck.

The bell above the door chimed, snapping me back to the present. I shouldn't be thinking about kissing Doug at work.

As I made a latte for the customer, I grinned. I'd been fantasizing about Doug for months. Only now my fantasies were based on reality, not speculation.

'Have a good day." I handed the latte over the counter.

Heat rushed to my cheeks. We had a date tonight. At his apartment. Doug was making me dinner, and if I didn't chicken out, he'd make me breakfast too.

But first I had to get through my shift at Grannie's. *And Chase's tee ball game.*

An hour before my shift ended, I got a text from Nina. She was sick and couldn't sit tonight. My heart sank as I read her text for the third time. I wasn't mad; she was reliable, and Chase liked her. But I was disappointed because there was no way I'd be able to find an overnight sitter at the last minute on a Friday.

"Everything okay?" Mary asked.

"Yeah, well, no. Nina's sick and can't watch Chase tonight, so I have to cancel my date with Doug."

"I'm so sorry. I'd offer to watch Chase, but John and I have dinner plans."

Mary understood how hard it'd be for me to find a replacement at the eleventh hour.

I thanked her before she tried to explain. "I just hope Doug understands." This was one of the reasons dating me, a single mom, was hard. Our dates were dependent on my babysitter.

"I'm sure he will." She asked, "Want to go call him?"

"Yeah, I should do it sooner rather than later." I walked to the break room with my shoulders slumped forward.

As expected, Doug understood. He was busy at work so we couldn't talk, but he said he'd call me later. I thought about asking him to come to my place but stopped myself. Chase would be there, and I wasn't ready to cross that line yet.

In an effort to forget my disappointment, I deep cleaned the dining room during our slow period. It didn't help. My mind kept replaying Doug's response, looking for clues that he was more upset than he'd let on.

Later, during Chase's tee ball game I got a call from Meg.

"Hey Beth. I heard Nina had to cancel."

Doug must have said something because I hadn't told anyone but Mary. Though it wouldn't have been out of character for Mary to tell Meg.

"Unfortunately." I couldn't keep the disappointment out of my voice.

"Well," she dragged out the 'e' for effect, "I just talked to Jack and he's good with us having a sleepover with Chase tonight."

Did she just volunteer to take Chase for the night? And save my date?

"Are you sure?" *Why am I asking?*

"We're sure." I could hear her smile through the phone.

There wasn't a word in the English language strong enough to express my gratitude.

"Beth?"

"Sorry, I just can't believe how lucky I am."

"Well believe it. What time do you want us to pick him up?"

"I can drop him off, along with his car seat, around six if that's okay." My legs had minds of their own and were bouncing up and down on the metal bench, eager to get up and jump for joy.

"Six is perfect. We'll see you then."

"How can I ever repay you?"

"Just have fun tonight."

That's the plan.

"Thanks Meg. I appreciate both of you."

"No worries, we love that kid. Now relax and enjoy the game."

As soon as the game was over, I asked Chase if he wanted to have a sleepover at Auntie Meg's. His enthusiastic excitement was exactly what I'd expected. For a second, I wondered why he didn't ask about it, having never stayed the night anywhere except his grandmother's.

Then I remembered he was five and he loved Meg, so all he cared about was the idea of spending the entire night at her house with Jack and Jamie.

"Come on, let's get you cleaned up and fed."

"Can I use my dinosaur suitcase and bring my water dinosaurs?" He refused to call them sharks.

"Of course."

Once I had Chase's seal of approval, *like he'd ever say no to time with Meg*, I texted Doug to let him know I'd found a babysitter and asked if he still wanted me to come over for dinner.

His yes was in all caps.

Chapter 23

Doug

She found a babysitter. I had no idea how she'd managed to find an overnight babysitter so late in the game, but I wasn't going to question my luck.

I only had about ninety minutes before Beth arrived, so I headed home and got to work. I'd done most of the cleaning and decorating the night before, so all I needed to do was take a quick shower and start prepping the food.

Before browning the chicken for the cacciatore, I lit the lavender candle I'd bought for the bathroom. Not knowing much about scents, I'd chosen lavender sage thinking Beth would like the light floral scent. As a bonus, the sage prevented the lavender from being obnoxiously strong.

The kitchen filled with the rich smell of chicken as I browned it. I chopped the onion first, knowing it'd make my eyes water. Then washed my hands and face before chopping the celery, peppers, and mushrooms. When the chicken was done, I plated it and put it in the microwave while I cooked the vegetables.

One of the things I liked about this recipe was it was all done in one skillet. One large, heavy cast iron skillet. Once the veggies were soft, I added in the tomatoes, tomato sauce and paste, a cup of the red wine I'd be serving with dinner, and some fresh herbs. And lastly, I placed the chicken thighs in the sauce and set the timer for forty-five minutes.

While it simmered, I made sure the apartment was picked up and turned on my country music station on Pandora. Then I checked my watch.

Beth should be here any minute.

I couldn't remember the last time I felt this nervous about having a woman over. Had I ever felt this nervous?

A few minutes later I got a text from Beth, she had just parked and was on her way up to my second story apartment. I opened the door as she reached the exterior landing, a huge stupid grin plastered on my face.

Her smile was more on the shy side, and her cheeks were pinker than normal.

She had a large purse in her hand, but no overnight bag. *Did she change her mind?* It didn't matter; we'd still have a good date with a great meal.

"Come in."

Her grin turned to a broad smile as she walked into my apartment. She was close enough for me to smell her bright, fresh, floral perfume reminding me of a spring morning after a rainstorm.

Beth looked around as I hung her coat on a peg near the door. From our position near the door, she could see most of my apartment. The open floor plan felt like a studio, except I had an actual bedroom. The kitchen was separated from the rest of the space by an island, creating a galley style kitchen space.

"Want me to hang your purse too?"

She shook her head as she walked towards the table, inhaling deeply as she did. "It smells amazing in here."

"Thanks, I'm making chicken cacciatore."

"Wow, that's impressive."

"Try it before you compliment me." I laughed.

"Is this your first time making it?"

"No, I've made it before."

"Then I'm sure it'll be delicious." Her smile lit up my kitchen, outshining the candles I'd lit on the table.

I changed the subject. "I'm glad you were able to find a replacement sitter."

Her nervous laugh before answering was unsettling. "You might not be when you hear who it is."

"Yeah?" I asked, thoroughly intrigued.

"Meg and Jack volunteered to a slumber party with Chase."

That explains her nervous laugh. I wasn't surprised Meg had volunteered. She loved Beth and wouldn't want her to have to cancel her plans.

"Ahh, so they know you're spending the night out."

"They do." She blushed as she reached into her bag and brought out a bottle of wine.

I laughed, curious about what else she had stashed in her purse. "You didn't have to bring anything."

"I know, but my mom taught me to never go to someone's house empty handed."

I could appreciate that; my mom had taught me the same thing.

"Thanks. Want me to open it? Or I can pour you a glass of the red I have open for dinner."

"That sounds nice, let's save this for later." She lifted her purse. "Where should I put my overnight bag?"

Overnight bag? I thought it was a purse. I pointed to the bedroom, just down the hall. "The bedroom's fine. Bath is on the right." *She still plans on staying.* The horny teenager in me did a little jig.

As she walked the short hall towards my bedroom, I took a second to appreciate how good she looked. Her short black skirt hung just below her knees, swishing back and forth as she walked. Her floral yellow button-down shirt displayed just a hint of cleavage.

I can't wait to kiss her neck as I undo those buttons.

Reluctantly, I turned away and adjusted myself before pouring her a glass of wine. Then I topped off mine before checking the timer. "Dinner would be done in about thirty minutes."

I grabbed the small appetizer plate from the refrigerator and set it on the table along with two small plates. I'd gone all out to impress Beth.

"Sorry it took so long, I wanted to wash my hands."

"No worries." I handed her a glass and lifted mine. "To finding a babysitter at the last minute."

Her smile lit up her whole face as she said, "Cheers." We tapped our glasses and sipped our Chianti Classico.

I didn't know much about wine so I Googled what red wine would pair well with the chicken cacciatore and had the friendly salesperson at the wine shop help me pick out a good one. I bought two bottles since I had to use a quarter of the first bottle in the dish.

"Your place is nice." She looked around. "Not quite the man cave I was expecting."

"Thanks. I'm not a neat freak, but I don't like clutter." I didn't tell her I'd gussied up the place over the last three days. *Hell, the throw pillows probably still smell new.*

We nibbled on cheese, meats, and crackers and talked while we waited for dinner to finish simmering. When the timer went off, I excused myself and checked the chicken. Thankfully, it was done because I was starving. I hadn't eaten much of the appetizers because I didn't want to be too full to enjoy one of my favorite dishes.

I heard Beth's chair slide back before she asked, "Anything I can do to help?"

"You can open the second bottle of wine; the corkscrew is in the drawer." I nodded in the direction since my hands were full.

I felt my body relax as we worked together in my tiny kitchen area; me plating our meals, Beth opening the wine. Everything else we needed was already on the table.

"It smells so good. Looks good too. I can't wait to try it."

I wasn't prone to blushing, but her compliments were enough to bring color to my cheeks.

I waited for her to take her first bite. When she did, she closed her eyes and made mmm sounds as she slowly chewed.

I blushed for an entirely different reason and turned my attention to my plate to avoid embarrassing myself.

As we ate, I told her more about falling in love with Italian food while stationed in Italy and the cooking class I took while I was there.

"Did you always like cooking?" She asked.

"Yeah, my mom taught my sister and I how to cook when we were young. She never really got into it, but I did." I sipped my wine. "How about you, do you like to cook?"

"I do, though I don't get to as often as I'd like. Chase is a picky eater and it's too much effort to cook two meals." She paused, a far away look in her eye, which cleared after a few seconds.

After a few minutes, Beth changed the subject when she asked, "Do you miss Chicago?"

Do I? I thought about it before answering, "Not really." I refused to dwell on why. "I might visit at Christmas." I laughed as I thought about December in Chicago.

Beth raised an eyebrow in question.

"Chicago winters are brutal, so it'll be a shock."

"I've heard it doesn't take long to acclimate to warm southern winters."

"It doesn't. When I went back last year it wasn't too bad because I'd only been gone a few months, and December is usually mild. Luckily, I missed the harsh January and

February storms last year. Well, I wouldn't say I 'missed' them since I was enjoying the mild Texas winter."

"We rarely get snow here, and winter storms are even rarer," she said softly.

I saw pain cross Beth's eyes. I hadn't meant to remind her of her Phil's death.

"I'm sorry, I didn't mean to-"

"It's okay." Beth smiled as she reached over and placed her hand over mine, squeezing it when I laced my fingers with hers. "Really, it is. I don't want you to feel like you have to be careful about what you say."

"Okay, just promise me you'll let me know if you don't want to talk about something." I made her make the same promise she'd required of me.

"I promise." She looked down at her lap, then back up at me. "Thanks for understanding."

"You're welcome." Feeling like the conversation was over, I stood. "Why don't you go to the living room and relax while I clear the table."

"Do you want help?"

"Nah, I got it. Want more wine?"

"Sure. I'll get more water. Want some?"

"Yeah, thanks. There's pitcher is in the fridge; the tap water here isn't great."

After refilling our glasses, Beth went to the living room and got comfortable on my couch. *She looks good there.* I made quick work of clearing the table, neatly stacking the dishes after rinsing them. I'd usually wash them right away, but they could wait, I'd rather spend time with Beth.

We talked for thirty minutes or so, before I asked her if she wanted dessert.

"You bake too?"

"No," I chuckled, "my cooking skills don't translate to baking. I bought a cheesecake."

"Sounds good, but I'm still pretty full." She patted her stomach.

"I'm glad you enjoyed dinner." I brushed the hair off her face and tucked it behind her hair. "You look beautiful tonight."

She blushed and looked down at her lap. "Thank you."

I put my wine glass on the coffee table, then took hers and did the same. I was dying to kiss her, but didn't want to risk spilling the wine. Not that I cared about the wine, or my old couch, but I didn't want anything interrupting us.

I reached up and cupped her face, my thumb gently caressing her lower lip and cheek. She turned into my hand and released a soft sigh that sounded like a purr. I leaned forward and brushed my lips against hers. The scent of her perfume filled my nose. I didn't know the name of it, but the scent was now burned into my brain and would forever be associated with Beth.

Her soft lips opened, inviting me to deepen the kiss.

I slid my tongue along her lower lip before she opened them further and her tongue darted out to meet mine. I could taste the wine on her tongue.

Our kiss was slow and exploratory. And hot as hell.

It'd been a long time since I'd kissed someone like this. Not rushing in, but letting the passion build slowly. Only the rest of my body didn't get the message. I was already hard and getting harder by the second.

Beth slid her hand up my arm and around my neck, pulling me closer, demanding more.

I was happy to give it.

She paused for half a second, just long enough for me to feel it, but not long enough for it to be a request to stop, when I put my other hand on her thigh.

I could feel the warmth of her leg through her skirt, then because I wanted to feel that warmth with nothing between us, I bunched up her skirt and slowly slid my hand under it, stopping just above her knee.

I rubbed small circles on her inner thigh but didn't move my hand any further. I wouldn't rush things with Beth.

Beth clutched my neck with one hand while the other slid to my waist, just above my beltline. She fisted my pale green polo and pulled.

Wanting tonight to be special, not rushed, I pulled back so we could catch our breath.

Chapter 24

Beth

This wasn't the first time I kissed Doug, so I knew he was a good kisser. *But damn!* This was intense. His kisses lit a burning desire in my core. A feeling I hadn't felt in a long time. *Since before Chase was born.*

Not that I was a monk, or nun, or whatever, but I was too busy grieving and then raising Chase to think about dating. When I finally did, I hadn't wanted more than a chaste good night kiss.

With Doug, every touch left a trail of fire on my skin. Every kiss sent shivers down my spine. Every sexy grunt caused me to clench my thighs.

I had a hard time believing someone as hot as Doug, who was almost a decade younger and could probably have his pick of gorgeous, young women, could be attracted to me.

But when he pulled away, the desire in his hooded eyes reassured me he was as turned on as I was. All doubt fled my mind. This might not last forever, but right now I wanted to enjoy the moment and not worry about the future.

"Beth." He half whispered, half growled my name. *God, that's sexy.*

Deciding I wanted to make the next move, I trailed my hand along his cheek and chin in a soft inviting caress as I stood up.

Doug closed his eyes and grabbed my waist, pulling me between his knees. Not breaking eye contact, I rested my hands on his shoulders as he caressed his way to my hips, sending goose bumps over my skin.

I had to step back and tilt my head up to maintain eye contact as he stood. The moment was surreal; neither of us spoke, but we communicated plenty with our eyes and our hands. Doug slid his hands up my sides, lifting my shirt as he went. Before reaching my bra, he lifted his hands and let the material fall back into place.

Not wanting to break contact, I ran my hands up and down his muscular chest. The rapid beat of his heart below my right palm, made me smile. I might feel self-conscious about my forty-year-old mom body, but there was no ignoring the signs that Doug wanted me as much as I wanted him.

Doug's eyes flared when I licked my lips.

I didn't hesitate when he reached for one of my hands and walked backwards, pulling me towards his bedroom.

It took me a moment to realize where I was when I woke up the next morning. The memories of the night before, the night I'd shared in physical bliss with Doug, flooded my brain and made me blush. I turned over and reached for him.

Empty. I looked at the clock on the bedside table; six-fifty-three.

I smiled, noting my sore abs and inner thighs, as I rolled out of bed—last night had been quite the workout. I grabbed a clean pair of panties and tugged the long pink and yellow striped tee I'd brought with me over my head. I wasn't confident enough to walk around naked, but I didn't want to get fully dressed just yet.

The smell of freshly brewed coffee hit me as soon as I opened the bedroom door. It felt luxurious to wake up to someone brewing coffee for me, since I not only had to brew my own, but I was the person brewing coffee for Grannie's early morning regulars during the week.

Before following the smell of coffee to the kitchen, I stopped by the bathroom to relieve myself and brush my teeth. While I was there, I splashed some water on my face and finger combed my sex-induced rat's nest of hair.

"Good morning." I said, as I padded into the kitchen on bare feet.

Doug's eyes looked down, then up, sending shivers across my skin as I remembered the feeling of his hands, caressing where his eyes were now wandering.

"Morning, Beautiful. Did you sleep well?" Doug asked, a smile on his face and a sparkle in his eyes.

"I did. It felt nice to sleep in a little." I leaned against the island. "How about you?"

"Like the dead." He winked. "Coffee will be done in a minute. How do you like your eggs, or would you prefer an omelet?"

"You're spoiling me."

"You deserve to be spoiled." Doug said as he put down the mugs he had grabbed before closing the small distance between us, wrapping me in a hug, and kissing my forehead.

I wrapped my arms around him as I said thank you into his chest. *He smells good.*

"So, how do you want your eggs?" He whispered into my hair.

"An omelet sounds good. Want any help?"

"Nope, I'm happy to let you sit and enjoy your coffee while I make breakfast."

I hesitated, debating whether I should take him up on his offer, which I had to admit sounded delightful, or offer to help again. The idea of relaxing while someone else did the work sounded wrong to me.

Because you're not used to someone taking care of you.

I hadn't decided when the coffee machine beeped letting us know our morning caffeine fix was ready. Doug filled the two mugs and nodded towards the fridge.

"Half and half is on the top shelf. Now go, relax for a few minutes." Doug reassured me that he brewed Grannie's coffee—I wasn't a coffee snob and wouldn't have said anything but I was glad he brewed it. It was the best around, and I would know; I drank it every day.

I won't lie or pretend I was upset he made the decision for me. Having a quiet moment to enjoy my coffee while someone else made breakfast felt like a vacation. I thanked him as I poured half and half into my coffee. Then I went and sat on the couch, as instructed.

Instead of relaxing, I pulled out my phone and checked my messages.

The only notifications I had were from Mary and Meg. Mary had only sent one, last night: Have fun tonight.

Meg had sent some pictures of Chase during the night. I looked through them quickly, and then downloaded them to my phone. It looked like he'd had a blast with everyone. My favorite was one of Chase on Jack's shoulders with a plastic dinosaur in each hand, roaring at whoever he was chasing.

Forgetting how early it was, I sent a thank you text to Meg and confirmed I'd be there at ten to pick up Chase. I didn't expect to get a reply right away, but I did.

Meg: No rush. With a wink emoji.

There wasn't a rush, per se, but I told Chase I'd take him to the museum this afternoon.

I wondered if Doug has plans this afternoon.

Am I really thinking of inviting him to join us? Yes, the night we'd just shared was special. Not because it ended a five-year dry spell, but because of the connection I'd felt.

We'd felt. I could tell from his touch, and the look in his eyes, Doug felt it too. Was I ready to take the next step in our relationship so soon?

It's just the museum, not—

"Breakfast is served." Doug's announcement interrupted my thoughts. He placed two steaming plates of food on the table then said, "I'll be right back."

I sat in the same place I had at dinner and waited. When he came back, he had the coffee pot, a potholder, and the half and half. "I figure we'll want refills."

He wasn't wrong. You'd think I'd grow to dislike coffee working full time as the manager of a coffee shop, but you'd be wrong.

The ham and cheese omelet was delicious. We talked. I refilled his coffee when I refilled mine.

As we ate, I worked up the nerve to ask him about his day.

"I was, um, wondering, do you have plans this afternoon?" Damn it, I sounded like a nervous teenager.

"Not really," he smiled as he answered. His charming smile teased me without words.

"I told Chase if he was a good boy for Meg and Jack, I'd take him out to lunch and then to the science museum." I paused to sip my coffee and build up courage. "If you wanted to, you could come with us, I mean I'd like it if you wanted to. Although I'm sure hanging out with a five-year-old probably doesn't sound like much-"

Doug cut of my rambling. "I'd love to."

He laid his hand on the table, palm up and I accepted the invitation. When I laced my fingers with his, he rubbed the back of my hand with his thumb. I felt heat rise in my cheeks at the intimacy of the moment.

We both understood the implications of me inviting him to spend the day with us, so it didn't need to be said.

Doug lifted my hand and pulled it towards him. Then he placed a soft kiss on the back of it before releasing it so he could collect our empty plates and carry them to the kitchen.

The tenderness of the moment brought tears to my eyes. I could be so sensitive sometimes. *I blame my hormones.* I'd read that women entering Perimenopause could be extra emotional, and blamed it on that.

What was I thinking? Did I make a huge mistake inviting Doug with us today? What if Chase gets attached and then Doug dumps me because I'm too old?

What thirty-year-old wants to be with a woman going through the change?

"You want to shower while I clean up?" Doug called from the kitchen, putting a stop to my thoughts before they caused me to change my mind.

"Yeah, thanks."

I grabbed my bag from the bedroom and hopped in the shower, letting the hot water wash away my doubts. I had to trust Doug when he said my age wasn't a problem. It was time to take the plunge and trust I could handle it if he changed his mind.

Right, that might be possible if it was only me, but I have to think about Chase.

Chapter 25

Doug

Beth wanted to drive, so I folded myself into her small, dark green four-door sedan. On the drive to Jack's, she laid out the ground rules: keep an eye on Chase at all times, he tends to wander when he gets excited or hyper focused, and we don't let him stop and look in the shop because he'll want to buy all the things, especially in the shop near the dinosaur exhibit.

"I usually hold his hand and drag him to the exit." She said, shaking her head.

"Anything else?"

"Be patient."

"Copy that." I reached over and squeezed her hand to let her know it'd be okay. I understood her nervousness, even if I didn't like it. Inviting me to join them today was a big step for her. She didn't have to tell me how worried she was about getting Chase involved; it showed in her actions. I didn't blame her. In fact, I respected her for it.

When she asked me this morning, I was surprised and honored. It was an opportunity I couldn't pass up. Chase was a good kid, and if I wanted to be a part of Beth's life, I had to be a part of his. And I was more than okay with the package deal.

Hell, I wanted it, because the only way I could be a dad was through adoption. Reality crashed down and rained on my parade. I still hadn't told Beth I wasn't quite the man she believed me to be. *I need to tell her soon, before I fall too deep.*

I asked Beth if she wanted me to wait in the car when we got to Jack and Jamie's, but she said no.

"It's not like they don't know we're dating, or that I spent the night at your place." Her voice wavered as she said it.

She was pretending it was no big deal, but it was. Because she wasn't just confirming she'd spent the night with me, she was broadcasting I was spending the day with her and Chase.

A declaration they wouldn't miss.

Knowing she was ready to shout it from the rooftops was an ego boost. *One that comes with a fuck ton of responsibility.* I held my head a little higher as Beth rang the doorbell.

When Jack opened the door, he acted like it was no big deal for me to be with Beth, picking up Chase. If it hadn't been for the quick rise of his eyebrow when he saw me, I would've thought he'd been expecting me all along.

Chase cut our greeting short when he came running to the door yelling, "Mommy Mommy Mommy." He wrapped his arms around her legs and said, "I had so much fun but I missed you and Auntie Meg let me help her make pancakes this morning and …"

He stopped when he saw me standing beside his mom. "Mr. Doug why are you here with my mommy?"

Kids. No fucking filter. I got down on one knee and held out a fist. "Hi Chase."

"Mr. Doug is coming to the museum with us."

"Yay!" Chase jumped up and down, clapping his hands. Then with the enthusiasm only a kid can have, he launched into a breathless list of things he wanted to show me. "I'll show you all the dinosaurs and the rocks and swords and there's a submarine and-"

"Why don't you let us come inside." Beth turned Chase around and ushered him into the room. She looked at me, raised her eyebrows, and shrugged. I snickered as I followed her into the living room.

When Beth asked, Meg said Chase was well behaved. Chase echoed his agreement.

I felt Jamie and Jack's eyes on me as Beth and Meg talked and tried to ignore them. I'd have to answer their questions eventually, but not today.

Beth thanked everyone for watching Chase, then grabbed his suitcase as she started saying goodbye. The gentleman in me couldn't let her carry bags while my hands were empty, so I took the suitcase. I didn't miss the nods of approval.

As we were walking out, Jack said, "Don't forget your booster seat, Chase."

"I'm a big boy, I don't need it." Chase pouted as he argued.

"Sorry bud, but you need it until you grow a little taller," Jamie said.

Chase put his hands on his hips and stood up on his tip-toes. "I'm taller now."

I wasn't the only one who laughed.

Chase eventually stopped arguing and got in his booster seat. On the drive over Chase asked me about working at SSI and if I'd ever been a cop. I said no, but I'd worked as a civilian for the Chicago PD, after serving in the Air Force.

"Do you want to join the military when you grow up?"

He shook his head back and forth. "I'm gonna work for Uncle John after I'm the police like my Daddy."

I could see Beth blinking back tears.

"I bet your dad would be proud to hear you say that."

Chase's smile revealed a gap where he'd recently lost a tooth.

Beth insisted on paying when we got to the museum. I thought about arguing, but Chase was watching, and I wanted to set a good example for him. I considered myself a gentleman and didn't usually let women pay for dates, but Beth's argument—she'd invited me so she should pay—was a solid one. *I'll buy lunch.*

Beth let Chase choose which exhibit we saw first, and of course it was the dinosaurs. I couldn't blame him, there was something magical about seeing the bones of creatures that lived so long ago it may as well have been on a different planet. He'd love Sue, the largest and most complete T-Rex fossil ever found, at the Field Museum in Chicago. *Maybe someday I'll get to take him.*

After lunch, I scanned the crowd as Chase and I waited outside the ladies' room for Beth. When I turned back to Chase, he was gone.

My head was turned for five seconds.

"Chase." I scanned the crowd, my voice projecting calm authority as I called for him. *Fuck.* The weekend crowd would make it hard for him to hear me without yelling, which would cause a scene. *Fuck.* My heart raced—I lost him.

Beth is going to kill me.

My height gave me an advantage, but Chase would still be hard to see.

Think like a five-year-old, Sharpe.

To the left was a line for a special exhibit, one he wasn't interested in. In front of me was the food court, where we'd just eaten. He may have gone back there, but I didn't see him. To the right was a stand-alone display of a giant turtle. *Jackpot.*

I was about to call out again when the crowd shifted. There he was, talking to the middle-aged guy pointing at the display. Without thinking, I marched through the crowd, grateful for my size.

I took a deep breath and released it slowly as I stopped next to Chase.

"Chase, whatcha doing Little Man?" I kept my voice as calm as I could as I put a hand on his shoulder and tucked him into my left side. I looked for some indication the guy might be an employee. No museum polo, no badge, nothing.

"Mr. Doug! Mr. Dale said turtles live a long time. And they sleep in their shells. Did you know they're related to dinosaurs?" Chase explained like he hadn't just given me a heart attack by wandering off.

I'd been assessing Dale while Chase talked and hadn't picked up on any obvious signs of ill intent, but that didn't mean he was innocent. *What grown man talks to a kid without asking about his parents?*

Dale opened his mouth to say something, but I wasn't interested in anything he had to say. "That's nice." I cut him off before turning to Chase. "Say goodbye to Mr. Dale."

Just then Beth ran up, clutched Chase to her side, and asked, breathlessly, "What's going on?"

Fuck. I'd hoped to be waiting for her, where she'd left us, so this wouldn't happen. I would have told her, and she would have been upset, but she wouldn't have experienced the fear she was currently feeling.

I let my hand fall from his shoulder and moved to a better position to intercept. Dale didn't look like he'd try anything, but I wanted to make it clear he'd have a bad day if he did.

Beth's chest was heaving, her eyes wide.

"Sorry ma'am, I didn't mean to worry you. I was just telling young Chase here about turtles. Thought he might be interested when I saw the dinosaurs on his t-shirt."

I wanted to believe him, but couldn't. Even if Chase had wandered off, what kind of guy would befriend him but not look for his parents?

The wrong kind. Keeping my voice neutral, I said, "We'll be on our way." Before Beth could say anything, I turned and stepped between her and Dale. Not wanting her to start a scene, I gently nudged them away.

Beth had every right to be scared and pissed, but yelling at the guy wouldn't solve anything. Plus, it'd upset Chase, who I was sure was about to get a lecture on stranger danger.

Chase stared at his shoes as we walked away, his fear radiating off him. I followed as she dragged Chase to the side of the room. Holding his hands, she kneeled in front of him.

"Chase, who was that?" Beth asked, her voice still a few octaves above normal.

I scanned the crowd while she talked to Chase.

Chase shrugged. "Mr. Dale. He liked my shirt and showed me the turtle."

"How many times have I told you not to talk to strangers?"

Chase looked confused; his eyes wet with tears.

Don't talk to strangers is one of those things we tell children, but it doesn't carry a lot of meaning for them. I'd attended a seminar on talking to your kids and keeping them safe, and one of the things they'd emphasized was that kids don't think the way we do.

A person offering them candy is a friend, not a stranger, because friends share.

A person looking for a lost dog or cat isn't a stranger; because they need help.

A person sharing information with them isn't a stranger, because they're like a teacher.

Beth could say, "don't talk to strangers," until she was blue in the face, but it wouldn't help.

"Beth," I placed my hand on her arm, "may I?" I asked softly. It wasn't my place to parent Chase, so I'd back off if she said no. Thankfully she didn't, because I could help them both. Not as a parental figure, but as a professional.

"Chase, you didn't think of Mr. Dale as a stranger when he offered to show you the turtle, did you?"

He shook his head back and forth, still looking at his mom with his hands shoved in his pockets. *Poor kid, he doesn't understand why he's in trouble.*

"You're not in trouble, Chase." I gave Beth a look begging her not to contradict me. I had a point to make. One I wish we could have discussed and made together, or she could have done it on her own, but I didn't want to miss this opportunity while their emotions were still high.

We remembered lessons better when they were tied to our emotions.

"Your mom isn't mad at you. She's scared, because when she came out of the bathroom we weren't where we were supposed to be and-."

"I'm sorry Mommy."

"I forgive you." Her tone was softer. Then she looked at me and added, "But Mr. Doug isn't done yet."

Her faith and trust in me would have dropped me to my knees, if I wasn't already on them.

"We scare the people who love us if we wander away without telling them. You don't want to scare your mom, do you?" I asked.

"No." His voice was barely above a whisper.

"That's good." I smiled, hoping to put him at ease.

"Chase, sometimes people who act nice are actually bad people. We have to be extra careful anytime we talk to someone we haven't met before. Do you understand?"

"Think so," He said sheepishly.

"Good." I put my hand on his shoulder like I was sharing a secret. "Here's what I want you to do. Any time someone you've never met before starts talking to you, I want you to ask your mom if it's okay to talk to them. Can you do that?"

"What if they need help?" Chase asked, looking a little more like himself.

"You tell them you have to ask if it's okay, and then you go to your mom."

"What if I'm at school?"

I looked at Beth for clarification, momentarily forgetting Chase called daycare school.

"Then you say you have to ask your teacher," Beth answered.

"Okay." He nodded.

"So, what do we do if someone we've never met before asks us if we want an ice cream?" It was a test; one I'd intentionally made difficult by including ice cream.

Chase looked from me to his mom and back to me. "I say I have to ask my mommy."

"That's right." I held out my fist and waited for him to bump it. "Or your teacher, if you're at school."

Beth got on her knees and hugged Chase, she mouthed 'thank you' over Chase's head as she held him tight. She didn't let go until he started to squirm.

Chase sounded like himself again. "Can we go see the rest of the turtles now?"

"Only if you promise to hold my hand." She smiled down at him.

The rest of the afternoon was less exciting. Chase wore himself out dragging us around trying to see everything and fell asleep five minutes into the drive home.

Once I was sure he was asleep, I turned to Beth.

"I'm sorry if I overstepped earlier today."

"No, thank you for handling it the way you did. I was too scared to be calm. Or rational."

"I get it." *Time to fess up.* "Beth, I'm sorry. I took my eyes off him for five seconds and almost had a heart attack when I realized he'd walked away."

Her jaw clenched and her death grip on the steering wheel turned her knuckles white.

"I told you he wanders off."

"You did. And I'm sorry. If I'm ever given the opportunity again, I'll hold his hand the entire time."

She nodded before glancing in the mirror to look at Chase. Her eyes shimmering with unshed tears.

"Beth, I'm so sorry."

"I know." She sighed. "And I forgive you. I'm willing to give you a second chance, but only because your apology included a plan to prevent it from happening again."

"Thank you." My shoulders relaxed as the tension drained from them. I'd almost blown my first chance to show Beth I could be a responsible parent by fucking up and losing Chase.

After some uncomfortable silence, she told me about a couple of times she'd lost Chase. Confessing it never failed to give her a heart attack.

It was scary how quickly it'd happened, despite all my training. *I'm just happy I found him right away.* A cold chill swept over my body as I thought of all the things that could've gone wrong. I offered to teach her what I'd learned in my class on child safety, and she gratefully accepted.

We spent the rest of the ride talking about more pleasant things. When she turned onto my street, I had her drop me off at my front door rather than park, so she could get Chase home.

"Thank you for a fun, and eye-opening, afternoon." I swore to myself I'd never make that mistake again. I wouldn't be able to live with myself if anything happened to Chase on my watch.

"You're welcome." She glanced back at Chase at the same time I did.

He was still sound asleep, so I leaned over and gave her a quick kiss on the cheek. "I'll call you later, okay?"

"Yes." She reached for my hand as I turned to open my door. "Despite the scare, I had a nice time, too. Thanks for coming with us."

Chapter 26

Beth

What a day! I was exhausted from the emotional roller coaster I'd just ridden. The highs of waking up in Doug's bed, the nervousness of asking him to join us, bringing him to pick up Chase, the fear when I couldn't see Chase at the museum, my anger when I realized Doug lot him, followed by gratitude for helping me navigate the situation when my anxiety made it hard to think.

Knowing it wasn't his fault Chase had wandered off, my initial anger at Doug had worn off quickly and I'd forgiven him. I spent the rest of the day worried I'd lose Chase and wouldn't let go of his hand except to let Doug take him to the men's room. Chase was excited to use the big boy bathroom, but I couldn't share his feelings. I'd hovered outside the door like a nervous nelly the entire time.

Much to my relief, Chase fell asleep on the ride home giving me an opportunity to talk to Doug. Chase would be disappointed when he woke up, because I'd promised him ice cream, but I could make him a sundae at home. He'd be disappointed Doug wasn't with us too, but, sensing I needed time with Chase, Doug had asked for a rain check.

I pulled into the garage and closed the door behind me before getting out of the car. It was one of the many safety protocols Phil had taught me and was now a habit. Much like locking the doors as soon as I got in or out of the car.

"Chase, time to wake up," I said as I unbuckled his seatbelt.

He blinked his eyes a few times as he came fully awake. "Where's Mr. Doug?"

"He had to go home, but he wanted me to thank you for telling him all about the dinosaurs."

"But we were supposed to get ice cream." Chase looked like he might cry.

"We can still have ice cream; we'll just have it here." I said as I helped him out of the car. "Mr. Doug said he'll take us out another time. You'll get twice as much."

"Yay." As soon as we were inside, Chase ran to the kitchen and climbed into his favorite chair.

I rubbed his head as I walked by him, feeling blessed today hadn't ended badly. I grabbed his favorite bowl and scooped some chocolate chip cookie dough into it. Then, because it'd been such a crazy day, and I was filled with gratitude induced generosity, I added some whip cream and chocolate sprinkles. He'd be on a sugar high for a while—and I'd enjoy every second of it.

"Here you go. I'll grab your suitcase while you eat."

"No ice cream for you?" he asked around a mouthful.

"Not yet, I'll have some when I come back in." I reached over and scooped a few sprinkles off his whipped cream with my finger.

"Hey!"

"It was too yummy to resist." I smiled around my finger. "I'll be right back."

As soon as he finished his ice cream, Chase wanted to color in his dinosaur book. I sat on the couch and watched as he opened several coloring books and dumped out his sixty-four pack of crayons, making a mess all over the floor.

I wouldn't change a thing, because he was safe and sound. And happy.

After getting Chase cleaned up and put to bed, I texted Doug to ask if he could talk.

My phone rang a few minutes later in reply.

"Hey, how are you holding up?" he asked instead of saying hello.

"Better now. Chase is finally asleep."

"Did he say anything about what happened?"

"Nah, he's pretty resilient. Though he was sad you didn't have ice cream with us."

"Did you tell him I was sorry?"

His voice sounded a little strange.

"I did, and that you offered to take us out another time. Sorry for volunteering you."

"I'm glad you did… Beth, I'm sorry." I could hear him struggling to hold back his emotions.

"I forgive you." I'd already told him that, but it sounded like he needed to hear it again. "Doug, please don't beat yourself up and don't drive yourself crazy thinking about what if scenarios."

"Thanks, I'll try."

"Good." It really wouldn't do him any good to wallow in what could have happened. I knew, because I drove myself mad the first time it happened to me.

"I had fun with you guys today, despite the hiccup, and-"

I interrupted him, "Oh, I like that. Makes it sound less scary."

"Yeah."

"I'm sorry, I cut you off. Continue."

"Just tell me when and I'll take you both to The Chocolatier."

We talked for a few more minutes before I started yawning, prompting us to say goodbye.

I took a shower before bed, hoping it'd help me relax so sleep would come easier.

It didn't.

Ignoring the advice I'd given to Doug; I kept thinking about all the things that could have gone wrong today.

Chapter 27

Beth

The next four days were blessedly uneventful. I worked. Chase played. Doug and I talked every night. I smiled, things were going well with Doug and I couldn't wait for our next date. Neither could Chase, because he wasn't one to forget that Doug had promised to take him out for ice cream.

Late Wednesday morning my phone buzzed—Chase's daycare. They usually sent texts throughout the day with updates, pictures and other mundane things. They only called for questions or problems, so I always answered.

I knew something was wrong the instant I heard Angela's panic-laced voice.

My breath caught in my throat.

"What happened? Is Chase okay?" Dreading what she might say, I walked to the break room for privacy.

"Can you come to the park? We can't find Chase. Weatherford PD is on their way." I felt the color drain from my face as my knees buckled underneath me. I landed in the chair with a thud.

The PD! He's been gone long enough for them to call the PD.

Terror stole my voice. Chase was missing. I jumped when I felt a hand on my shoulder.

Mary's touch startled me out of my paralysis. I forced myself to take a deep breath before answering Angela, "I'm on my way."

When I told Mary I had to go to the park because Chase was missing, she said, "Go. I'll call John."

My sweaty hands shook as I untied my apron. Mary took it from me and handed me my purse. I dug out my keys as I ran to my car.

I'm going to be sick.

I didn't have time to be sick, so I swallowed down the impulse and started my car. The park was less than twenty minutes away, but it might as well have been on the other side of the state given how desperately I needed to be there.

I drove as fast as I safely could, praying the entire time I'd get a call telling me Chase had been found.

It wasn't hard to figure out where Chase's teachers were because of the crowd gathering. Parking as close as I could, then prying my hands off the steering wheel, I jumped out of my car and ran towards the crowd, flexing my stiff hands along the way.

I stopped at the nearest officer and choked out, "Did you find him yet?" I held my ribs as I sucked air in, willing myself not to hyperventilate and pass out.

"You must be Chase's mom. No ma'am, but we're still looking."

I turned when I heard my name.

Angela ran over, her mascara staining her cheeks. "Oh Beth, we're so sorry. One of the kids fell and scraped his knee. It was bad, and I needed Shawna's help. We told the kids to gather up." She wiped tears off her cheek. "When we finished and took a headcount, Chase was gone."

Chase was known to wander off. He loved chasing ducks or frogs and even the occasional butterfly. But he rarely went far, and he always came running back to tell me about his adventures. It wasn't hard to imagine he'd come running back any second, excited to see all the policemen and tell me all about the animal he'd chased.

It took me more than fifteen minutes to get here. Shouldn't he have come back by now?

Especially since there were cop cars with flashing lights everywhere. Chase was drawn to flashing police lights like a moth to a flame. His obsession with policemen was second only to dinosaurs.

He's really missing. My stomach dropped as the playground started to spin.

The officer grabbed my elbow to support me. "I assure you, Mrs. Wyatt, we're doing everything we can to find your son."

Turning my head left and right, I searched for any sign of Chase. It took every ounce of strength I had to stand still and not run off screaming his name.

The officer put his hand on my shoulder and offered comfort with a gentle squeeze. I reached up and placed my hand on his, grateful for the support. I took a deep breath and released it slowly, but it did nothing to slow down my racing heart as I looked around again. *I can't just stand here.*

"What can I do? Should I call for him?" I asked.

"Yes. We have uniforms looking for him, but he may be scared of getting in trouble. If he hears your voice, he may come out into the open, or call out if he's stuck somewhere."

Chase had never been afraid of the police. *But he might be now, Doug and I talked to him about wandering off four days ago.* The park was fairly large for such a small town, with a baseball diamond at one end and a field for soccer and football at the other. In between was a playground and a gazebo surrounded by grass and benches. There were houses and apartment complexes on three sides.

There were a million and one places Chase could have gone.

The fall air felt like lead in my lungs.

Chase would've returned by now, if he could.

Which means he can't. My heart sank.

Where is he? I stepped away from the crowd and yelled. "CHASE!" I yelled until a wave of nausea forced me to stop.

Hoping to suppress it, I put my hand on my stomach. *If I can't get myself under control, I'll end up vomiting.*

Shawna handed me a bottle of water. "Here."

Grateful for the distraction, I took the bottle and brought it to my lips with trembling fingers. In an attempt to not drop it, I squeezed too hard and spilled water down the front of my shirt.

That was the straw that broke the camel's back.

"Chase." I sobbed as the dam broke and tears flowed down my face. Visions of Chase being kidnapped, tortured, beaten, never to be seen again, flashed through my mind as I sank to the ground.

This can't be happening.

But it was. I'd been married to a cop, so I knew it could. It could happen to anyone, anytime, anywhere.

To me, today, in our small, quiet, safe town.

Shawna sat down beside me and pulled me into a hug, rubbing my back the way I often did to comfort Chase. Her voice was soothing as she said, "I'm sure we'll find him soon. He probably followed a bunny into a bush and he can't see the lights or hear us yet."

I didn't believe her. After taking a few deep breaths, I thanked her and stood up.

I turned to the officer and asked, "Which way should I go when I call for him?" There was no point in screaming my head off in the wrong place.

"He was last seen walking in that direction." He pointed towards the other end of the playground, near the baseball diamond.

The diamond where Chase played tee ball.

"Thanks," I said as I ran off in the direction of the field. After almost tripping, because I was looking around instead of watching where I was going, I forced myself to slow down to a brisk walk. When I got to the officers at the other end, I introduced myself before I started shouting Chase's name.

Before long, my throat was sore, and my voice was hoarse from screaming steadily while searching. I asked the nearest officer if they'd heard anything, despite knowing the answer.

"No ma'am, not yet," the tall female officer answered. "We'll let you know as soon as we do."

When her radio crackled with an incoming message, I held my breath and prayed. *Please let it be someone reporting they've found him.*

Instead, it was another officer asking her to tell me John Sheppard was here.

John. My knees buckled in gratitude. John would find Chase. I just knew he would.

He has to.

The officer started speaking, but I was already running back towards the playground. In my mind I heard Chase say "manners," so I yelled thanks over my shoulder.

Chapter 28

Doug

When we heard John's booming, fear-laced voice yell, "Lobby, now!" AJ and I jumped from our chairs, shared a look—John never yelled—and ran out.

The expression on his pale face stopped me in my tracks; I'd never seen him look so rattled.

It was nothing compared to the look on Meg's face. She was pale and her eyes were frantic as she waited for everyone to assemble.

"Drop anything that isn't an emergency. We're going to the park to help search for Chase."

Chase is missing? Fear gripped my heart. *I have to get to Beth. She must be losing her mind with worry.*

The room buzzed as everyone started asking questions.

John turned to Sammie. "Campbell, get in touch with someone from the department. Let them know we're on our way."

"Yes, sir." Samantha Campbell was one of our part-time security personnel, and a full-time Weatherford cop.

"Chase is lost at the park. Beth is on her way there now. WPD is working under the assumption he's wandered off and not treating it like a kidnapping."

"Are we treating it the same, sir?" I asked. Beth told me Chase had a habit of wandering off. Hell, I'd witnessed it for myself. However, from what she'd said, he rarely went far.

"No." He ran his hand through his curly short brown hair. "Until he's found we'll work under the assumption he's been kidnapped. We'll search for clues while we help look for him." The Sheppards had known Chase his entire life. John added, "It's not normal for him to be gone long enough to inspire a man hunt."

Jack was standing beside Meg, his arm around her. She asked, "What do you need me to do?"

"Stay here for now." He softened his tone to answer her. When he turned back to us, he was all business again.

"Janerek, you're with Jamie and Jack. Sharpe, you're with me. Campbell, we'll take any help you can give us before your shift starts. Gear up, we leave in three."

We all nodded and returned to our respective offices to grab our search gear.

Jack gave Meg a hug before we left, promising her we wouldn't stop until Chase was found, as he wiped a tear off her cheek.

A wave of jealousy washed over me; I want a love like that. I chastised myself for focusing on the wrong thing and steeled my mind to the task at hand.

Finding Chase. It was the only thing that mattered.

John confirmed my fears on the drive over; Chase was most likely hurt or had been kidnapped. He said Chase rarely went far when he wandered, and he usually came running back eager to share the story about whatever it was that had caught his attention.

"And he never misses a chance to talk to a cop. If he didn't come running to see them, we have to assume he couldn't."

Knowing he was right, and having nothing to add, I nodded.

"Beth will be a nervous wreck, so don't take anything she says too personal."

"Thanks." Beth and I hadn't been dating long, but I'd already seen how she acted when she was worried about Chase. The museum incident happened less than a week ago, but it was nothing compared to what she must be going through today.

I prayed we'd find him, safe and sound, sooner rather than later.

The first thing I did when we got to the park was look for Beth. I wanted, needed, to be there for her as much as I needed to help with the search. When I finally found her, talking to an officer a few yards away, I strode over as fast as I could without actually running. John was close on my heels.

When she saw me she flew into my arms, buried her face in my chest and sobbed. I held her close, stroking her back to offer what little comfort I could while John talked to the officer.

Beth stepped back and said between sniffles, "We can't find him. I can't lose him too."

Her fear and desperation tore my heart to shreds. I wanted to promise her we'd find him, and everything would be okay, but I couldn't lie.

What I could do was promise I wouldn't stop looking.

John finished talking to the officer and joined us just as Jamie, Jack, and AJ arrived.

"Beth," he pulled her into a hug, "we're going to do everything we can to find Chase and bring him home to you."

"Thank you." She pulled away and wiped her nose on her arm.

"Weatherford PD is calling out the search and rescue volunteers. Me and the boys are going to start a search in the direction he was last seen." He looked at Beth, then at me. "Do you want one of us to stay here with you?"

"Can't I come with you?"

"No, it's best for you to stay here since this is where he'll return, if he can. Plus, this is command central, so if he's found by another team you'll want to be here when they bring him back."

"Okay." Beth had drifted back to my side, so I put my arm around her. It was the only way I could think to offer her comfort.

"Do you want someone to stay?" John repeated the question.

"No." She shook her head. "You all need to look."

"I can call Emily and have her come stay with you," Jamie offered.

"Mary will be here as soon as she can," John added.

Beth put on a brave face. "Thanks, but I'll be okay until your mom gets here."

John reached out for Beth's hand and led her back to the commanding officer on scene.

When he returned , he said, "We're doing a standard neighborhood search. We're not leaving any bush, tree, or back yard uncovered. Understood?"

"Yes, sir."

"Chase was last seen walking towards the baseball diamond, so we're going to cross the street there," he pointed, "and start the search. I'll take point and stay in touch with Sgt. Walker, who'll be taking command of the search and rescue team when they get here. Any questions?"

"No, sir."

"Let's move."

Not long after we started, the Sgt. notified John that Mary had arrived on scene and was with Beth. Not surprisingly, she'd closed the shop early and asked her part-time baristas to set up a table with coffee and bottles of water.

We searched for ninety minutes before the volunteers arrived and started their search.

The sky turned orange and pink as the sun started to set. We kept looking.

We had high-powered flashlights, so we continued searching after the sun had set.

Two hours after sunset, Sgt. Walker called in the volunteers. We kept looking.

Chase was family; we weren't giving up.

John called in a favor with WPD and asked for an officer to be assigned to stay Beth and Mary.

Two hours later, John made the command decision to call off our search. By that time, we'd collectively searched a large enough area that we had to accept the probability Chase hadn't 'just wandered off'.

We walked back in silence—None of us willing to give voice to reality.

I need to be with Beth.

Mary and Beth had gone to the SSI office and were waiting for us there, along with Meg and Emily. Campbell was there, having been assigned to stay with Beth after clocking in for her shift.

Once we were in the car, John called Mary to let her know we were on our way back and asked her to order food. Most of us hadn't eaten since lunch.

We'd need calories to get through the night, because I knew, beyond the shadow of a doubt, none of us would sleep.

Chapter 29

Beth

I paced back and forth, clutching my hands together as I waited for updates. Mary kept me company, held me when I cried, and made sure I stayed hydrated.

Officer Campbell stayed with us after the volunteers were called back. Once everyone was gone, Campbell encouraged me to wait back at the SSI office, saying, "There's nothing more you can do here."

I shook my head, no. I wasn't ready to hear it. Leaving meant giving up.

"Beth, honey, she's right." Mary talked to me like she would a scared child. "Let's wait at the office. John will keep us updated."

What if Chase comes back? He wouldn't. Couldn't. Not after so much time had passed.

Sammie, as Officer Campbell told us to call her, said she could start the paperwork to get access to the traffic cams if we went back. "I can also file the missing person's report."

Missing person's report.

My son is missing.

The world started spinning. Bile rose in my throat as my legs gave out. I might have hurt myself, but Sammie caught me before I hit the ground.

She and Mary helped me back to my feet and walked me to Mary's car.

I panicked. "I have to have my car. His booster seat is in it. What if I need to pick him up?"

"It's okay, we'll take your car, but I'm driving," Mary said.

Knowing I was in no condition to drive, I handed her the keys.

Waiting back at the SSI office wasn't any better despite the added support of Meg and Emily. Meg was still working, getting regular updates from WPD and relaying information to John and the guys in the field, and Emily was offering friendly support.

I wore a path in the rug of the lobby as I paced, glancing at my phone every couple of minutes to see if I'd gotten a message from Chase. I'd made him memorize my phone number as soon as he was capable, and he knew to ask an adult to call me if he got lost.

It was after eleven when John called Mary. He told her they were stopping for the night, and asked her to order food. It was too late to order delivery, so Emily went to the store and stocked up. When I tried to give her my credit card; she refused.

I started crying again as I thanked her. There was no way I could have handled this without these women. My friends.

They're family.

When John and the rest of the SSI team returned, they looked exhausted. *Defeated.*

I thanked each of them with a hug as they came in.

When it was his turn, Doug apologized softly. I told him not to apologize; I didn't blame him, them, for stopping for the night.

When John said, "We've stopped the ground search, but we're not done." Everyone nodded and agreed. "We'll eat, then do what we can from here."

Jamie glanced at his phone. "Emily's on her way back."

Sammie came out of her office. "I've filed the missing person's report, and put in a request for access to the traffic cam footage around the park for the two hours before and after the 9-1-1 call came in. We should get access first thing in the morning."

"Campbell, thank you for staying, but we've got it from here."

"Copy that. Holler if you need me before my scheduled time tomorrow."

As soon as the door closed behind her, John turned to Doug. "Sharpe."

"On it." Doug dropped his hand from my back before taking my hands in his. "You can come sit with me anytime you'd like." Then he kissed the top of my head and went to his office.

I didn't want to distract him from whatever assignment he'd been given, so I stayed in the lobby.

"Meg, do you think you can contact Agent Jones and see if he'd be willing to help us out?"

Agent Jones. I'd never met him, but I remembered Meg telling me he was the FBI agent who'd helped her change her identity and relocate after she testified against a mob boss in Boston. She'd mentioned he'd recently transferred to Dallas.

My breaths started coming faster and faster.

"Sure thing." Meg answered. Her voice sounding like she was underwater.

The FBI. If we needed the FBI this was bad. *John thinks Chase has been kidnapped.* Which meant he was in grave danger. *I may never see my son again.*

"The FBI?" It sounded like a whimper as I sank onto the couch. I put my face in my hands and tried to calm down, but I couldn't slow down my shallow breaths.

John kneeled in front of me and pried a hand from my face, taking my pulse as he said, "Jack, bring some water and a wet cloth."

"Got it."

"Beth," he pried my other hand away, "I need you to take a few slow deep breaths. Can you do that for me?"

I nodded, but my breathing didn't change.

"Here, do it with me. Breathe in, nice and slow. There you go. Hold it for two, three, four. Good. Release it, nice and slow."

We did that a few more times, the staccato rhythm of my heart calming down with each repetition. After the last one he put a cold cloth on my forehead and handed me a bottle of water.

"Beth, I'm sorry I scared you. I'm reaching out to Agent Jones to see if he'll do us a favor, not because we need the FBI. They have access to information and systems we don't." He paused as I looked at him through blurry eyes. "And it won't hurt to get him involved early, just in case."

I stared at him, hearing his words but not fully grasping them.

When he asked, "Beth? Are you with me?" I nodded, unable to speak.

"Can you talk to me? Tell me you understood what I just told you?"

I blinked a few times and tried to remember what he'd said. "The FBI is, is, is just in case." I leaned into him and sobbed.

He held me as he patiently reiterated the stuff I'd left out. "And they have resources we don't. We have a good working relationship with Agent Jones, so he may be willing to help us."

He leaned back and lifted my chin, forcing me to make eye contact.

"Okay?"

"Okay." It was anything but okay, but it wouldn't help anyone if I broke down again. *I need to stay strong for Chase.*

I heard, "here, try to eat something," as a sandwich was pressed into my hands. I glanced up to see Mary. In my panic, I hadn't heard Emily come back in.

"Thanks." I took the sandwich and stared at it, trying to decide if I should bother unwrapping it.

"Let me help." John unwrapped it and handed it back to me. "Try to eat a couple of bites, it'll help keep your strength up."

It was what I needed to hear. I needed to keep my strength up so I could help find my son.

Please, God, bring Chase home to me.

The package said ham and cheese but all I tasted was cardboard.

Mary and Meg sat on either side of me as I forced myself to eat a few more bites of the sandwich and a few baby carrots.

Everyone else, including Doug who'd come out for food, scarfed down their sandwiches, along with chips, vegetables, and cookies before going back to their offices.

When Doug went back to his office, I accepted his invitation and followed. I needed to hide away for a few minutes. Everyone meant well, and I appreciated everything they were doing for me, but I was overwhelmed and terrified and needed some solitude.

"Can I close the door?" I asked after I walked in.

"Of course." He sat at his desk.

"What are you doing?"

"I'm accessing footage from traffic cams around the park."

"You can do that?"

"I'm capable, yes. But I shouldn't be, so it's a secret."

"Thank you." Doug was breaking the rules to look for Chase.

"You're welcome. Let me know if you need anything, okay?"

"Okay."

I sat in one of the leather chairs reserved for clients and prayed Chase was safe, and we'd find him soon. I knew the first twenty-four hours were crucial in missing person's cases. Because I'd taken the self-defense class John taught, I also knew a person's chance of survival was halved if they were taken to a second location.

All this knowledge is killing me. I clutched my hands to my chest as panic set in again.

"Beth?" Doug was by my side in a flash. "What's wrong?"

"They, they took him to, to a second location." Was all I could say between sobs. Terror had a vice grip on my mind and wasn't letting go.

"I wish I could tell you everything will be okay; that Chase will be fine." He kneeled in front of me and wiped the tears off my face with his thumbs. "But I won't lie to you. Every hour he's gone-"

"The harder it'll be to find him." My heart shattered as I finished his sentence.

His nod was expected but unwelcome. "I'm so sorry Beth, I wish I could make this all go away."

"Thank you for not lying." The truth sucked, but I had to deal with reality, not rely on false hopes.

"You're welcome." He stood. "Want to sit with me and help me look? It might help to be doing something."

"Please."

I spent the next hour scanning footage from the three cameras located around the park. Doug isolated the fifteen minutes before and after Chase went missing. Nothing new.

Doug expanded the search to an hour before and after Chase was reported as lost.

While he pulled them up, I went to the bathroom. The face staring back at me in the mirror had aged considerably since this morning. I rinsed my face in cold water before going back to the lobby.

Please God, watch out for Chase and bring him home to me.

I checked in on everyone, and grabbed two bottles of water.

"You should try to get some rest. I know it's hard, but you won't do yourself any favors if you're dead on your feet." Mary added, "You can stay with us, if you don't want to be alone."

I glanced at John's open office door. He was talking to Jamie and Jack. I looked in Jack's office and saw AJ working at Jack's desk. Meg had paused her work to check on me but would start again once I left.

"Everyone is still working, the least I can do is stay awake and help as much as I can."

"Okay, but I'll ask again when we leave." Mary hugged me. "I love you."

"I love you, too."

Chapter 30

Doug

When Beth broke down, I offered to let her help me search the park videos. She might not be much help, but it'd keep her mind busy. Right now she needed to do something, anything, other than sit and ruminate. When she asked why I didn't need permission, I had to explain I was hacking the footage. Though none of us would say it in front of Campbell—Plausible deniability and all that. It wasn't legal, but time was of the essence, and I wasn't willing to wait until tomorrow morning for permission.

Neither was John.

I asked Beth to tell me if she saw anyone who seemed familiar, especially if she'd seen them at the park or near the daycare. She didn't know traffickers often scouted an area before taking a child, so I kept that part to myself.

We came up empty-handed during our initial search, so I widened the parameters, going back an hour before and an hour after Chase was reported as missing.

We watched the video from the first camera but hadn't seen anything. I wasn't ready to give up, I still had an hour of footage from the second camera and two hours from the third to review.

Beth dozed off, her head resting on her forearms on my desk.

When my phone buzzed with a text from John, just after two, I gently shook Beth awake so we could join everyone in the lobby.

John was sending us home. We didn't want to stop working, but John put his foot down.

"None of us will do Chase any good if we miss a vital clue because we're exhausted."

"Beth, you can stay with us tonight if you'd like." Mary offered.

Beth shook her head. 'Thanks, but I want to be home. Just in case."

"Want us to stay with you?" Mary asked.

I didn't give Beth a chance to answer. "I'll stay with her."

Heads turned my way, but no one looked surprised.

I put my hand on Beth's shoulder and turned her, so she was facing me.

Realizing I shouldn't have spoken for her, I asked, "If it's okay with you." Giving her the chance to speak up.

"It's okay. Thank you."

Out of the corner of my eye, I saw Mary and John exchange a look and a tired smile. It felt like a sign of approval.

"Let me grab my stuff and I'll drive you home."

"I can drive, I need my car if I need to pick up Chase." The panic in her voice was palpable.

"We'll move his booster to my truck. You're not safe to drive, and I need to have my gear on hand."

Beth looked like she wanted to argue, but didn't. Instead she nodded before saying, "I'll go get the booster out of my car."

"I'll go with her," Mary said. Meg stood up and said, "Me, too."

I'm not the only one who's afraid to leave her alone.

AJ was in our office, packing his laptop and gear, when I walked in.

"I probably won't sleep much tonight, and I know you won't, so call if you need anything," he said as he slung his bag over his shoulder.

"Thanks, man. Appreciate it" I said as he walked past me and clapped my shoulder, the way men do when they aren't sure what to do and a hug feels weird.

When we were all packed up and back in the lobby, John asked for a final update on everyone's progress.

"Meg?"

"I haven't heard back from Jones yet. I'll try again first thing in the morning. I posted a BOLO on the SSI Facebook page, since we have a lot of local followers."

That was good thinking.

"Sharpe?"

"Nothing yet. But I have at least three more hours of footage to review." Which I'd be doing as soon as I put Beth to bed.

"Jamie?"

"Jack and I sent a BOLO, along with several photos, to every PD and private eye in a hundred-mile radius."

"Janerek?"

"I did the same for every hospital, clinic, and security company."

"Beth, we'll do everything in our power to find him," John said before giving her a hug.

Mary hugged her goodbye and said, "Call, no matter what time it is, if you need me. For any reason."

Beth nodded, then let me lead her out the door. She was on autopilot, and I was grateful she'd agreed to let me stay. She didn't want to admit it, but she needed someone to take care of her.

Beth put Chase's booster in my back seat while I put my bag in the bed. As soon as I closed the cover, Jamie and Jack pulled me aside and told me the same thing AJ had, only Jack added, "welcome to the family," before shaking my hand. He pulled me into a one-armed hug and pounded me on the back. Jamie did the same.

In that moment I realized I finally had the family I'd always wanted. A family who had my back, without question or judgment.

Chapter 31

Beth

Doug tried to convince me to go to bed, but I couldn't. There was no way I could rest while Chase was missing. My head throbbed and my chest was tight with fear, making sleep impossible.

So I'd thought.

After we got home, Doug sat on the couch with his laptop and patted the space next to him. "Want to help me search some more?"

I nodded and sat down. One second, I was waiting for Doug to pull up the footage from the third camera, and the next I was waking up in a panic as the memories rushed back in.

Chase is missing!

If he'd been found, someone would have called.

Maybe I slept through it ringing. I grabbed my phone and checked my messages.

Nothing. I checked the time: six-forty-seven.

When I heard my name, I jumped up, snapping my head towards the kitchen.

How had I forgotten about Doug?

"I'm making coffee. If I scramble some eggs, will you try to eat?"

"Yeah, okay." I answered without thinking. My bladder needed emptying. When I said, "I'll be right back." He nodded.

I washed my face and pulled my hair into a ponytail. *I can't believe I fell asleep.*

When I came back to the kitchen, Doug handed me a mug and told me to sit while he finished making the eggs.

"Doug, thank you for all your help." I wanted to say more but couldn't find the words to express the depth of my gratitude. Not only was he searching for Chase, but he was taking care of me.

"You're welcome."

We ate for a few minutes in silence, Doug's mostly closed laptop sitting beside him.

Even though I knew the answer, I had to ask. "Did you find anything on the videos yet?"

"I'm sorry." He glanced at his laptop. "I dozed off before I finished. I'll start again as soon as we finish breakfast."

"No need to apologize. You need sleep," I said hoping to put his mind at ease. He had no reason to feel guilty after doing so much.

"I did. The few hours I got will help me think more clearly." He finished the last bite of his eggs before continuing. "Do you want to stay here, or go to the office?"

I couldn't stop the tremors in my voice when I answered, "I think I'd rather be at the office, trying to be useful." I was blinking a lot, trying to hold back my tears and failing. "Can I take a shower first?"

"Of course." Doug picked up our plates. "Mind if I take one too?"

"No. I'll get you a clean towel." I forced myself to do and say the things I knew I was supposed to say and do.

And tried not to fall apart as I showered faster than I ever had before. *Every second matters.*

Chase had now been missing for eighteen hours.

Chapter 32

Doug

As Beth showered, I started re-watching the last hour of footage in case missed something before dozing off.

Don't let your guilt distract you.

Thank God I did. About ten minutes in, I saw Chase. A woman had her hand on his neck and was leading him away from the park. A few seconds later she turned.

Gotcha!

I didn't. Her hat and sunglasses obscured her face, so I couldn't make out any identifying features. *And I can't run facial recognition.* I grabbed a screenshot and emailed it to everyone at SSI. I summed up what I'd seen and told them Beth and I were heading to the office. I'd go back and look for the woman entering the park after we got there. If we were lucky, I'd find her car. More importantly, her license plate.

Beth had just come down, so I called her over to look at my screen. I asked, "Do you recognize this woman?"

She gasped and put her hand over her mouth when she saw Chase. After squinting at the screen, shook her head no as she brushed away her tears. "I've never seen her before. At least I don't think I have. It's hard to tell because I can't see her face."

Hope bloomed in Beth's eyes. I wanted to encourage it, but wouldn't give her false hope. "I already emailed SSI her photo. Give me two minutes to shower and then we'll head out."

"Okay. Should I bring anything?" she asked, clearly needing to do something.

"Maybe some clean clothes for Chase, and his favorite stuffed toy."

She nodded and headed up to Chase's room to pack while I showered.

On the ride to the office, I told Beth my plans to look for the woman entering the park, hoping to see her face more clearly and maybe find her car and get a license plate. Not wanting to eliminate her hope, I didn't tell her it was a long shot. "I'll do everything I can to ID her."

Beth picked at her nails and nodded, clinging desperately to what little hope I could offer. *I wish I could offer more.* I reached over and held her hand.

We we arrived, John was there and brewing coffee. While he greeted Beth, I pulled up the section of video for him to watch. Then I poured three cups of coffee.

"Do you recognize her?" I asked as I handed him a mug.

"No, but then again it's hard to tell."

He said he'd round everyone up as soon as they were in, and we'd create a game plan.

That settled, I went to my office and got back to work. Beth came with me, hoping she might recognize the woman if we got a clear shot of her face.

It didn't take me long to find her entering the park. Unfortunately, her face wasn't visible, and there was no footage of her getting into or out of a car.

By then, everyone else from SSI was in. When we gathered in the lobby for an update, Meg told us Agent Jones was on his way and he was bringing a profiler.

Once again, I saw Beth struggle to control her panic at the mention of the FBI. I pulled her into a hug and reminded her we were asking for a favor, not involving the FBI on a professional level. I held her face and forced her to look at me.

"Beth, please tell me you understand?"

She nodded, but I could still see fear in her eyes, but at least it wasn't panic.

Jamie, Jack, and AJ had checked all their BOLOs but had nothing new to report.

While we waited for Agent Jones, Meg printed pictures of Chase for everyone. We'd go to the local businesses around the park, asking if they'd seen him. We'd also ask to see the tapes from any cameras they had.

John called WPD to let them know what we'd found and fill them in on our plans. We didn't need their permission to run our investigation, but it helped if we all played nice and shared information.

WPD wasn't happy to hear the FBI was getting involved, so John had to smooth their ruffled feathers by explaining Jones was a friend of the family and helping us out as a personal favor. He promised the FBI wouldn't take over or interfere with their investigation.

When Agent Jones arrived a few minutes later, he introduced Agent Maxwell as he greeted everyone.

Agent Maxwell was a short, serious woman with thick, curly red hair and piercing blue eyes. She was nice enough as she shook each of our hands, but I had the feeling she was a take-no-shit kind of woman. She was a profiler for the special victims unit, so we asked her to look at the tapes to see if anything stood out to her.

She watched the grainy videos over my shoulder, then gave us her assessment.

"There isn't much to go on. Despite the fact she hid her face, I don't get the feeling she's a criminal mastermind. I can't quite put my finger on it…" she trailed off, tapping her chin.

"I trust your gut," Jones said to her, then addressed the rest of us. "We'll keep working with the worst-case scenario as we plan."

Hope for the best, prepare for the worst.

I checked on Beth to make sure she was still doing okay—as okay as she could be—while Maxwell watched the footage of the mystery woman again.

John wanted lists of every gas station and home security camera, as well as the license plate number of every vehicle at the park. It'd take a while, but once we had the plates we could use them to pull the owner's driver's licenses and look for a match to our mystery woman.

It didn't take us long to compile a list of the businesses in a six-block radius around the park.

John made sure we all had pictures of Chase before assigning each team a portion of the list. I'd be working with Jack, AJ with John, and Jaime with one of our part-timers, Dean, a retired Dallas police officer. Eric and Campbell would be in later and help where needed. Jones and Maxwell would stay behind with Meg and Beth, and run the plates from the park.

We went from station to station, starting with the ones closest to the location where she'd entered and left the park. She hadn't used the same street to leave the park as she had to enter it, but they were close enough for us to triangulate where she might have parked.

We'd focused on that quadrant first, and work our way out from there.

It wasn't always easy getting shop owners to cooperate, but the threat of FBI involvement was enough to convince them.

Less than two hours later, Jamie and Dean got lucky. A station, a few blocks from the park, had hidden outdoor cameras. While reviewing the video, they recognized her hat as she gassed up. We now had a clear image of her license plate. But still not her face. Not that we'd need it if the owner of the vehicle matched the general description of the woman in the video.

When they called it in, we all raced back to the office, eager to start looking.

By the time we got back to the office, Jones had already used the license plate number to identify the woman and was doing a deep dive into her background. *This is why we wanted their help.* I had to hack into a secure government site to get information he had legal access to.

It wasn't hard for Maxwell to build a profile based on the information they'd found. Jill Smith, thirty-two, had lost her husband and her son in a car accident seven months ago. "She's been treated for mental illness most of her adult life. It's likely the loss sent her over the edge."

"That poor woman." Beth whispered as she wiped away tears.

That was why I loved her; despite the pain and fear Smith had caused, Beth sympathized with her. It shouldn't have surprised me. Beth was a remarkable woman: caring, passionate, compassionate, and so much stronger than she realized.

Maxwell showed us a picture of Smith's son. There was a collective gasp in the room; his resemblance to Chase was uncanny.

Beth covered her heart with her hands, sympathy and fear written all over her face. "My God, they could be brothers," she whispered.

"Given what I read, I believe Mrs. Smith is trying to replace her late son with Chase." Maxwell looked around the room, hesitation written all over her face. "It's also possible she thinks Chase is her son."

"Go on." John encouraged her.

"I don't want to get your hopes up," she addressed Beth, "but I don't think she'll hurt him. There's no indication she was a bad mother. And while we can't rule it out altogether, I don't think she'll harm him. The evidence suggests she's had a psychotic break."

Beth wobbled as Maxwell's words sunk in, so I put my arm around her to steady her. She turned in my arms, buried her face against my chest and cried in relief. I could hear her thanking God Chase would be okay.

Looking over her head, I made eye contact with Maxwell, trying to judge her confidence in the profile. She was looking at Beth with compassion in her eyes, and there was nothing there to make me doubt her faith in her skills. For my peace of mind, I looked at Jones for confirmation. It felt like he was reading my mind as he held eye contact.

"I'll say it again, I trust Maxwell's instincts and her skill set," Jones answered my unasked question.

"That's good enough for me," John said, looking around the room. If any of us had questions, doubts, or something to add—now was the time to do it. "Bring your laptops to the conference room." He gave the order, then took Beth aside.

I waited as he talked to Beth, offering what little support I could.

"Beth, I need you to stay here with Meg."

"But I need-"

"I know, but we need to focus on the job at hand and that'll be easier if we don't have to censor ourselves." He hugged her and laughed as he added, "You know how heartless we cops can be when we're working."

His attempt to lighten the mood didn't work. Beth nodded her understanding, but didn't laugh.

She hated being left out while we made our plans, but John was right. It was for the best. We had to plan for every possibility, including not finding Chase or finding him dead. Worrying about being gentle or censoring ourselves would be a distraction.

As we settled down to work, I realized I didn't have anything to do. Jones and Maxwell ran her personal history, tracked her phone, and checked her credit card and bank accounts for activity. Watching them do the things I normally did felt weird, but they could do a faster, more thorough, job than I ever could. *And it's legal.*

After a few minutes, Jones spoke up. "Smith might not be a criminal mastermind, but she knows enough to turn off her phone and not use her credit cards. The last purchase was at a grocery store just after Chase went missing, and her last bank activity was at the ATM in the same store."

We'd hoped to find evidence Smith had taken Chase to her home, so we could have him home within the hour, but if she was smart enough to avoid using her phones and cards, she was probably smart enough to avoid going home. Not that we wouldn't check.

"No point in waiting. Gear up. We'll check her home first. We go in armed, but remember, we're dealing with a distraught woman, not a violent criminal here. We aren't barging in with guns blazing."

We said, "Yes, sir," as we stood.

Chapter 33

Beth

Jill Smith. I didn't recognize her name or her face when Agent Maxwell showed me her picture. Her son was, had been, the same age as Chase, but we'd never crossed paths. I wanted to hate her but having lost my husband in a car accident, I understood her grief.

What I couldn't understand was her going so far as to kidnap my son. Chase could never replace her son or lessen her grief. He was just a little boy. A little boy who was probably terrified.

If he's still alive.

Was Maxwell right? Would she be kind to him, or would she get frustrated when Chase didn't act like her son and do something horrible to him? Would she drug him? Hurt him? Kill him?

A sob escaped my throat as I paced in the lobby. It took every effort for me to not pepper Meg with questions while she worked.

I picked up my phone and looked at the screen for what felt like the thousandth time since waking up. No messages or calls. Well, none that mattered. The daycare left a message with more apologies, to ask if we'd found him, and to offer help in any way they could.

And a text message from Mary sending her love and support.

I replied to Mary with a brief update and thanked her.

I wasn't ready to talk to Chase's daycare teachers yet. I was terrified for Chase and blaming them for the situation, even though there was a little voice in the back of my mind reminding me it wasn't their fault. Maybe it wasn't, but I wasn't ready to forgive them yet, and I didn't want to say something I'd regret later. My text message reply was borderline rude as I told them Chase was still missing.

Feeling angry, even if misplaced, felt better than feeling scared.

I went back to pacing, glancing at the stairs every thirty second to see if Doug, John, and the others were coming down. They weren't.

"Beth, do you want to sit and talk?" Meg asked.

I'd been so engrossed in my thoughts; I hadn't heard her get up or walk over.

I do. "I don't want to interrupt your work." She was helping find Chase.

"There's nothing more I can do right now." She gently grabbed my elbow and led me to the couch. "Let's sit. Do you want anything to eat or drink?"

Afraid I'd start sobbing again if I answered, I shook my head. After taking a few deep breaths, I asked Meg in a shaky voice, "Do you think Maxwell is right? Do you think she'll hurt Chase?"

It was terrifying to know Chase was in the hands of a woman who was mentally unstable, willing to kidnap an innocent child to replace her own.

"Jones said she's one of the best profilers he's ever worked with, and she has a great track record for being right."

I nodded, praying this wouldn't be one of the times she was wrong.

Meg continued, "If she says Smith is probably caring for Chase, not hurting him, then we have to trust her."

"I can't stop thinking about how scared he must be." I felt the sting of fresh tears in my eyes. When I looked at Meg, I saw tears in her eyes too. She loved Chase. So much so she'd asked him to give her away when she married Jack. I smiled at the memory of how proud Chase had been when she asked him, and how grown up he'd looked when he walked her down the aisle and then told Jack, "You better take good care of my Auntie Meg."

That was what, five, six weeks ago? It didn't matter. Today he was missing, and his Auntie Meg and everyone he loved and admired was doing everything in their power to bring him home.

"He's a tough kid, he'll get through this."

I couldn't help but notice she didn't say he'd be okay.

Because she can't know that, none of us can.

"If they find him, I don't think I'll ever let him out of my sight again."

"When. Everything Maxwell said gives me reason to believe he's alive and well. Let's not give up hope yet."

I didn't resist when she hugged me.

Meg had grown so much in the past year. It was probably condescending for me to be proud of her, but I was. She'd been through so many horrible things in her twenty-five years, some of it just last year. It was amazing to see her thriving. Thinking of how much she'd healed in the last year with help from Jack and a loving family, gave me hope for Chase.

If, when, I corrected myself, when they bring him home, he'll be surrounded by people who love him, and we'll help him heal. No matter how long it takes.

Chapter 34

Doug

Jones knocked on the front door, Maxwell beside him. Jack and I were covering the back. Jones knocked again, louder this time, announcing himself.

Still no answer. We weren't ready to kick in the doors, but that didn't mean we couldn't search for a key or an unlocked window.

"Or try the door," Jack said as he reached for the handle. Unlocked. *That was unexpected.*

As expected; Smith wasn't there. Maxwell looked around, determining Smith's state of mind from the mess she'd left behind. It wasn't promising.

Back at the office, Jones updated everyone on what we'd found. He then asked Maxwell to share her new evaluation.

As Maxwell filled us in, I could see sympathy mingled with fear in Beth's eyes. She'd lost a husband and understood Smith's grief, and now she deeply understood the pain of losing a child. Even if he was found safe and sound, Beth would never forget the terror she'd experienced.

Her sympathy for the woman who took her son showed just how strong she was. *I don't think she realizes it.* I made a mental note to tell her, once this was all over.

Maxwell stood by her earlier statement, she didn't believe Smith would harm Chase. However, given the state of her home, we should expand the search. "There's some indication she planned for this and is likely in hiding."

"I'll search further back in her bank records to see if there's any indication she was stockpiling cash, and I'll freeze her credit cards." Jones turned to me and said, "Sharpe can you check her phone, see if she's turned it on?

"Yes, sir." I opened my laptop, started the program, and turned the screen so Beth couldn't see it.

"I'll check for a passport for Smith and her son," Maxwell paused when Beth gasped. *Beth shouldn't be here for this.* I held Beth's hand and nodded. Maxwell continued, "Sheppard, have your team send BOLOs to airports, and transportation terminals in Texas and the surrounding states."

Beth's nails dug into my skin as she squeezed my hand in a death grip. I squeezed back to let her know I was there for her.

Maxwell wasn't without empathy, but she had a job to do, and she delivered information the same way she issued orders—with authority and without emotion. John was the same way when we were on a mission. Understanding the necessity for law enforcement to detach themselves didn't make it any easier for Beth.

I rubbed Beth's back to comfort her as her panic set it. All of this was speculation and worst case scenario because we couldn't ignore any possibility, no matter how unlikely. We should have gone to the conference room, though Beth wasn't one to sit on the sidelines, no matter how hard it was to hear the truth.

Once the updates were done, Jones and Maxwell set up shop in the spare office. They'd be filing an FBI missing person's report. *Thank God they didn't say that in front of Beth.* Having an open case allowed them to use the full power of their badges going forward in the investigation.

While they did that, John and Jamie called every relative listed on Smith's background check. They'd ask nicely, once, but if her relatives were uncooperative the gloves would come off. I had no doubt they'd be creative with the list of things they'd threaten to charge them with if they didn't cooperate.

Chase had now been missing for twenty-four hours and our window to find him was closing. Fear was driving us, and our patience was thin.

John said, "Conference room," as he and Jamie walked into the lobby. Jamie stuck his head in Jack's door and said the same thing.

"I'll be right back." I said as I closed my laptop and stood up.

"Can I come?" Beth asked, desperate to hear any, and all, news.

"I'm sorry, but no," John answered her, his voice soft and full of empathy.

After seeing her reactions to Maxwell's updates earlier, none of us wanted her to be in the room for initial briefings. In a short text chat, we agreed it'd be better if we summed up the information and presented it to her in a way that was less blunt and shocking.

My heart ached as new tears formed in her eyes. I had no doubt she was assuming the worst. "Beth, I know this is hard, but please, trust me. Trust us."

Maxwell was the last one in the conference room, so she closed the door behind her. Jamie started talking before she took her seat. "No one has seen or talked to Smith in days, but her brother said she goes to a friend's cabin when she wants to get away."

"Did you get an address?" My fingers were poised over my keyboard, ready to type as he answered.

"No, he didn't know it, but he gave us the friend's name."

It didn't take long for Jones to find the address. I pulled up a map and shared my screen on the projector, so everyone could see it while Jones looked for more information on the home owners.

Using the terrain map feature to assess the cabin's location, our confidence soared. It was isolated in a wooded area, with a long dirt driveway. Smith didn't have a passport, and hadn't bought any airline tickets recently. The FBI had flagged her driver's license so she couldn't go anywhere requiring an ID, and her accounts were all frozen, so she had limited funds.

Jones looked up from his laptop. "The homeowners are on a cruise. They'll be home Tuesday, at the earliest."

"Do you have access to a drone?" I asked. After a recent case, in which a drone would have been helpful, I'd purchased one. I had my recreational license, but not my commercial one. John had signed Jack, AJ, and I up for the next available class being offered for first responders. The next time we needed a drone, we'd have our own, but that was months away.

"I'll the sheriff and see if he has an operator available." John answered.

Maxwell cleared her throat and all eyes turned to her. "Given what we know, we don't need to wait for the drone. The cabin makes sense. It's secluded and familiar to her, so she'll feel comfortable and safe.

Not for long.

We finalized our plan to storm the castle, so to speak, with John emphasizing Chase's safety as our top priority. We weren't going in guns blazing, but we weren't taking any chances so we were going in hot.

Before gearing up, John talked to Beth to tell her what was going on. She wouldn't like it, but we'd decided it'd be best for her to wait at the office with Meg.

She argued she couldn't wait here without losing her mind. After John broke the news, it fell to me to comfort her. She tried to use our relationship to persuade me, but I couldn't, in good conscience, agree to let her come with us. We had no idea what we were walking into, which made Beth a liability.

I knew Beth well enough to know she wouldn't stay out of harm's way if she thought Chase was hurt, and we couldn't afford to split our focus between managing her and finding him. Beth was willing to risk her life for Chase, but I wasn't willing to let her.

And we don't need the distraction. Though I was significantly kinder when I explained it to her.

"We have a team of trained professionals ready to fight and die, if needed, to bring Chase home. Including me." I grabbed her hands and brought them to my chest. She winced when she felt my soft armor under my polo.

"It's standard procedure, Beth." I wrapped my arms around her and whispered a half-truth, "We aren't expecting any trouble."

We always expect trouble.

As we reconvened in the lobby, Beth badgered John relentlessly until he offered a compromise. She could wait nearby, at a location of his choosing, with Dean. John made it clear Dean wasn't to bring her on site until he gave the all clear.

"You aren't to let her out of your sight," he ordered Dean, "Cuff her if you have to." There was no bite behind John's bark, but it added weight to his threat nonetheless.

"Yes, sir." Dean answered, as Beth thanked John.

That settled, we paired up, with Maxwell and Jones joining us this time, and left for the cabin. Dean was told to wait five minutes after we left before escorting Beth to the agreed upon location.

I kissed her forehead before breaking the hug. I wanted nothing more than to promise her this would all be over soon and we'd bring Chase home safe and sound, but I couldn't.

Beth reached up and touched my cheek. "Thank you."

On site, John let Jones take command. It felt weird taking orders from the FBI, but it made sense. This was now an open FBI case, even if Jones wasn't treating it as such. If they had; SSI would've been benched.

We parked on the road, near the end of the driveway, did a comm check, and made our way on foot to the edge of the tree line surrounding the cabin. It wasn't a thick forest, but there were enough trees to provide a natural cover line. From our position we could see movement inside, but the curtains prevented us from making a positive ID. John, Jamie and AJ circled around back.

"Smith's vehicle in back. Curtains closed. No visual on Pan." John's voice was scratchy in my earpiece.

"Copy that," Jones replied.

He gave our team quick orders.

Jones and Maxwell would take the lead, and breach if necessary. Jack and I, Sierra Three and Five over comms, would be right behind them. The guys in the back would cover the door, but not enter unless ordered to. We were concerned about Smith's reaction if we breached both doors at once. She might not want to hurt Chase, but she was unstable—panic and desperation could make a person erratic. And dangerous.

We were doing this by the book, giving her a chance to turn herself in. We wouldn't break down the door unless we had to. Our goal was to take Smith alive, with minimal violence. She was a grieving mother who needed help, not a hardened criminal.

And the last thing any of us wanted was for Chase to see someone get shot or killed.

"Foxtrot moving to front door, Sierra Three and Five on our six. Sierra One, hold your position. No one leaves this house." Jones started moving as soon as he gave the order, Maxwell close on his heels.

We crouch-jogged across the driveway, scanning the windows as we went. If she happened to look out and see us, we'd lose the element of surprise. The plan was for Jones to knock politely and ask her to come out, hoping the presence of the FBI at her front door would be enough for her to realize there was no way out.

Jones knocked on the door. His voice politely authoritative, "Mrs. Smith, it's the FBI, open up."

No response except a silhouette moving inside. Still no sign of Chase.

Jones pounded on the door, and yelled, "FBI, open up!"

More movement in the house, but she didn't answer the door.

"Sierra One, confirm your position," Jones' voice echoed as I heard him live and over comms.

John confirmed, "Sierra One in position."

Jones tried one more time, hammering on the door and yelling like a cop in a movie, "We have the cabin surrounded. Come out with your hands up."

No response.

Jones tested the doorknob, just in case. Locked.

"Sierra Five, on three, kick it in," Jones said as he moved out of the way.

I got in position, nodded, and waited for his count. My pulse pounded in my ears as Jones and Maxwell moved into position on opposite sides of the door. They'd have a line of sight into both sides of the room when I kicked the door open. Their eyes were already focused beyond the door.

I shut down my fear and focused on the job.

"Foxtrot One breaching, on my mark," Jones' voice was low but clear.

I waited, like a cat ready to pounce, as Jones counted. "Three. Two..."

On one, I put my weight behind my leg and knocked the door open with one solid kick. We heard a muffled scream as the door swung open violently. I stepped back, giving Maxwell and Jones room to enter. I drew my gun and held it close to my body with the muzzle pointed at the ground as I followed Jack in.

The cabin had an open floor plan; the living room and kitchen were to the left, and there were two closed doors off to the right. Jones and Maxwell took the door at the far end while Jack and I took the other one.

We took up position on either side of the second door, covering it and the open space, while Jones and Maxwell searched their room. We heard, "clear," a second before they exited.

Chase is in this room.

My heart beat faster as sweat broke out on my forehead.

He has to be.

Foxtrot One took up position to cover the living space so we could search our room.

When Jack and I turned towards each other, he signaled he'd open the door, and I'd go in first. I nodded and waited for his signal.

Please, God, let us find Chase safe and sound.

When he nodded, I counted off the longest three seconds in my life.

Focus.

Jack opened the door and I rushed in, gun at the ready. Jack was right behind me.

It took us less than half a second to see her huddled in the corner, holding Chase with her hand over his mouth. Smith's scream pierced the silence as soon as she saw our guns.

Relief made my knees weak but I couldn't stop. We'd found Chase but he wasn't out of the woods yet.

Tears streamed down Chase's face as he tried to wiggle out of her grasp. He looked scared, but unharmed, his eyes wide with shock and fear.

We lowered our guns but didn't holster them—we still weren't sure if she'd resort to violence.

I saw the instant Chase recognized us. His tear-filled, red-rimmed eyes doubled in size, and he tripled his efforts to break free, punching and kicking at Smith.

She had the strength of a woman possessed as she held him to her chest. One arm was wrapped like a vice grip around his tiny chest while her other hand covered his mouth to keep him from screaming.

I took a deep breath before whispering, "cover me," without moving my lips.

As soon as I heard Jack say, "covering," I holstered my gun and held my hands out in front of me. Smith looked confused as she looked from me, to Chase, to Jack.

"It's over Mrs. Smith. Let Chase go." I used his name, reminding her he wasn't her late son, as I sank to one knee.

"Scotty?" Her voice shook with grief and fear.

Maintaining my posture, I slid a little closer every time she shifted her focus away from me. She didn't register the change.

I need to get closer. Close enough to physically restrain her if I needed to. I doubted it'd come to that. I could see the pain and confusion in her eyes. It wasn't hard to find compassion for her, despite everything she'd done. "Mrs. Smith, Jill," I held out my hand, palm up, and pointed to Chase, "that's not Scotty. His name is Chase."

She blinked a few times, tears rolling down her face as she looked for answers in Chase's hair.

I slid closer still. *I can reach her if I lean forward.* But would I be fast enough?

She dropped her hand from his mouth and asked, "Where's Scotty?"

As soon as she did, he yelled, "Uncle Jack. Mr. Doug," and started squirming again. I slid a few inches closer when she looked at Jack, struggling to grasp the reality in front of her.

"It's okay, Jill. It's time to let go."

With a sob, she let her arm fall slack and crumpled in a heap on the floor, burying her face in her hands. I could see her shoulders shaking as I instructed Chase, "Run to Uncle Jack."

This time, I let the relief flow through me. *Thank you, God.* Chase was safe.

Chase scrambled to his feet and ran to Jack. "Uncle Jack!"

Jack quickly holstered his gun and sank to his knees before Chase crashed into him. I left my gun holstered as I watched Smith. She wasn't a threat anymore. I also knew Jones and Maxwell were covering us from the doorway, based on the chatter I'd only been half listening to in my earpiece.

Jack announced, "Scene is secure. Pan is safe." He hugged Chase close to his chest and stood up.

Maxwell relieved me so Jack and I could remove Chase from the room. The sooner he was away from her the better.

As we left, I heard them talking to Smith, promising her they'd get her the help she needed, over the sound of her sobs.

Poor woman. I opened the back door for the rest of the team, while Jack carried Chase to the living room and set him down on the couch.

As soon as he was in the door, John took command again, "Jamie, you and Janerek find out what Jones needs from us." Relief washed over his features as he glanced at Chase, then turned to me, "Sharpe, call Beth."

"Yes, sir," we answered in unison as I took out my phone. I wanted to be the one checking on Chase, comforting him, but I had my orders.

Chase turned towards the sound of John's voice, and cried out, "Uncle John!" a split second before escaping Jack's hold and running over.

"Hey, Kiddo, are you hurt anywhere?" John asked as he kneeled in front of him, running his hands over Chase's body as he hugged him.

He shook his head as he cried into John's shoulder, "I want my mommy."

"She'll be here soon," John said as he made eye contact with me over Chase's head.

I nodded as I gave Dean the all clear and hung up. John said to call Beth, but Dean had specific orders to stay put until he heard directly from one of us.

I bowed my head and thanked God as relief washed over me. *Chase is safe and Beth is on her way.* Smith hadn't hurt him. Not physically, at least. He'd need a psych evaluation to find out what emotional damage she'd caused during the twenty-seven hours she held him captive. He'd need therapy, but at his age, and with the support of his family, he should bounce back without long-term repercussions.

John was holding Chase tight enough to crush him.

More tension left my body when Chase said, "You're squishing me, Uncle John."

"Sorry, I'm just so happy to see you," John answered with a laugh as he released him.

I still hadn't had a chance to hug him, so I got down on my knees and opened my arms. I choked on the words as I asked, "Can I get a hug too, Little Man?"

Chase didn't hesitate. "When will my Mommy be here?" he asked into my chest.

"She'll be here any second now," I answered without releasing him.

Jamie and AJ were tasked with contacting the local PD and securing the scene. It was a given none of us wanted Smith and Chase in the same room, so Jones held her in the bedroom until we left. Jamie made sure he got a hug from Chase before ushering us outside. After I picked Chase up, AJ gave him a fist bump and told him he was brave, and then took up position at the back door. Jamie would cover the front.

We'd underestimated a threat once, with Emily, and it'd almost cost her life—we wouldn't do it again.

Chase craned his neck as far as he could, without letting go of me, to look left and right as I walked down the porch steps. "Where's my mommy?"

"She'll be here soon, I promise." I rubbed his back to soothe him. He wasn't crying any more, but judging from his vice-like grip he was still more than a little shaken.

I prayed Beth would get here before the police, allowing her some time with Chase before they had to talk to him.

I turned around when I heard tires crunching on gravel. Beth.

"Your mom is here," John said as he rubbed Chase's hair.

Chase pushed against my chest, but I refused to put him down until the car stopped.

Chapter 35

Beth

I tapped my fingers on my thighs while I waited in the car with Dean. I'd wanted to go with them to the cabin but John insisted I stay at the office. I argued I wanted to be there for Chase but John counter-argued, they didn't know what they were walking into and he couldn't risk having me on site.

His argument was stronger, which pissed me off. I couldn't just sit around the office waiting. I'd go crazy. Begging Doug hadn't helped either; the traitor sided with John. When John suggested Dean take me closer to wait, I hadn't hesitated to accept the compromise.

I wanted to be there, but I understood why I couldn't be. *Doesn't mean I'm happy about it.* They didn't want to risk my safety. Truth was, I couldn't guarantee I wouldn't get in the way if my emotions got the better of me.

I'll only be a few minutes away.

Dean drove us to a gas station near the cabin, where we waited for John's call. *Fucking John told Dean to cuff me if necessary.* I'd given him a look so scathing it could have put Medusa to shame. I loved the man, and appreciated everything he was doing, but in that moment I could have punched him. *Handcuffs? Really?*

Dean tried to make small talk, but I wasn't in the mood.

I didn't meant to be rude but I wasn't in a good head space. He was just trying to help, but I didn't have the energy for small talk. Every nerve in my body was screaming in fear.

Would Chase be there? Would he be alive? What did she do to him?

Before long I didn't recognize where we were. The GPS on the dash showed our location as south west of Weatherford, but I'd never been out this way before.

Visions of Chase flashed through my mind. His smile. Trying on his first tee ball cap. Sitting on Meg's desk. Looking handsome and grown up as he walked Meg down the aisle. Playing with his dinosaurs in his pool.

I sniffled. *I'd give anything to hear him laugh right now.*

I had to stop the flood of images before I was swept away by fear and grief, so I asked Dean how he liked working for SSI.

He said he loved it. "It's the perfect post-retirement job." He'd retired from Dallas PD two years ago and was bored until he started at SSI. He answered my questions but didn't ask me any. I couldn't blame him, given my previous behavior.

Dean pulled into a gas station and parked at the edge of the lot.

We're close to Chase. But not close enough.

I fiddled with the strap of my purse and forced myself to make polite small talk. It had to be better than staring out the window and worrying. "Do you have a family at home?" I asked, it probably wasn't the safest topic, but it was a socially acceptable one.

"I do, a wife and three kids."

I tried to guess how old Dean was and figured he was about John's age. Of course, he could be quite a bit younger. *I'd thought Doug was older than he looked.*

"How old are your kids?"

Hearing the love and joy in his voice as he talked about his wife and kids was the perfect distraction. It's how I imagine Phil would have talked about Chase and me.

I kept looking out the windows even though I couldn't see anything. Just like I kept checking my phone knowing I wouldn't be the one getting the call.

John said he'd call Dean when it was safe for me to go to Chase.

When Dean's phone beeped, my heart skipped a beat.

Did they find Chase? Is he okay?

He answered it, but didn't put it on speaker. Not that I would have expected him to. I held my breath as I waited for a sign.

Dean's shoulders relaxed as he said, "Copy that, Pan is safe."

Pan is safe. I looked up, hand on my chest, and thanked God.

"We're on our way." Dean turned and smiled before turning the key in the ignition.

I sagged against the window as relief surged through my body.

Pan is safe. The words echoed through my mind. They'd found Chase.

My heart raced in anticipation of seeing him, holding him in my arms again.

Chapter 36

Doug

Beth jumped out of the car before it came to a full stop and ran to Chase. He started squirming as soon as he saw her, so I quickly put him down.

"Mommy Mommy Mommy," he cried as he ran to her.

Tears of joy filled my eyes as Beth fell to her knees a half second before Chase crashed into her. She hugged him close as tears streamed down her face.

"Mommy, you're crushing me."

She relaxed her grip, and said, "I'm sorry, I'm just so happy to see you."

"Uncle John and everybody saved me," he said as he pushed away from her.

"He did," she said as he asked why she was crying.

"I was scared because I didn't know where you were." She brushed his hair off his face then straightened his t-shirt. Her head tilted to one side when she noticed the construction truck. She put her hand on Chase's chest as fresh tears filled her eyes.

"The crazy lady gave it to me."

"Chase." Beth choked on his name as she hugged him again.

"Mommy, who's Scotty?'

She looked up at me, then at John. I could tell she didn't have it in her to answer. Before I could say anything, John answered. "Scotty was Mrs. Smith's little boy. She misses him so much it made her sick."

Chase looked confused but the police car coming up the long driveway distracted him.

"More police." He pointed.

"Let's go wait in Mr. Dean's car," John said. He gently led them back the car, motioning for me to follow. He whispered, "Stay with them while I talk to the officer in charge. They'll need to talk to Chase eventually, but I want to buy Beth a little more time."

"Of course." I had no intention of leaving them.

"Beth, Doug and Dean are going to stay with you while I talk to the officers. Have Doug reach out if you need anything."

Beth nodded and looked at the cabin before saying, "Okay."

I helped Beth and Chase get in the backseat, then got in with them. John's voice was soft in my ear, "I'm going to ask them to take Smith out the back, but they'll still have to drive by. Keep them distracted so they don't see it."

I couldn't answer without Beth hearing, so I tapped my mic twice to let him know I'd heard.

We thought it'd be better for everyone involved if Beth and Chase couldn't see Smith, and Smith couldn't see them. There was no telling what kind of a scene any of them might cause, given how high emotions were running.

My attention was split between Chase telling his mom what happened, and John's conversation with the local LEOs. When the officer questioned the presence of the FBI, John explained, "They're here as a personal favor to us, the missing child is family."

The officer sounded skeptical, but let it slide. We were all on the same team, and that was all that really mattered.

Ignoring my desire to hold them, I watched them as Chase said, "She said I could have ice cream anytime I wanted, but I didn't like her kind."

In my ear I heard John say, "They're pulling around front now."

"What kind did she have?" Beth asked

I shifted my position to block their view of the passing police car.

"The pink kind."

Pink kind?

"Do you mean strawberry?"

"It was yucky. She said I like it, but I don't."

When Beth started crying again, Chase wiped her tears as he said, "Please don't cry, Mommy."

Beth pulled him onto her lap. "They're happy tears because I'm just so glad we found you."

"Uncle Jack and Mr. Doug saved me." I puffed up a little at getting credit, even though it was a group effort.

"Yes, they did." Beth looked at me over Chase's head.

"We had lots of help," I added, knowing he'd named us because we were the first two friendly faces he saw.

"Mommy, can we go home now?" Chase asked as he burrowed into her chest.

I saved Beth from having to disappoint him. "Not yet, Little Man, you'll have to talk to a nice policeman first."

A few seconds after I said it, I heard John in my ear. He was telling the officer he wanted Chase to get checked by a doctor. "We'll bring Chase and Beth to the station after Chase is medically cleared."

The officer's grumbling response wasn't clear, but it sounded like he was complaining about the delay, worried Chase's memory wouldn't be as good.

"You have our statements and enough evidence to convict without a statement from a scared five-year-old." John's tone ended the argument. "We'll bring him to the station after he's seen a doctor. If that's a problem for you, you can speak with Agent Jones."

"What's going on?" Beth's question interrupted my eavesdropping.

"John's pushing his weight around," I answered with a laugh. When I heard, "watch it, Sharpe," in my ear, I laughed again and made a mental note to be more careful while my mic was on.

John and I took them to the hospital.

I demonstrated Herculean control and kept my hands to myself, while we waited for Chase to be seen by a doctor. There was nothing I wanted more than to wrap my arms around Beth, and let her know I was here for her. But I couldn't, this wasn't about me. It was about her and her needs.

I have to let her come to me.

John took out his phone and held it towards Chase while he told us all about the crazy lady who took him from the park. When I raised my eyebrows in question, he mouthed, "video." He'd have Chase's unofficial statement recorded. *Clever.* I shouldn't have been surprised, John had thirty years of experience

Chase looked scared when he explained how he tried to tell her he couldn't go with her, "just like you said," but she wouldn't listen. John and I listened while Beth reassured Chase he wasn't in trouble, and praised him for trying to do the right thing. He let her words sink in for a minute then told us the rest of the story.

After Smith grabbed him, she'd forced him in her car and made him drink some water. He didn't remember anything else until he woke up in the cabin.

John and I made eye contact—she'd drugged him. Probably crushed a sleeping pill in the water. We'd ask the doctor to check for drugs in Chase's system. He wasn't showing any signs of drugged-up behavior, but it was still best to check.

"She made me soup and strawberry milk. She said they were my favorite, but I don't like strawberry milk." He crinkled his nose in disgust, making Beth chuckle.

He doesn't like strawberries, noted.

He said she kept calling him Scotty and wouldn't listen when he told her his name was Chase. She locked him in the bedroom as punishment. "She said I had to stay until I stopped hurting her and called her Mama." Chase yawned. "Why'd she do that?"

Beth rubbed his back as she looked at John then me, her eyes pleading.

"Mrs. Smith got confused when she saw you because you look just like her little boy, who went to heaven." John answered with practiced ease. Raising four kids and his law enforcement experience made him an expert at handling situations like this.

I couldn't have come up with an answer half as good, even if I'd had twice the time.

"Like my daddy?" Chase asked his mom.

Yes," Beth whispered, "like your daddy."

"It's so sad that her little boy died," Chase said, looking sad.

Just then a nurse came out and called for Chase. I waited while John and Beth went back with him. Beth had readily agreed when John had asked earlier if he could go with them. He'd phrased it as offering support and a second set of ears, which was true, but he also wanted to hear anything else Chase might say, and to ask the doctor to test for drugs.

Chapter 37

Beth

I almost had a heart attack when John asked the doctor to run a blood test for sedatives and sleeping pills. Had she drugged him? What had she given him? I didn't have to ask because the doctor did.

"We think she may have drugged him yesterday afternoon," John looked at me, sympathy written all over his face, while he answered the doctor, "and possibly last night."

"Whatever it was is likely out of his system by now, but we'll check just to make sure."

"Thanks, Doc."

The rest of the appointment was standard for a physical or checkup. Except it wasn't in his pediatrician's calm, colorful, kid-friendly office, but in the cold, sterile ER. Chase was brave and answered all the doctor's questions. John helped him take the urine test for the sedatives. When it was time for the nurse to draw his blood, I held his hand because, as brave as he was, needles scared him. John stood near the door, offering quiet support.

I wish Doug was here. I appreciated John's presence, but wanted Doug to hold my hand and tell me everything would be okay. To take care of me the way I was taking care of Chase.

"Can I have a lollipop?" Chase asked when the nurse thanked him for being so brave.

The nurse apologized, she didn't have any.

Not getting a lollipop was the last straw. The flood gates opened as Chase lost his shit.

A fucking lollipop. It wasn't even close to the worst thing he'd been through in the last thirty-six hours, but he was five and his reserves had run dry.

So had mine. Tears flowed down my cheeks.

John stepped up and calmed Chase down when I couldn't.

I took a deep breath, reminding myself I had to be strong for Chase.

Chase stopped crying when John promised him a banana split with extra whip cream.

I used the tissues John handed me to wipe my face, while he wiped Chase's.

"Can we get ice cream now?" Chase asked between sniffles.

"Not yet, Baby. We have to see the doctor again," I answered. "Then we can go."

"Before ice cream, we get to go talk to the nice policeman who came to help us today." John phrased it in such a way as to make it sound fun. And to be fair, it usually was for Chase. "If you want, we can stop and buy him a donut."

"Can I have one?" Chase asked.

John winked and answered, "Of course, but only if you get one for your mom too."

Chase looked at his feet and asked in a shaky voice, "Am I in trouble?"

"No, he just wants to ask you some questions about what happened." John used his most soothing dad voice. It was hard to believe this was the same guy who used nothing but his tone of voice to snap everyone at SSI to attention.

Chase loved going to the police station, but this time was different— they'd be asking him to relive his kidnapping.

"Will you come with me, Uncle John?" Tears were forming in Chase's eyes again. He still believed he was in trouble.

I wished we didn't have to take him to the PD, but the sooner it was done the sooner we could go home and start healing.

"Of course I will." He high-fived Chase before ruffling his hair. "Then we'll get ice cream."

Chase smiled as he moved his head away from John's hand. The normalcy of his action calmed my overwrought nerves. *He'll be okay.* It might take some time, but he'd be okay.

After the doctor confirmed there were trace amounts of a sedative in Chase's system, and reassured me there'd be no lasting side effects, he released us. John scooped up Chase and carried him to the waiting room, where a patiently waiting Doug stood as soon as he saw us.

He opened his arms as I walked up, my need to be in his arms written all over my face. "Shh, it'll be okay. I'm here," he whispered near my ear as he stroked my hair.

I let a few tears fall before pulling myself back together. There'd be time to cry tonight, after Chase was asleep, safe in his own bed.

"Thank you," I said as I wiped my tears, "I needed that."

He smiled softly as he brushed my hair off my blotchy face, calming my nerves and adding a little energy to my depleted well.

"Uncle John said we can get donuts." Chase interrupted the moment.

I turned just in time to see John's smirk; the one with a 'what took you so long' vibe to it. Doug had been here the whole time, ready to hold and comfort me, but I'd been so focused on Chase I hadn't noticed.

Doug didn't miss a beat. "That's good news because I'm starving." He slid his hand down my arm to hold my hand before looking at John. "I talked to Meg, everyone's gone back to the office to wait."

"Thank you," John answered. "Can you stay in touch and send updates?"

Doug nodded. "Of course." He squeezed my hand as he talked to Chase. "You're Aunt Mary and Auntie Meg want me to tell you they can't wait to see you."

"Can we bring them donuts too?" Chase asked John.

"I'm sure they'd like that," John answered with a laugh.

My kid was going to buy out the bakery if he added anyone else to this list, because we couldn't just buy donuts for Mary and Meg, we'd have to buy them for everyone at SSI.

True to his word, John let Chase pick out two dozen donuts to take to the station, and one for himself. Chase remembered to ask me what I wanted, then asked Doug if he wanted one too. John added three large coffees to the order. When Chase asked about the donuts for SSI, we told him we'd come back and buy more later. I tried to pay, but John insisted it was his treat. I was too exhausted to argue.

The chocolate glazed donut I ate on the short drive to the station was literally the best thing I'd ever tasted. It represented my son being home, safe and sound, and the loving people who surrounded us.

Chase told Doug all about his hospital visit in between bites of his powdered donut. John's back seat would be a mess, but I didn't think he'd mind.

I hadn't had a chance to talk to Doug during all the chaos, but he'd been the entire time. I couldn't stop thinking about seeing Chase safe in Doug's arms. The warmth of his hand on my lower back. The soothing effect of his thumb rubbing the back of my hand. He stuck by my side, taking care of my every need, sometimes before I even knew I needed it. And I loved him for it.

Love? It happened fast, but I was definitely in love with him.

More than once I could have sworn I saw love in his eyes when he looked at me. It was all a bit too much to deal with at the moment so I tried pushing it to the back of my mind, but it kept creeping back to the front.

I'd been worried about falling for another protective male who risked his life to help others, but it turned out I had a type because it was one of the things I loved about him.

Watching Doug give Chase his full attention, and seeing Chase so comfortable with Doug, was enough to melt my heart. I caught Doug's gaze over Chase's head, smiled, and mouthed, "thank you." His brief nod was interrupted by Chase, but not before I saw it.

Chase wanted everyone to go with him to give his statement and refused to let go of Doug's hand as we walked across the parking lot.

Doug got down on one knee and explained, "We can't all go with you Little Man, but I promise I'll wait inside, near the door."

Chase looked at me, and then at John, who nodded, and then back to Doug. Chase stared at his feet as he said, "Okay," in a soft voice. He wouldn't admit it, but he was afraid. *God, I just want to hug him.* I wanted to reassure him, but also didn't want to embarrass him when he was trying so hard to be brave in front of the guys.

"You've been so brave through all of this." Doug asked, "Can you be brave and hold your mom's and Uncle John's hands, so they feel brave, too?" He addressed Chase's fears in a way I never would have thought because I couldn't see past my maternal need to comfort.

He'll make a great dad.

John took the cue. He balanced the boxes of donuts on one hand and held the other out for Chase.

Chase released Doug's hand and asked, "Will you be okay without me?"

"It'll be hard, but I'll be okay," Doug answered.

"But who'll watch out for you?" Chase asked, clearly wanting to avoid going inside.

"Chase, we have to go in now." John used a subdued version of his command voice. He wiggled his fingers at Chase in invitation. "The sooner we start, the sooner we'll finish."

Chase lifted his chin and squared his shoulders.

No doubt he learned that from the guys at SSI.

Chase took my hand. "Let's go Mommy." The only outward sign of his fear was the death grip he had on my hand. I was sure he was holding on to John's just as tight.

You'd be so proud, Phil. He's terrified, but he's not letting it stop him.

It took less than thirty minutes for Chase to give his statement. It would have taken less time, but once Chase met the officer, who he conned into letting him have another donut, he relaxed and turned into his talkative self. The officer was patient as he answered more questions than he asked. He gave Chase a mini plastic badge after Chase said, "I'm going to be a policeman someday."

Chase needed to use the bathroom, so John took him. Before he did, he handed the officer his phone with a video queued up for the officer to watch while they were gone.

A few seconds in, the officer looked at me and said, "You have a remarkable son, Mrs. Wyatt."

"Thank you." This time, the tears filling my eyes were from pride.

When the door opened, he stopped the video. He handed John a business card and asked him to email a copy of the video before shaking his hand. "We have everything we need. You're free to go."

Thank God. All I wanted to do was go home and hug my son.

"You're a very brave little boy–"

"I'm a little man, Mr. Doug says so."

I laughed. *That's my kid.*

The officer hid his laugh with a cough. "My apologies. You're a very brave little man." He held out his hand for Chase. "It was nice to meet you."

Chase shook his hand, "Nice to meet you too."

Before we left, John gave the officer his business card and told him to call if he needed anything else from SSI.

I wanted to ask the officer what would happen to Mrs. Smith but not in front of Chase, so I asked John to take him out front. I was furious with Smith for taking Chase, but I also felt sorry for her. I knew what it felt like to lose a husband and could only imagine how much the grief would be multiplied if I'd lost a son at the same time. She deserved to go to jail for what she did, but she needed a level of professional help and care she couldn't get there.

"What will happen to Mrs. Smith?"

"She'll most likely be released to a mental hospital for evaluation before going to trial. Beyond that, I don't know."

I nodded. A mental hospital wasn't much better than jail, but at least they could help her.

On the ride home, Chase reminded us about getting ice cream. Under normal circumstances I wouldn't let him have ice cream after eating two donuts, but today I was more than happy to get him all the ice cream he could eat. *I'll worry about the belly aches later.*

"Why don't we go to the Ice Cream Palace and get ice cream for everyone, then go back to the SSI office. What do you think, Chase?" I asked, hoping he'd forget about the donuts he wanted to get them.

He nodded so enthusiastically I thought his head would break off. "We can get ice cream for Auntie Meg and Uncle Jack. And Uncle Jamie. And Mr. AJ. Will Aunt Mary be there? Because she'll be sad if we don't bring her something…"

Chase went on for awhile, talking about what we should get for everyone. My thought had been to get him whatever he wanted and grab a few half gallons for everyone else to share. But no, Chase was on a mission to get everyone what he thought their favorite flavor would be. I made a mental note to add Agents Jones and Maxwell to the list, just in case.

I could hear John chuckling from the front seat as I made eye contact with Doug and shrugged.

His ear-to-ear smile mirrored my own.

Having to spend a small fortune so my son could buy everyone ice cream was a problem I was happy to have.

Chapter 38

Doug

Chase had a blast ordering for everyone. We apologized more than once to the couple behind us, grateful they understood. When I offered to pay, Beth refused saying it was the only way she'd be allowed to pay SSI for everything they'd done. I couldn't argue with that; we both knew that as Chase's godfather, John wouldn't charge her.

"But you can help me carry all this stuff," she added as she signed the receipt.

"Happy to." I handed the cashier thirty bucks. "For the couple behind us." *It's the least we can do.* I thanked them again for their patience.

John and I carried the bags of assorted sundaes and the two half gallons Beth had chosen in case anyone didn't like what Chase had picked for them. Beth had her hands full herding Chase, who was too busy eating his banana split, with extra hot fudge and whipped cream, to pay attention to where he was going.

Chase was done eating by the time we got to the office, so he insisted on carrying a bag in his hot fudge smeared hands.

I wasn't surprised everyone, including Jones and Maxwell, was still there. Plus, Sammie and Eric had stopped by to offer what assistance they could, and stayed to celebrate after hearing Chase was safe.

"I got everyone their favorite ice cream!" Chase announced as he walked in.

Eyebrows around the room rose; it was unlikely Chase knew anyone's favorite flavor let alone everyone's.

Not that any of them would complain.

Chase stopped short when he spotted Agents Jones and Maxwell talking to Meg. "Are you new?" he asked, his head tilted to one side like a confused puppy.

"Hello, Chase. I'm Agent Jones." Jones held out his hand. "It's nice to meet you."

"Hello, Agent Jones." Chase mimicked him. "It's nice to meet you too. Do you work for my Uncle John?"

"No. I work for the FBI. Agent Maxwell," he pointed to her, "and I wanted to help him find you."

Agent Maxwell held her hand out for Chase, who shook it.

"Chase, what do you say to someone who helps you?" Beth nudged him.

"Thank you." He looked down at the bag, "I'm sorry I didn't get you any ice cream."

"It's okay," Maxwell answered.

"We have two half gallons: vanilla and chocolate. Help yourself," I said over Chase's head.

"Chase, why don't you pass out the ice cream before it melts." John encouraged him.

Chase talked to everyone as they ate their sundaes. He didn't notice a few people swapping out, or Jamie giving his to Emily then getting a bowl of chocolate for himself. He was too busy telling them all about his rescue, visit to the hospital and police station, and how brave he'd been the entire time.

He told everyone who would listen, "I'm going to be a policeman and work at SSI and save people when I grow up."

Before long, Chase's energy started to wane, so I offered to drive them home. I expected Beth to argue, but thankfully she didn't.

It took another thirty minutes for her to thank everyone again and say her goodbyes. While I waited, John asked if I was planning to stay the night with them.

"Yes, if she'll let me."

"Good. Let me know if you need anything." He shook my hand and pulled me into a one- armed hug. "Take care of them."

"Yes, sir." I blinked away the sting of tears. I'd never questioned John's trust in me on a professional level, but this was different. This was his godson and his wife's best friend and his trust in me to protect and take care of them was overwhelming.

Back at Beth's house, I boiled water for tea while she gave Chase a bath and put him to bed. I expected it to take a while, so I took out my phone and checked my emails while

I waited. Beth was in a t-shirt and pajama shorts when she finally came back down.

"Chase got me soaking wet," she explained with a shrug.

"Want some tea?" I asked.

"Please."

"Chamomile?" It wasn't hard to guess what she might want.

Beth nodded and reached for the cabinet.

"I got it." I walked her to the couch. "Sit."

I made two cups and brought them to the living room.

"Thank you." She held the mug close to her nose and inhaled. "For everything. I know I didn't say it enough, but I appreciate everything you've done the last few days."

"You're welcome." I wanted to say more, but now wasn't the time to confess my love.

"I..." She trailed off, tears forming in her eyes.

"Come here." I pulled her close and wrapped my arms around her, rubbing her back in slow strokes while she cried.

She'd cried a little over the last two days. Tears of fear, of pain, of frustration. Even a few tears of relief. She'd been so focused on finding, then comforting Chase, she hadn't released her pent-up emotions. It was time for her to let it all out.

Our tea was lukewarm by the time she stopped crying and pulled away. I offered to warm them up while she washed her face.

We drank in silence for a few minutes when I realized I hadn't told her I was staying the night.

"Beth, I'm going to stay with you tonight."

Her eyes opened wide as she processed my words.

"What? You–"

Fuck. That wasn't what I'd meant.

"Not like that. I'll sleep on the couch. I want to be here in case you need me." Then I added, "If it's okay with you?"

I should have started with that.

"Oh, okay," she stared at her tea, "I thought…"

"I'd never do that to you. I just want to stay close by." For me as much as for them.

"Thank you. I'll get you a pillow and blanket."

"No rush. Finish your tea." I held my arm out in invitation, and she leaned into my side. She fit perfectly, like she was meant to be there. I couldn't have kids of my own, but I could see a future with Beth and Chase, if they'd accept me, a broken man, into their lives.

Now isn't the time to tell her, but it needs to be soon.

Beth fell asleep before finishing her tea. I felt bad waking her up, but she needed a good night's rest, in her bed.

"Beth, honey, let's get you to bed."

She was only half awake as I carried her up to her bedroom and tucked her into bed. I kissed her on the forehead before going to check on Chase.

This is the life I want.

Chapter 39

Beth

Mary gave me the rest of the weekend off. Normally I'd be excited for a three-day weekend, but I was too exhausted and too nervous to let Chase out of my sight to enjoy it.

I slept okay Thursday night, probably because I was beyond exhausted and Doug was downstairs watching over us. He left early Friday morning after making coffee and breakfast, to go home and change before going to work.

Not long after Doug left, Chase got up. I was shocked he'd slept so long but given what he'd been through the last couple of days I shouldn't have been.

We didn't leave the house. I didn't have the energy to deal with anything or anyone and Chase's energy was low. He clung to me like white on rice, any time I was out of sight for more than a few minutes, he'd come looking for me and give me a hug.

I didn't mind—I needed to be near him, too.

After eating the sandwiches and salad Doug had delivered for lunch, Chase and I napped through a movie. Doug offered to come by and make dinner for us, but I declined. I wanted more time alone with Chase. And now that I was better rested, I needed to start acting like a mom again.

Which meant cooking and cleaning. Doug called later that night and asked if I wanted him to stay on the couch again, offering to come over after Chase was in bed.

"Wouldn't you rather go do something fun on a Friday night?"

"No."

That was it. One word, but it meant everything. Thinking back to what I'd seen with other guys from SSI, I asked, "Will you watch over the house if I say no?"

"Yes." After a pause, he added, "I want you to feel safe."

"Okay, you can stay on the couch." Then because it had sounded like I was doing him a favor instead of him doing one for me, I said, "Thank you for offering. I'll feel safer knowing you're here."

"You're welcome."

"Call me after Chase goes to bed."

"Thanks. See you later."

I almost changed my mind and didn't call him, but I wanted him here.

I also wanted to tell him how I felt, but worried about trapping him in a relationship that would deny him his own kids. *Even if he says he's okay with it now, will he still be okay with it later?* Could I survive losing my heart again?

We had so much to talk about, but I was still too emotionally raw to deal with it so I suggested we watch TV instead. It didn't take long for me to fall asleep, safe in the comfort of his arms.

He made breakfast before leaving. I felt bad for not inviting him to stay, but John and Mary were coming over for lunch and I needed to take care of things around the house before they arrived. *And I don't want him here when Chase wakes up.*

"How are you holding up?" Mary asked once we were alone. Mary and I were sitting on the back patio, sipping sweet tea while John played catch with Chase in the backyard.

It felt good, normal, to spend time with them. Normalcy was what Chase and I needed.

"Okay. Mostly. I'm still scared to let him out of my sight. The constant anxiety is exhausting." I paused to sip my tea and watch Chase run after a ball he missed, giggling. "But this is helping."

"Any time. You know we love both of you and we'll always be here for you." Mary patted my arm.

"I know. And you guys know I'm here for you too."

She nodded. "How are things with Doug?"

"He's been a lifesaver. Staying over at night so we feel safe, feeding us. Did I tell you he surprised us with lunch on Friday?" I could feel my smile growing as I talked about it. "He's been so helpful."

"Mm hmm." Mary looked at me with a wicked grin and one eyebrow raised.

I laughed. She knew me too well. "Okay, okay. It's been nice having him around, period. It feels good to have someone looking out for us."

She looked at John before answering, "I know."

John and Mary. Mary and John. I couldn't imagine either of them without the other. They challenged each other daily, often driving each other crazy, but they loved each other completely. It didn't matter how big of a fight they were having—if you went after one of them, you'd face both. John liked to say he was the protector of the family, but everyone knew you didn't mess with Mama Bear Mary.

Would it have been like that for Phil and me? Can have something like it with Doug?

I shook my head to clear it. Dwelling about the past and worrying about the future wasn't going to change the present. In the present, all I wanted to do was spend time with my precious son.

Chapter 40

Doug

When Chase invited me to dinner Sunday night, I hesitated. *Is he inviting me with or without his mom's consent?* Having dinner with them was a big deal, and I didn't want to overstep if Beth wasn't ready yet.

Maybe I should decline. I didn't want to disappoint Chase, but it'd be worse for him if we got close and Beth left me. It'd suck for me too—I was already attached.

I looked at Beth, half hoping she'd shake her head no or give me some other indication it wasn't a good idea. Not that I didn't want to have dinner with them, but I hadn't found a good time to bring up my inability to reproduce and letting myself enjoy time with them, *like a family*, was a bad idea.

She nodded. If I wanted to get out of dinner, it was all on me.

I stayed.

Beth cooked a simple meal of cheeseburgers and mac and cheese. She apologized, explaining they were Chase's favorite foods.

"Who doesn't like mac and cheese, right?" I took a big bite and smiled.

"It's my favorite." Chase said with a mouthful, spitting food in his enthusiasm.

"Chase, please don't talk with your mouth full. I'm sure Mr. Doug doesn't want to wear your half-chewed dinner." She corrected him.

Chase was on his best behavior the rest of the meal.

I was on my best behavior, too. More than once I caught myself before a swear word slipped past my lips. The last thing I wanted to do was upset Beth by having a potty mouth in front of Chase the first time we had dinner together.

I could get used to this, having dinner like a family. I shoved the thought to the back of mind knowing it was stupid to think about it before talking to her.

Which I planned to do tonight, after Chase was asleep. It had to be tonight, because the longer I waited, the harder it got.

I'd spent the last three nights on her couch, wishing our relationship had progressed to the point I could stay in her bed. Of course, given the circumstances, it was probably a bad idea since she'd told me Chase had ended up in her bed every night since being rescued.

I wanted to spend the night with Beth, but wasn't ready to freak out her son if he found me there. *Hell, he still doesn't know I'm sleeping on the couch.*

It was probably for the best. She may not want to see me anymore after I confess my shortcomings.

I told myself I'd calmly accept her decision. If she turned me away, I'd do my best to make sure things weren't too awkward at SSI and Grannie's. Because, unless I quit my job and left Weatherford, there was no way Beth and I wouldn't run into each other once in a while.

Chapter 41

Beth

Doug had looked like a deer trapped in headlights, looking to me for confirmation, when Chase invited him to dinner. I'd agreed, because it'd be rude to do anything else.

Dinner was awkward, at least for me and Doug. Chase didn't seem to notice the two adults in the room were less talkative. Then again, he'd never been with us when the conversation flowed easily between us.

After dinner, Doug said he'd wait for me in the living room while I put Chase to bed. It'd only been three days since the guys from SSI found him, safe and sound, and he was still struggling to sleep. *So am I.* I put him in his bed every night, and every morning I woke up with him in mine. Not that I minded; I slept better after he crawled into bed with me. I think he did too. But the disrupted nights were catching up with us.

Doug had stayed with us every night, which was a huge comfort to me, emotionally and physically. But I had a feeling he wouldn't stay tonight.

Not only did I have to address the reality of being too old to give him kids, but thinking about Jill Smith's tragedy had re-awakened my fears of losing someone else I loved. Doug had a dangerous job so the likelihood of him dying and leaving me, us, was higher than average. I might be attracted to protective alpha male types, but that didn't mean it was a good idea to fall in love with one.

I thought back to the fear I'd felt when Chase was missing, and didn't think I could live with the fear of losing Doug every day.

I can't do that to myself, or to Chase. He'd never known his birth father, so he hadn't mourned him, but he missed him. Even if he didn't say it, he expressed it every time he mentioned wanting a dad.

Doug would be a great dad.

No. I stopped the thought cold in it's tracks.

I convinced myself we couldn't have a future, even though I'd been leaning on him, relying on him, for the last few days. *He's ten years younger.* And while we hadn't had a chance to talk about it yet, I knew he'd want kids of his own someday. Kids I can't provide for him. It wasn't fair for me to string him along just because he helped me feel safe.

I'll talk to him tonight. It's the right thing to do.

When I walked into the living room, Doug wasn't there. Anxiety washed over me before I heard his soft footsteps.

Good God, I'm wound up tighter than a Yoyo.

"Here," Doug handed me a mug, "I made you some tea, with a splash of whiskey." The mug felt warm as I cradled it in my shaking hands. *I'm going to miss him and all the thoughtful little things he does.*

"Thank you." My voice sounded shaky. *I need to calm down.* This would be hard enough as it was. I didn't need to make it worse by being a nervous wreck.

"You okay?" Doug's hand on my arm felt warm, supportive. "Come on, let's go sit," he said as he led me to the couch.

"Still processing it all." My laugh sounded bitter. "Chase asked if the women who took him would be okay, and it was hard to answer."

Doug nodded but didn't say anything. I sipped my tea, appreciating the touch of smoky flavor the whiskey added.

"I mean, what do I say to that. I know she didn't intend to hurt him, and I know she had a mental breakdown and needs help, but I'm just so fucking mad she did this to us." Even though I understood how grief could overwhelm someone and drive them to act out of character.

Doug massaged my shoulder as he answered, "You know it's okay to be mad at her for what she did, and to feel sympathy at the same time."

"I know. It's just hard to reconcile all the emotions raging at the same time." Not to mention the anxiety I felt knowing my talk with Doug would probably end things.

"What'd you tell him?"

"I told him she's getting help and can't hurt him anymore. Then he reminded me she didn't hurt him, just scared him."

My laugh sounded forced. She may not have hurt him physically, but she'd hurt him emotionally.

"He's a good kid, surrounded by loving, caring people. He'll bounce back." It was like he'd read my mind.

"Probably faster than I will." My nightmares would last longer than Chase's; I didn't think they'd ever stop.

Doug took the half-empty mug out of my hands and put it on the table before pulling me into a hug. His arms wrapped all the way around me creating a protective blanket. *I'll miss his hugs.*

I always felt safe, and calm, in his arms. Except tonight. I had to have 'the talk' with him, and I was dreading it.

After a few minutes I moved out of his embrace, wiped the few errant tears that had tricked down my cheeks, and picked up my now lukewarm tea. "I do feel for her." I still couldn't bring myself to use her name, despite my sympathy. "I remember losing Phil. One of the only things that kept me going was knowing I was pregnant with Chase. I could barely function when I thought I'd lost him too." I took a few breaths and wiped away a few more tears before continuing, "But to lose them both at the same time? Who's to say I wouldn't break completely too?"

"Beth," Doug gently turned my face, forcing me to look him in the eye, "she had a history of mental illness, losing her husband and son sent her over the edge. That wouldn't happen to you." He paused. "It'd be hard, devastating, but you have so many people who love you and would support you through it. They'd never let you get to the point where you'd hurt someone else." He addressed my unspoken fear;

that I could end up so emotionally overwrought that I'd hurt someone else.

I couldn't find the words to respond, so I nodded instead. Doug wiped the tears off my cheek with his thumb. *He's so gentle for someone so big.*

Doug changed the subject to something less stressful and we talked for a few more minutes.

I decided tonight wasn't the best night to have the talk with him. It was selfish, but I needed him.

Our conversation was flowing, like it so often did between us, when I heard myself ask, "Do you want kids of your own someday?"

My breath caught in my throat—I'd just opened the can of worms I'd decided to keep closed, at least for tonight.

"I've always wanted kids, but–"

Chase's high-pitched scream cut him off.

My heart pounded as I jumped up and ran upstairs to Chase's room. "I'm here. It's okay." I whispered as I sat on his bed and pulled him into my arms. "Shh, it was just a bad dream, you're okay." I rubbed his back and smoothed his hair, knowing it had calmed him in the past.

"Mommy?" His voice sounded so small, it broke my heart all over again.

"I'm here." I didn't need to look to know Doug was standing in the doorway, offering his quiet support. *I can feel his presence.*

"You're squishing me." I heard what sounded suspiciously like a muffled chuckle from behind me as Chase wiggled out of my arms. The tension drained from my body; he was okay.

"Sorry." I brushed a few strands of damp hair off his face. "You want to tell me about it?"

He shook his head back and forth. "I don't remember." He looked at me with his father's big blue eyes and asked, "Can I have some chocolate milk?"

This time Doug's chuckle wasn't muffled.

"Mr. Doug!" Chase leaned forward and looked around me.

"Hey Little Man." Doug waved but didn't move from his position in the doorway. He cared about Chase, and wanted to be there for him, for both of us, but he never inserted himself into a situation without an invitation.

An invitation I'd been hesitant to offer, but Chase had no such problem. He'd been the one to invite Doug to dinner, and once it was asked, I couldn't say no. Chase had loved every minute of it. *I have a feeling it's already too late to prevent Chase from getting hurt.*

I'd let things go on too long.

When Chase asked Doug if he wanted to have chocolate milk with us, I laughed. I hadn't said yes yet, but that didn't seem to be an issue for Chase.

"If your mom says it's okay." He winked at Chase.

As soon as I said, "How can I say no." Chase scrambled out of bed.

"But only a little, it's late and I don't want you up all night."

As I watched Chase reach for Doug's hand, three things flashed through my mind: there was no maybe about it, Chase was already attached to him, Doug would make a great father someday, and Doug saying he wanted kids of his own.

Kids I can't give him.

After everything Chase has been through, I'd have to tell him Mr. Doug wouldn't be around anymore. There was no way he wouldn't be sad.

I was distant, stuck in my head, while we drank our milk. I was sure he'd noticed, but would likely chalk it up to stress.

Doug said goodbye after we finished, leaving before I put Chase to bed. I wasn't sure if he was coming back. *Maybe it's for the best.*

After putting Chase back to bed, and reading him another bedtime story, I made myself a cup of tea and contemplated the last thing Doug said, "I've always wanted kids." He might not think the age gap was a big deal now, but he would as time ticked on and he realized he'd never have his own children if he stayed with me.

We need to break up. It's the only option. I could probably live with the fear of losing him. After all I'd managed with Phil, but I couldn't live with the guilt of knowing I'd deprived him of the family he wants. The sooner I dealt with it, the sooner we could all move on.

Just rip off the band aid.

Chase and I would both feel the loss when Doug left, but loss was a part of life. A painful, unavoidable part. Tears slid from my eyes and rolled down my cheeks. I didn't want to push him away—I was in love with him.

But I just don't see how this can work.

Chapter 42

Doug

When Chase screamed, I instinctively followed Beth upstairs with my hand on my pistol. Luckily, it was just a nightmare. Not that Chase would consider himself lucky, but he wasn't the one with a hundred and one bad scenarios racing through his mind as he sprinted up the stairs.

I relaxed my shoulders after scanning his room, confirming there was no external threat. Then I stood in the doorway while Beth comforted him.

I hadn't meant to attract his attention but couldn't help chuckling when he asked for chocolate milk. *He's milking this for all it's worth.* But I did, and when he invited me to join them, I couldn't say no.

After we finished, I said goodbye and left for the night.

I had intended on staying the night to offer what little comfort my presence brought but, given the circumstances, wanted to give them their privacy. Beth didn't ask me to stay.

Damn it! I shoved my truck into reverse. *Chase's timing sucks.* Not that it was his fault.

I was finally going to tell her I'm sterile, and was halfway through the sentence before Chase's screams cut me off.

When Beth had casually asked if I wanted kids, I'd been ready to answer. Unlike every other time I'd tried to bring it up and tell her in the past, this time hadn't felt awkward or forced. It was time to share my secret. Reveal my shame.

She might send me away, not wanting a defective man to raise her son.

She might tell me she didn't care because she was past childbearing years.

Or she might tell me it's okay, then one day suddenly decide it's not and rip my heart out.

That'd be the worst outcome. Of course, the first one wasn't ideal either, but at least it would be immediate.

"I'll talk to her tomorrow," I said to my steering wheel.

Then I cranked up the volume on my radio to drown out my thoughts.

Later that night, I tossed and turned as I thought about all the possible reactions Beth might have when I finally told her my secret. I argued back and forth with myself. My fears and insecurities on one side, my knowledge of, and trust in, Beth on the other.

Beth wasn't the type to judge someone and get rid of them just because they had a physical defect.

"I have to trust in that, in her."

What if she lies?

"She's not a liar."

Or changes her mind down the line?

"That's a risk I'm willing to take."

The revelation shook me to my core. I finally fell asleep, comforted by the knowledge—Beth was worth the risk.

Unfortunately, I didn't get to talk to Beth the next day. She sent a text early in the morning saying she was taking Chase to her mom's for the day. *That's fine.* Hell, it was probably a good idea, they needed some downtime and from what she'd told me about her mom, they'd be loved and spoiled all day. *Good for her.*

I sent a quick reply: Have a good day.

I reread her text throughout the day, and each time I did, the more off it seemed. It wasn't her normal energy.

Was she just overwhelmed and not feeling like herself?

Or was she pushing me away, and avoiding me so she didn't have to tell me?

Chapter 43

Beth

Chase was thrilled when I told him we were going to see Grandma. She didn't know about our recent ordeal; I'd intentionally not told her because I didn't want to risk making her declining health worse. So, I waited until Chase had some time to recover before bringing him for a visit.

And I want to avoid seeing Doug. No doubt about it, I was being a coward.

I was sure my mom was curious why we were making an unexpected visit on a Monday, but I couldn't tell her over the phone. It was better to tell her in person, so she could see Chase was safe and sound, eliminating her need to worry.

And it did, but it didn't stop her from being angry at me for not telling her when it was happening.

"I could have been there for you," she said.

"I know Mom, but I didn't want to worry you." She couldn't drive anymore, so there wasn't much she could have done except call and offer support, or express concern.

"I forgive you. Just don't do it again." Her voice was weak but still held authority. "It's my job to worry about you. And I'm not so sick I need you protecting me from scary news."

"I promise. Hopefully, we never have to go through anything like that again."

Luckily, Mom was having a good day and in high spirits. She hugged Chase a little more than usual, but Chase didn't mind. He didn't see her nearly enough. *That's my fault.* Not wanting to miss out on what was left of her life, I made a vow to visit more often.

More than once my mom asked me why I seemed distracted, and every time I blamed it on what had happened.

She nodded and said, "uh huh," each time. I half expected her to badger me with questions, but thankfully she let it go.

We headed home after lunch, so my mom could take a nap. As we were leaving, I promised we'd be back soon. She told me to call when I was ready to talk about what was really bothering me.

I didn't think I'd ever tell her about Doug. There was no point since I had to let him go.

After we got home, I gathered my courage and called Doug, asking if he could come over after Chase went to bed.

When Doug arrived, I led him to the kitchen table rather than the living room. I wanted the table between us as a buffer. Not because I thought he'd hurt me, he wouldn't, but because I was afraid I'd lose my resolve if he was close enough to touch. To feel his comforting warmth radiating off his body. To smell the clean leather and pine scent he so often wore.

His greeting was formal. His expression reserved. Not like his normal stoic work expression, or the smile he always wore when he was with me.

He knows something's wrong.

It wasn't like I'd done a good job of hiding it. I hadn't answered his phone calls, and my text messages were short and impersonal. It didn't take a PI to know something was up.

"Beth, is everything okay?"

The concern in his voice made me want to reconsider, but I couldn't. I couldn't condemn him to a life without kids.

"Do you want something to drink? Tea? Coffee?" I avoided his question as I fidgeted in the kitchen. Doing anything to avoid making eye contact.

"No, what I want is for you to sit down and talk to me." His voice had an impatient edge to it. It was a tone he'd never used with me before. But I deserved it after being so distant and rude. I was a grown woman, a mature adult. Even if I wasn't acting like it.

Time to face the music. I sat across from him, clasped my hands together, and rested them on the table.

"Doug, this isn't going to work." I couldn't look him in the eyes, so I stated at his chest. His strong, warm chest that always felt so good, so safe, to relax into as he held me.

His chest lifted as he inhaled sharply, then fell when he released his breath. When he reached for my hands, I pulled them away and set them in my lap.

"What happened? Did I do something? Say something to upset you?"

I could feel my lower lip trembling as I shook my head. Now that I was sitting down and actually doing it, breaking up with him, all the things I'd rehearsed to make this easier flew out of my head.

"I, we, this isn't going to work," I said, instead of answering his question.

"Why? Is it because I stayed when Chase asked me to have dinner with you? Did I overstep by accepting." He was struggling to keep his voice calm, but I could hear his confusion.

"No, that's not it."

"Beth, please?"

It was time to put on my big girl panties and do this. "Doug, I can't give you what you want."

And even if I could, I'm afraid of losing you. I hadn't fully recovered from the fear of losing Chase, and the memories of losing Phil were back in the front of my mind.

"What the hell does that mean?" Doug raised his voice then looked at the stairs. He couldn't know he hadn't been loud enough to wake Chase.

But he was loud enough, and his frustration obvious enough, that I cringed.

"I'm too old to have kids." My nails dug into my hands as I spoke.

His shoulders relaxed as he said, "I know that, and it's not a problem–"

I cut him off. "You say that now, but you'll change your mind." I blinked back the tears threatening to fall. I needed to be strong, or at least not look like a blubbering fool, while I got through this.

"Beth, please lis–" The frustration was back in his voice.

I cut him off. "You deserve the life you want, the family you want."

Why won't he listen to me? I'm doing this for him. If anyone should be frustrated, it's me. I'm trying to save us a lot of heartache down the road.

"Will you please–"

I shook my head as I cut him off. Nothing he could say would make me change my mind. "No, this is for the best."

Doug stood up and put his hands on the table. His sudden movement knocked his chair over, forcing him to shout over the sound of it crashing. "Beth, will you please be quiet and list–"

"Mommy?" Chase's scared voice reached us from the stairs. *Shit.*

"Chase, everything's okay." I turned to Doug and said, "You should leave." I couldn't deal with him and calm Chase down at the same time.

"Beth, please?"

"Just go." I brushed away the tears I could no longer hold back as I watched him leave.

"I'll be right there, Baby." I said as I walked to the front door to lock it behind him. Out the window, I could see

Doug's shoulders slouching forward, making him look small. Defeated. He glanced back at the house before getting in his truck, but I couldn't read his expression in the dark.

Watching him leave tore at my heart, but doing so bought me some much-needed time to compose myself before I talked to Chase.

The last week had been hell. Chase and I had been through so much, and now I had to wipe the tears from his face yet again while I explained why Mr. Doug was upset.

He's upset with me for doing what's best. How was I supposed to explain that to Chase?

"Mommy, why are you crying?" One look at Chase's crest-fallen face and I changed my mind.

Fuck the truth.

Chapter 44

Doug

What the fuck just happened? Beth hadn't been acting like herself, but I'd chalked it up to stress. Never in a million years did I expect her to break up with me.

And to make matters worse, Chase overheard me lose my cool and raise my voice at Beth. *Not my finest moment.* Shame washed over me and settled like a rock in my gut. Chase had been through so much in the last week, seeing me yell at his mom, making her cry, was the last thing he needed.

Fuck. "I need to make this better."

If she'd only listened to me, we could've avoided this. But she wouldn't let me finish a single sentence.

This is my fault. I should have told her sooner.

I ran my hand through my hair. How could I fix this?

I had half a mind to send her a text: I'm sterile. Can we talk?

But that wasn't the right way to deal with this. I had to find a way to talk to her, to get her to listen. And it had to be in person.

Deep in thought, I drove home on autopilot and parked in front of my apartment. I sat behind the wheel, my mind locked in problem solving mode.

I could steal a move from Jack's playbook and send flowers with a note asking her to talk. Or maybe bring the flowers to Grannie's myself. *No, I can't put her on the spot at work.* Plus, I wasn't the kind of guy to make grand gestures or bold declarations in public.

It has to be in person, and in private.

I could keep calling and asking her to see me so we could talk.

A couple caught my attention when they walked by my window, interrupting my train of thought. When I instinctively turned my head toward the movement, they waved. I waved back. *No need to be rude because you're having a shitty day.*

Not wanting to look like a stalker, I waited until they were inside before I got out of my truck and went home for the night.

I poured a finger of whiskey, then doubled it, before collapsing on the couch. The throw pillows, the ones I bought so my apartment was more appealing to Beth, taunted me.

Twice I pulled up the website for the local florist, and twice I browsed without buying.

I thought about calling Jack and asking for some advice, but pride wouldn't let me.

Calling my parents was out of the question. I needed help, not judgment. *I could call Meg.* She'd have good advice. But it was probably too late. At least that was the reason I gave myself, until I looked at the clock. It wasn't even nine yet. She'd be up, but it was probably best not to involve her.

When I got up and refilled my glass, I only poured one finger. No need to risk being hung over at work.

I couldn't stop thinking about Chase. How was he doing? What did Beth tell him after I left?

Does he hate me because I scared him? Because I made his mom cry?

The thought made my eyes sting.

I'll figure this out. I had to, because now that I'd let them in, I couldn't imagine my life without Beth and Chase.

Chapter 45

Beth

I chickened out and lied. It wasn't my finest moment, but given the circumstances I didn't berate myself too much for it. Seeing tears in Chase's eyes when he asked why I was crying was too much for me to bear.

I hugged him and told him I was sad, but there was nothing for him to worry about.

"Is Mr. Doug mad at me?"

"No, Baby, he's not mad at you." At least that wasn't a lie.

"Why'd he yell at you?"

"Sometimes adults yell when they don't mean to, but everything's okay." Maybe not the truth but it wasn't a total lie either. *The mental gymnastics I'm doing to justify my answers is dizzying.*

When I tried to put him to bed, he asked if he could sleep with me. *Does he realizes I need it more than he does.* Of course,

I said yes, because regardless of who needed it more, it'd help us both sleep better.

Before drifting off to sleep, I convinced myself it was all for the best. Not only couldn't I give Doug what he needed, but I couldn't live with the risk of losing him. Chase deserved to have a dad who'd stick around, not leave because he was unhappy or because he died in the line of duty.

I was wrong, neither of us slept better. Chase tossed and turned throughout the night, no doubt plagued by nightmares.

My night wasn't much better, not just because of Chase, but because I couldn't shake the feeling I'd made a huge mistake by stubbornly kicking Doug out before hearing what he had to say.

I dozed fitfully between bouts of calming Chase down and replaying the breakup conversation over and over in my mind.

Doug had tried to tell me something, but I kept interrupting him.

Knowing he was gone for good, not just tonight, contributed to my sleeplessness more than Chase's restlessness.

It's all my fault. I'd chased him away.

In the wee hours of the morning, before the sun started peeking over the horizon, I finally admitted to myself that being with a man who could help me feel safe, and protect Chase, was worth the risk of losing him to an early death.

But did realizing he was worth the risk even matter? It was only half the reason I thought Doug and I couldn't have a future together.

The next morning at breakfast Chase was tired and crabby, which did nothing to help my already crappy mood. I was exhausted and stressed. Not to mention a bundle of nerves because today was Chase's first day back at daycare.

I couldn't blame them for what had happened. Chase knew better than to wander off, and they'd only lost sight of him because they were helping a little boy who'd gotten hurt. It certainly wasn't their fault Smith thought Chase was her son and had convinced herself he'd run away.

They were good women, and great with Chase, so it never crossed my mind to send him somewhere else. Besides, he adored them.

Breakfast helped Chase's mood, but not mine. It was going to take a lot more than cereal to cheer me up.

"Mommy, you look sad. Is it because Mr. Doug yelled at you?"

Damn it, Chase. Why'd he ask that when I was trying so hard not to think about Doug?

"That's not it. Mr. Doug didn't mean to yell," *best to just say it,* "but he won't be coming over anymore."

"Why?" he asked, his expression a mix of sadness and confusion. "Don't you like him anymore?"

How could I explain it to him in a way that made sense? *You don't have to.* He didn't need to know the reason; I could just tell him it didn't work out.

"I do like him, but we can't…" I paused. Chase didn't know we were dating "We can't be friends anymore." I turned away, hoping to hide the tears of sadness and frustration forming in my eyes. I wasn't ready to talk to Chase about this. Not when I was already a nervous wreck about dropping him off at daycare.

"Finish your breakfast while I pack your backpack for school." He liked calling it school because it made him feel like a big kid.

"Okay." He lifted his bowl to drink the sugary milk and spilled some on his shirt. "Oh no. My dinosaurs." His lower lip trembled.

He's still struggling too. He seemed like his normal self, most of the time, but the smallest things were setting him off. *I hope talking to a therapist will help.* I'd asked his pediatrician for a referral, and Chase's first appointment was the following week.

Neither Chase nor I were fit to interact with people today. If I hadn't called off work the day before, I would've stayed home with him. *I can't abuse Mary's compassion and patience by calling off again.*

"It'll be okay, let's find a different dinosaur shirt for you to wear."

He sniffled and wiped his nose on his arm before nodding. Then he hopped off his chair and pulled his shirt over his head as he walked towards the stairs.

I picked up his discarded top and followed him.

It's going to be a very long day.

When I dropped Chase off, Shawna assured me they wouldn't be leaving the house, then added "I'd be happy to send you updates throughout the day if it'd ease your mind."

She understood my anxiousness at leaving Chase for the first time. She didn't know it'd be the first time he'd be more than a few feet away from me since he crashed into me in the cabin driveway almost a week ago.

We agreed to hourly text updates, at least for this week. I hoped to need them less frequently as we returned to our normal schedules.

"Thanks." I kissed Chase goodbye, and reluctantly left for work.

I wasn't my normal happy-go-lucky self, but I did my best to put a smile on my face and add cheer to my voice for the customers. During a lull, Mary sent Amber to clean the dining room and asked me what was wrong.

"I'm just nervous about Chase." *More half-truths.*

"And?" she asked. "I know you well enough to know there's more to this." She drew a circle in the air in front of my face.

"I broke up with Doug last night." *Do not cry. Do not cry.* My tear ducts didn't get the message.

"Oh Beth." Mary hugged me before asking, "What happened? I thought things were going well."

"I'm too old for him."

"Did he say that?" There was a hint of protective anger in Mary's tone.

"No, but he wants kids, and I'm too old." I had zero control over the tears forming in my eyes.

Mary took my arm and led me to the break room. "Amber, we'll be back in a few minutes."

"Okay," Amber answered without taking her eyes off the sweetener packets she was refilling.

Mary patiently listened while I told her what happened, including the part about me not letting him get a word in edge-wise.

Then she asked the tough question, "Do you love him?"

"I think I might." I wiped my face on a napkin. "But it doesn't matter. I don't want him to end up miserable because he gave up his chance to have a family."

"Beth, why are you assuming he'd be miserable? If the two of you got married, you and Chase would be his family."

"What if that's not enough for him?" Could it be enough? Why was I so convinced it couldn't be?

"Why don't you ask him, instead of assuming." Mary's Mama Bear tough love wasn't just for her kids.

I had made a mess of things and totally, one hundred percent, deserved it. I laughed, not a chuckle or a giggle. More of a cackle.

I sound like I've lost my mind.

"What?"

"Nothing." *Just tell her.* "I was just thinking I probably deserve the Mama Bear treatment."

"Only because I love you and want you to be happy."

"Thanks. I love you too."

"Do you want to take the rest of the day off?" Mary asked.

"No, I need to get through a 'normal' day and the sooner I do it, the better." I picked up my phone and smiled at the text message from Angela. She'd included a close-up picture of Chase laughing. I showed it to Mary.

"If my five-year-old son can get through the day, then so can I."

"Then get back to work," Mary said, but there was no bite to her bark. After rinsing my face with cold water I got back to work.

Towards the end of my shift, Mary asked, "Are you going to call him?"

I nodded. "Tonight, after Chase is asleep. I don't want to risk him overhearing any more conversations not meant for him."

"Good, it may not work out, but at least you'll know you tried."

"Exactly," I said with an enthusiasm I didn't feel.

Chapter 46

Doug

I felt like shit the next morning, and it wasn't from the whiskey. I'd slept like crap, and still didn't know how to convince Beth to listen to me. I decided to call her after work, and if she answered, I'd beg her to talk to me. It wasn't clever, but it was all I could think of.

I was finishing up a report when my cell phone screen lit up two seconds before the phone on my desk rang. The message on my phone said: It's Chase.

I grabbed the phone and slammed it to my ear as I stood up. "Chase, are you okay?"

Please, God, let him be okay.

"Yes." His voice sounded small, hesitant, over the line.

"Where are you?" I could hear voices in the background.

"I'm at school."

I released the breath I'd been holding. *Thank God.*

"Can you come get me?"

Do I detect anger in his voice?

"Why do you need me to come get you? Is your mom okay?" *If she isn't, why am I the person he's calling.* My mind tripped over itself trying to figure out why he was asking me for help when he'd talked to Meg first.

"My mommy is sad and it's your fault. I want to talk to you."

Well doesn't that just fucking suck? I already felt like Beth had shoved a knife into my heart, and now I had to go talk to Chase and let him twist the blade. Because no way in hell would I say no to him. Nor would I hide from the truth.

I just have to be careful how I say it.

"Alright, I'll come. But we have to stay there, okay?" I didn't think Shawna or Angela would let me take Chase without Beth's permission.

Nor should they.

"Are you coming now?" His voice kept wavering between scared and mad.

"I'll leave as soon as we hang up."

"Okay. Bye." The phone went dead.

I grabbed my cell and keys off my desk. When I got to the lobby, I waved my cell as I called over my shoulder, "Call if you need me." She'd transferred the call, so she knew I was going to see Chase. *Did he tell her why?* I'd find out later, but right now I had to face the music.

"Will do." Meg's reply reached me as I walked out the door.

Halfway to the daycare guilt washed over me for not telling Meg where I was going. I didn't want her thinking something was wrong, given I'd run out of the office a few minutes after she transferred Chase's call.

I dialed the office.

"Sheppard and Sons-"

"Hey Meg, it's Doug. Chase is okay but he wants to talk to me so I'm going to the daycare."

"I know. He told me, but thanks for letting me know." I could hear the humor in her voice. *What did he tell her?* No one at SSI knew Beth dumped me last night.

And if I have it my way, we'll be back together before they know it even happened.

The kids were playing in the yard when I parked. I saw Angela as I crossed the street. Before talking to Chase, I introduced myself and handed her a business card. We'd met before but that was the day Chase had gone missing and it was possible she didn't recognize me.

Chase stood up and crossed his arms over his chest when I first got there but didn't move any closer. He just stood there, staring at me. *Am I really intimidated by a five-year-old?* I was, because he was going to give me hell for hurting his mom, and I deserved it.

I told her Chase wanted to talk to me and asked if it was okay as long as we stayed close by and visible. Angela and Shawna were being extra cautious, and I didn't want to give them cause to worry.

Angela nodded and called Chase over.

"Mr. Doug." He put his hands on his hips and squared his shoulders.

"Chase." I stuck out my hand and waited for him to take it. "Let's go sit over there," I pointed to a patch of grass away from everyone else, "so you can tell me what you want to talk to me about."

As soon as we sat, he asked, "Why'd you make my mommy cry."

"I didn't mean to..." I wasn't sure what to say next, but it didn't matter, Chase had another question.

"Don't you like us anymore?"

I took a deep breath, then another. Navigating this conversation felt like walking through a minefield.

"I do like you. A lot."

"Then why can't you be friends with us anymore?"

That was what she'd told him? I could work with that.

"She, I, we," crap, maybe I couldn't, "Chase, it's complicated."

"Nuh uh."

Not helpful kid.

"If my mommy likes you and you like my mommy then why can't we be friends?"

I'd bitten off more than I could chew. Maybe I shouldn't have come.

Don't be stupid, Sharpe. This is perfect.

"I really like your mommy. And you. I want to be friends again. Will you help me fix my mistake?"

I'm taking a huge risk by asking Chase to help.

This plan would either be a rousing success and we'd get back together, or it'd crash and burn, and I'd have to leave town.

Chase's demeanor changed from worried and sad, to cheerful as he jumped up. "Yes."

I had to think fast to come up with a plan on the spot or lose Chase's attention. And it had to be something we could do right away, preferably tonight.

"Chase, do you like ice cream?" I asked with a mischievous grin.

"Duh."

I would have thought five was too young for eye rolling.

"Do you think you can convince your mom to take you out for ice cream after school?"

"What if she says no?"

He had a point, today was her first day back to work since the kidnapping, and more stressfully, Chase's first day back at daycare.

"Tell her you think it'll cheer her up." It might work, today would be stressful and she wouldn't want to say no to him.

"It'll cheer me up." He sounded gleeful at the idea of getting more ice cream.

"Ice cream cheers everyone up." We agreed he'd ask to go to his favorite ice cream shop right after school, and I'd meet them there.

"Chase?" I pulled him close, so he was standing between my legs, and we were eye to eye. "Can you keep this a secret? I want to surprise your mommy."

"I can, Mr. Doug." He crossed his heart. "I promise."

"Good boy." I ruffled his hair which made him squirm away.

"I'm a little man." He put his hands on his hips and tried to make himself taller.

"Yeah, you are. Come here." The tension in my shoulders relaxed for the first time in days as I pulled him into a hug.

I looked at my watch, two-eleven. Beth would be here to pick up Chase in fifty minutes. I had to hurry. I walked a much happier Chase back to the group before talking to Angela.

"We want to surprise Beth, so please don't mention I was here," I said.

Thankfully, she agreed without hesitation.

I waved goodbye to Chase. *Please God, don't let this backfire.* If it did, Chase would be devastated.

So will I.

I jogged across the street to my truck and drove directly to the florists where I picked out the biggest bouquet of red roses they had. I asked the florist to wrap it in a ribbon and skipped the card. My plan was to tell her how I felt, not slip her a note.

I got to the ice cream shop ten minutes before I expected Beth and Chase to arrive.

Hoping to see them before they walked in, I chose a booth allowing me a view of the door and the big picture windows facing the sidewalk.

Every second I waited felt like an hour in hell. I second-guessed every detail of the plan. Was it wrong to ambush her like this? Was I a bad person for getting Chase involved? Would Chase tell her I'd be here? Would she be so pissed she wouldn't listen to me?

Fifteen minutes of self-inflicted torture ticked by before I saw Chase dragging a tired looking Beth to the door.

Maybe this wasn't such a good idea.

Too late now. She'd seen me and was shaking her head back and forth in disbelief.

I stood up, holding the flowers by my hip. The huge bouquet made a statement, but it wasn't the only statement being made today.

"Look Mommy, it's Mr. Doug." Chase's high-pitched voice drew a lot of attention.

"I can see that." She sounded exasperated, but not mad.

I took it as a good sign. Her eyes shifted to the bouquet—my version of a grand public gesture.

"I'm sorry to surprise you like this, but I need to talk to you and was afraid you wouldn't take my calls."

I saw the moment she realized Chase and I had planned this. Her expression turned dark.

Not a good sign. *Shit!* Then corrected it to crap because I'd gotten used to correcting myself when Chase was around.

"Doug, this isn't a good idea. I told you I-" Her voice was flat, and I could tell she was barely holding it together.

I held up my flower-free hand as I cut her off. "Will you please give-"

"What's the point? I can't give you the kids you want."

God, give me strength.

"I'm sterile!" My voice was high pitched, and in my frustration a lot louder than I'd intended.

So much for not making big declarations in public.
You could've heard a pin drop in the ice cream shop.
Beth's jaw fell open, her eyes widened to saucers.
"I tried to tell you Sunday, but we got interrupted."
"You're…" her voice trailed off.
"I am. I've always wanted kids, but I can't father them. I know it makes me less of a man-"
"No, it doesn't." She took a step towards me. "I'm sorry I wouldn't listen to you."
"I forgive you." I took a small step forward.
In for a dime, in for a dollar. I held out the flowers and said, "Beth, I love you. I love Chase. If you'll give me a chance, I know I can be a good husband to you and a good father to your little boy."

Chapter 47

Beth

Did Doug just propose in an ice cream shop? *What the hell do I say?*

Doug stood there, staring, waiting for me to say something, and looking more nervous than I'd ever seen him.

Chase was pulling on my arm telling me he wanted Doug to be his dad.

Everyone in the ice cream shop was clapping and cheering.

I hadn't actually said anything after Doug's declaration of love and sort-of proposal, but it didn't seem to matter. I was so shocked I hadn't even accepted the gorgeous bouquet he was holding out to me.

The sound faded away as I looked in Doug's eyes. Big, strong, quiet Doug had just admitted he was sterile to a room full of strangers, before telling me he loved me. *He's probably dying of embarrassment.* He was holding it together so well, you'd never know by looking at him.

"Mommy, why are you crying?" Chase tugged on my arm again.

I brought my other hand to my face and wiped away the tears I hadn't felt rolling down my cheek.

"These are happy tears."

A slow smile spread across Doug's face at my words. He asked, "Can we go outside and talk for a few minutes."

I nodded, but Chase crossed his arms and stomped a foot. "What about my ice cream?"

Doug and I both laughed, and just like that the tension between us evaporated.

"I thought we were here to get an ice cream to cheer me up?" I asked. It was the excuse he'd given when he begged me to come here. *Now I know why he was more relentless than usual.*

"I'll buy everyone an ice cream. If we can eat them outside," Doug said.

"Yay!" Chase clapped and started towards the line.

When Doug held out his hand, I didn't hesitate to slip mine into his. It felt like coming home after a bad day.

Ice cream in hand, we sat outside at one of the red metal tables.

"I'm sorry I ambushed you," Doug said while Chase focused on devouring his hot fudge sundae.

"Forgiven. I was going to call you later tonight so we could talk anyway." God only knew why I'd been so harsh with Doug when I first arrived. I chalked it up to being surprised after a stressful day.

"So, I didn't need to embarrass myself in a shop full of strangers to win you back?" There was a twinkle in his eyes, and no malice in his voice.

"No, but it was quite the romantic grand gesture." I teased him. "It puts every grand gesture I've ever read about in books to shame."

His laugh sounded more like a sigh. "I don't mind if you tell everyone about today, but can we keep the sterile part to ourselves?"

I'd never tell anyone, but I understood why he felt the need to ask. I could see in his eyes he was struggling with what it meant to his definition of manhood.

"Of course."

"What does stairall mean?" Chase's mispronunciation was cute.

"It means I can't be a dad," Doug answered.

"But you said you'd be my daddy."

Doug clearly didn't understand the mind of a five-year-old. *It's okay, he'll learn.*

His eyes rounded as he looked at me.

"What Mr. Doug means is, he can't make a baby. But he can be a daddy to babies already born."

"I'm not a baby."

"No, you're not. Not anymore." I agreed.

Chase went back to eating his ice cream.

"Beth, I didn't intend to say it the way I did, but I meant every word. I love you." He reached across the table and held his hand out to me, palm up.

"I'm not going to lie, it was a bit shocking." I placed my hand over his, palm down. We weren't quite holding hands, we were barely making contact, but it felt intimate. "I have a confession to make."

He waited, his eyes locked on mine, as I gathered my nerves.

"I love you, too."

His smile was brighter than the sun.

So was mine.

Doug asked if he could take us out to dinner. Chase said yes before I could answer, but I didn't mind. Today had been a whirlwind of emotion, and I was exhausted. Being relieved of cooking duty was a blessing.

"Would it be okay if we got takeout? I'm not up for going out," I asked. *Not only can I relax, but we'll have more privacy.*

"That's fine. Preferable actually," Doug answered, the side of his mouth lifting just a hint. "What do you want?"

"Pizza!" Chase answered.

"Chase, I think Mr. Doug was asking me."

Chase had the good sense to look ashamed as he apologized.

"Is pizza okay?" I asked, much to Chase's pleasure. Pizza was a treat in our house. Not only did I not want Chase getting used to having takeout or delivery too often, but I couldn't afford the effects on my hips and waist.

"Of course? What would you like on it?" His grin did funny things to my core. We'd only spent one night together, and until today I'd thought it might end up being our one and only, but now I could look forward to many more.

Doug's waiting for an answer.

"Pepperoni and green peppers." I rushed out. I had to at least try to get Chase to eat a few veggies.

"Salad?" There was a glint in his eye, like he knew I hadn't been thinking about pizza toppings.

Oh God, am I blushing? "Please."

"I'll pick up the pizza and meet you at your place. Need me to grab anything else?"

I didn't.

While we waited for Doug, I arranged my bouquet in a vase and set it on the table while Chase changed out of his fudge-stained shirt.

As we ate, I reminded Chase not to talk with his mouth full as he told me how he'd called Doug to yell at him for making me cry. It was sweet how protective he was. *He'll grow up to be just like you, Phil.* And he'd have a lot of help getting there from his stepdad.

Did I really just think that?

Chase took all the credit for getting us back together. Doug let him have it—praising him along the way for being protective of me, for being smart enough to see we belonged together, and clever enough to plan the surprise at the ice cream shop.

Chase beamed at Doug's praise. Watching him puff his little chest out caused my heart to fill with so much pride I thought it'd burst out of my chest, like cartoon characters when they see the love of their life.

Now that I knew my age wouldn't ever be a problem; the fear of 'what if he dies and leaves us' took hold again as I thought back to the devastation of losing Phil.

A large, warm hand on my thigh brought me back the present.

What am I thinking? It'd be a crime to deny us what Doug was offering—love, companionship, and family.

Of course I'd always be scared of losing him. How could I not be? But at the end of the day we'd be better off having him in our lives, even if it didn't last forever.

I was done standing in my own way.

It's better to have loved and lost, than never to have loved at all, and all that. And I'd get to experience it twice.

I hoped it'd be a good long time before any of us had to say goodbye forever, but I refused to let the fear of loss rob us of the joy of today.

Chapter 48

Doug

I hadn't meant to propose to her in the same breath as telling her I loved her for the first time. In a fucking ice cream shop, no less. Sure, I'd meant to confess how I felt, quietly, privately, but I hadn't intended on telling her I wanted to be her husband or Chase's father. *Not yet anyway.*

And I sure as hell hadn't intended on practically screaming, I'm sterile, to a room full of strangers.

In a fucking ice cream shop.

I was the guy who tried to shrink down and hide behind a monitor in high school. The guy who sat back and observed during parties. I was quiet. Reserved. Shy.

What was I thinking, asking Chase to bring her someplace public?

Christ, I hope no one recorded or live streamed it. The last thing I wanted was for it to go viral. Beth and Chase had been through enough recently; they didn't need the added notoriety that comes with going viral in a small town.

I'll write a program and scour the internet.

I was an idiot. I'd walked into an ice cream shop carrying a gigantic bouquet of red roses, then sat staring at the door, obviously nervous—and thought no one would notice.

In a fucking ice cream shop!

Anyone who noticed probably hung around, hoping to see some big romantic proposal, like a scene from a movie. Instead, they got a six-foot-four redhead impatiently yelling about his failures as a man.

Just fucking great.

I thought I'd fucked up six ways to Sunday, but Beth thought it was romantic, like something out of her favorite rom-com. While I was thrilled she didn't hate me for teaming up with Chase and surprising her, I didn't love being compared to a rom-com.

I wanted to be romantic. I didn't want to be a comedian. It wasn't who I was. No one called me the life of the party. I liked to think of myself as calm, cool, and collected. Some called me serious, others stoic. Both suited me.

At dinner, Beth and I got to hear Chase's telling of the day's events on repeat. He told the story out of order, and with a few embellishments that raised my eyebrows. One thing remained the same; he was the hero in every version. I couldn't disagree there. He called me at the office to find out why I hurt his mom, helped me plan the surprise, played his role getting her to the shop, and kept our secret. He deserved a cape.

I took a good long look at Chase while we ate, trying to imagine what he'd look like as a teenager. It wasn't hard, having seen pictures of Phil and knowing Chase looked just him. *He'll be a good-looking kid.* And with his good heart and protective instincts he'd be very popular with the ladies.

Beth and I finally had a chance to talk after dinner. She told me she didn't think any less of me because of my limitation. I must have looked uncertain because she listed all the things that made me a man.

I did my best to control the feelings bubbling up inside but lost it when she told me I wasn't just a good man, I was a great one. For the first time in a long time, I truly felt like one.

"That's why I love you," she said.

I'd been resisting the urge to kiss her all evening because Chase was glued to our sides right up until Beth put him to bed. *No reason to resist the temptation now.* I reached over and stroked her cheek with the back of my hand before saying, "Thank you." Then I wrapped my hand around her neck and gently pulled her towards me while I leaned in.

When our lips were half a breath away from touching, I paused and whispered, "I love you." Then I kissed her, pouring every ounce of love I had for her into the kiss, claiming her as I gave myself to her.

Waiting two days to see her again sucked, but I'd kept myself extra busy at work, scouring the internet for videos of my embarrassing outburst. So far, I hadn't found any. *Thank God.*

The wait would finally be over when we were had dinner tonight. After Chase went to bed, Beth and I would make out like teenagers on the couch, like we had every other night since getting back together. Though I hadn't spent the night, yet.

We'd decided it was best to wait awhile before I started staying the night, wanting to take things slow, for Chase's sake.

Last night, we finally talked about my impromptu, half-assed proposal. I told her I hadn't actually meant to say it, at least not yet and not like that.

She understood. In the end, we decided on a pre-engagement. When I asked if she wanted a ring, she laughed and said, "We're not there yet."

What a relief. It wasn't because I didn't love her or want to marry her, but things were moving so fast it was making me dizzy. I was the kind of guy who needed time to think, research, and plan. I'd jumped headfirst into this relationship based on nothing but raw emotion. I didn't have any regrets or doubts—I just needed some time to adjust.

My relief must have shown on my face because Beth asked, "Are you having second thoughts?"

"No. Not at all." Then I confessed what I'd been thinking.

"Thanks for telling me. Now I know it's weird for both of us to be moving so fast." She squeezed my hand.

I'd expected the conversation to be awkward. But thankfully, we were on the same page and the conversation wasn't just relaxed, it was fun as Beth joked about what Mary and Meg's reactions would be.

When the visual of John dragging me into his office to interrogate me popped into my head, I burst out laughing. Then, in a move totally not like me, I acted it out for Beth.

Beth brought out parts of me I didn't know I had. I always felt awkward and insecure, and had hidden behind a wall of aloofness. But not anymore.

And it's all Beth's fault.

Friday was a crazy day at work, and I was looking forward to our monthly gaming session at Jamie's. I was disappointed I wouldn't see Beth, but she'd be at the monthly Craft and Booze night so even if I didn't have plans, I wouldn't get to see her.

Chase was excited he'd get to spend the night with Uncle John and tell him all about what happened at the ice cream shop, again. *Please, God, don't let him mention the sterility part.* It was a prayer I found myself repeating daily.

We'd hoped to keep the blip in our relationship to ourselves, but Chase hadn't been quiet when he whisper-yelled to Meg how he'd saved the day by getting Beth and I back together. Which meant everyone in the area heard him, and anyone who hadn't, heard it through the grapevine as the day went on.

Thanks, Kid. It was going to take some getting used to; having a kid around to hear, and repeat, everything.

There'd been a few raised eyebrows, and even more questions, but I'd managed to put off answering most of them.

I couldn't avoid them tonight. I hadn't even closed the door behind me before Jamie, Jack, and AJ cornered me. They fired questions at me faster than Robin Hood shot arrows.

"Damn, at least let me crack open a beer." I laughed.

More than one eyebrow raised as I brushed past them, towards the fridge.

Chris, Jamie's best friend and Emily's big brother, arrived as I popped the cap off my beer.

"Doug, you remember Chris?"

"Yeah," I answered as I walked back into the living room, "How's it going?"

He shook my hand. "Can't complain."

We made small talk for a few minutes before AJ said, "Don't think you're getting out of it so easily, Sharpe. Fess up."

I summed up the events in the ice cream parlor, leaving out the details of why we split up and the part about my issues. I had a feeling it would get out eventually, but so far it was still a secret.

"Are you really engaged?" Jack asked. Chase was loudest when he told everyone I wanted to be his dad, and Beth's husband. He'd even gone so far as to tell Meg he'd walk his mom down the aisle just like he did for her. My heart had almost exploded with joy as I watched; I wanted me to be his dad as much as he did.

"We've decided on pre-engagement since we've been dating less than two months."

"Good for you," AJ said, clapping me on the back.

"Congrats." Jack shook my hand. "I have say, happy looks good on you."

"Thanks. It feels good."

Chris added his congratulations.

"You're a lucky guy. Beth's a great woman." Jamie shook my hand before pulling me into a one-armed hug. "And Chase is a great kid."

"I am." I felt like a new man. "I never could've guessed how much my life would change when I took the job at SSI. There hasn't been a single moment I've regretted leaving everything behind in Chicago."

"Dude, I don't think I've ever heard you say so many words at once, or sound so alive." AJ saved me from waxing too poetic.

"Thanks, I think." I shrugged; grateful he'd interrupted me. I wasn't used to being the center of attention.

"Do you think you'll move in with her?" Jamie asked.

"Not yet. We're going slow because of Chase."

"He seems eager for you to be his dad," Jack added.

I was pretty sure I blushed when I smiled. The curse of being a redhead. *If I'm lucky, it isn't visible under my tan.*

We talked for a few more minutes while we waited for the pizza to arrive. After a year in Weatherford, these guys were no longer just colleagues, they were friends. Family, I corrected myself.

We cracked open another round of beer after cleaning up—Meg would kill us if she came home to a messy kitchen—then sat down to play.

You'd think we wouldn't want to spend hours playing violent video games given our histories, but we found it relaxing. And we weren't killing humans, we were killing aliens who were hell bent on destroying humans.

During one particularly chaotic scene I unleashed hell and obliterated a room full of aliens.

"Damn, Sharpe, you cleared that room faster than you proposed to Beth," AJ said, his voice laced with respect and humor.

"Maybe next time you could slow down and let the rest of us have some fun," Jamie added.

"We can't wait for you Jamie, you're as slow at killing the enemy as you are at proposing to Emily." AJ was on a roll. He was the resident SSI funny man, and now the only eligible bachelor.

"Only compared to Doug." Jamie defended himself.

"And Jack," I added. He'd proposed to Meg three months after meeting her. "If I remember correctly, Jack blurted out his proposal too," I said, trying to turn the focus away from me.

"But I didn't do it in an ice cream shop."

Touché. He'd proposed here, last New Year's Eve. Jamie, AJ, and I had been here, but it was still, more or less, a private proposal.

Jamie had a lop-sided grin on his face, a family trait he shared with John and Jack. *Does Jaden have it too?*

"Who would have thought Doug would get engaged before you?" AJ asked, sarcasm dripping from his voice as he egged Jamie on.

"Yeah, about that…" Jamie's grin spread into a toothy smile.

We didn't bother acting like we didn't know what he'd just implied. We demanded to know when, and asked if he had anything romantic planned.

"Well, I thought about blurting it out in an ice cream shop, but Doug beat me to it."

More laughing and clinking of beer bottles. If you'd told me six months ago I'd be laughing at jokes made at my expense after a humiliating experience, I would have called you crazy. *But here I am, doing just that.*

"I'm taking her out next Friday."

"So, if she says yes," Jamie blanched at AJ's use of the word if, "you'll be engaged before the Hallo-"

"Dude, don't listen to him. You have nothing to worry about, she'll say yes." Jack put Jamie at ease.

The color returned to Jamie's face.

Figuring Jamie was as uncomfortable being the center of attention as I was, I said, "Let's go kill some aliens."

Chapter 49

Beth

I left Chase in John's capable hands; grateful he'd volunteered to be my regular babysitter for Craft nights. It'd save me the hassle, and money, of hiring a babysitter every month.

At first it surprised me he didn't want to hang out with the guys, but he said he wasn't a video game kind of guy, adding, "They'll have more fun without their boss hanging around."

Another benefit of John watching Chase was quality stand-in father time. John and Chase both loved their monthly dedicated time together, and it was good for Chase to have one-on-one time with a strong male role model.

Soon he'll have one full time. Though Chase would still want time with his Uncle John—My kid worshiped the ground John walked on.

Wanting some time to talk before the others arrived, Mary and I met half an hour before Craft and Booze was scheduled to start. You'd think working together every day would be enough for us, but we were never really alone, and our conversations were prone to interruptions. Not wanting to be overheard, I'd been pretty reserved the last few days when talking to Mary at work.

But not tonight, tonight I'd fill her in on the details. *Well most of them.* And we'd giggle like schoolgirls. Only we'd do it over wine instead of coffee or tea.

Mary was thrilled Doug and I had worked things out; and didn't miss the opportunity to remind me not to jump to conclusions the next time we had an argument.

I could have saved myself, all of us, a lot of heartache and tears if I'd just listened to Doug that first night instead of stubbornly refusing to let him speak. *Lesson learned.*

"How is Chase doing with the changes?"

"He's thrilled to see Doug almost every day. Though I'm sure that'll wear off in time." I laughed. Chase had the same level of excitement when he saw Dough each night as he had whenever we went to the SSI office. The novelty of it would dissipate, eventually. *At least I hope so.*

"I'm sure it will." Mary had a shit-eating grin on her face.
"What?"

"You look happy. Content." She picked up her wine and held it up for me to tap mine against. After I did, she said, "It's been a long time since I've seen you this happy."

"I was happy before," I countered.

"It's different, you're more than just happy," she tapped her finger on the rim of her wine glass as she searched for the right words, "you seem more at peace now."

We were on our second glass of wine when Meg, Emily, and Anne arrived.

I had to start at the beginning and share a less detailed version of what happened at the ice cream shop. Meg had heard Chase's version, which apparently was riddled with exaggerations and out-of-order events.

As expected, everyone oohed and aahed when I told them about the bouquet and unexpected declaration of love. I left out the sterile part, as promised. I hadn't even told Mary. So far, Chase hadn't mentioned that bit, and I prayed every night he never would.

We talked as we filled our plates with Meg's bacon mac and cheese, snacks, and veggies, then migrated to the table. Emily looked a little wistful as we talked about my pre-engagement. We all knew she was desperately in love with Jamie, and wanted to marry him, but she was being patient while he worked through his fears.

Jamie lost his wife, Isabelle, not long after I lost Phil. But where Phil's death was an accident, Isabelle's wasn't. She'd been murdered and Jamie was the first police officer on site. The image still haunted him.

Thank God I didn't have to go through anything like that.

Meg updated us on her house situation. She and Jack were still living with Jamie, but planned to move out before the holidays.

"If everything goes according to plan," she said with a sigh.

They'd found the perfect plot of land, but the house needed some serious work to be livable. They decided to have it gutted by a professional, who was also doing all the construction. Jack and Meg would do the cosmetic stuff, like painting, themselves. With a lot help from all of us. They warned us we'd be recruited for painting, decorating, and unpacking, which we were all more than happy to do. I even volunteered Chase, though there wasn't much he could do.

They'd received a lot of items for their home as wedding gifts, most of which were currently stored in Madi's old room since there wasn't enough space at Jamie's.

"Do you think Jamie will ask you to move in, once they move out?" Mary asked.

Emily shrugged, then blushed when Meg said, "She practically lives there now. She has a key and a parking spot."

"She never comes home anymore." Anne added, "Not that I'm complaining." She reached over and squeezed Emily's hand. Anne loved Jamie and was excited they were dating.

"I don't know, he hasn't said much about it. It might be weird for him to ask me to move in with him." Emily shrugged. "He built that home with Isabelle."

"But you'll say yes if he asks." Meg stated the question like it was a forgone conclusion.

"Duh. Like you said, I'm there most nights, anyway. Half my clothes are already there."

"And quite a few of your books." They laughed as Meg held up her wineglass and Emily tapped hers to it.

They shared a deep passion for reading, and realizing they shared the same tastes, started swapping books. I liked to read, but only read four to six books a year. *Like a normal person.* These two, they read that many in a month.

They often joked about writing a romance novel together, and they'd bounced ideas around a few times, but so far, they hadn't put pen to paper.

That's one book I'll buy instead of getting at the library.

We worked on our crafts while we talked. This month, we were making Halloween decorations for the Wyatt Foundation fundraiser, being held a week from Saturday. We had black, purple, and orange streamers we folded together to make fancy garland, and foam ghosts and goblins we decorated with googly eyes and felt accessories. We punched holes in them so we could hang them around the shop. If we had time, we'd also make some themed bracelets for the trick or treat bowl. It was an ambitious idea since we rarely finished most projects.

When I asked Mary where she got the stuff to make the ghosts, wanting to pick up some supplies and make some with Chase, she said I could take all the extra stuff home with me.

"I'd rather see it put to good use than get tossed. God knows I don't need to collect more stuff."

"Thanks, I'll send you pictures of him creating his masterpiece." We laughed, knowing Chase would end up with more felt pieces glued to himself than his ghost.

Chapter 50

Doug

Beth, Chase, and I came home to change after helping set up Grannie's for the Wyatt Foundation fundraiser. I had to wear a cowboy costume this year, just like everyone else. Except John. His job was to mingle and help raise funds, alongside Mary.

Everyone else from SSI would be sharing bartending duties, while Grannie's Girl's, as Mary liked to call her baristas, would man the raffle tables. Because everything was donated by the generous people of Weatherford, all proceeds from the night went to the foundation. The growth of the foundation meant they helped more families every year.

I lucked out last year because John wanted to introduce me to everyone and hadn't thought the costume would be appropriate. The Wyatt Foundation fundraiser was a big deal in Weatherford. Politicians, local and county cops, business owners, friends, and family all attended.

Phil Wyatt had been a respected member of the Parker County Sheriff's Department, and a beloved member of the Weatherford community— everyone wanted to contribute to the foundation started in his honor. John and Mary had helped a lot of families in the last couple years because of the generosity of everyone involved.

The sound of Chase's plastic spurs as he ran down the stairs brought me back to the present.

"Hey, Little Man, you look great." I scooped him up and swung him around, knowing how much he loved it. When he started to squirm, I put him down. "Where's your mom?"

"Upstairs. Where's your hat?"

My straw cowboy hat was on the table, along with the black pleather chaps that came with the costume. I flat out refused to wear them. I wasn't the kind of guy who dressed up in costumes. Give me a uniform and I'm good to go, but silly costumes, no thank you.

"I'll put it on when we get to Grannie's."

His pout made me consider putting it on, but Beth came downstairs.

Making my breath catch in my throat. The cowgirl mini skirt was shorter than anything I'd seen her wear, and it was sexy as hell as it swung with the sway of her hips. The cowgirl hat hung down her back and she'd tied the ends of the blue gingham button-up at her waist.

"You look-"

"Mommy, Mr. Doug doesn't have his hat on."

I was getting used to not finishing sentences when Chase was around. It could be frustrating, but it was the price of admission to be a part of Beth's life. It turned out I was willing to dish out cash left and right for the ticket.

"Chase, what do we say when we interrupt someone?"

He looked at me, shoulders slumped forward. "I'm sorry."

Beth waited for me to make eye contact before asking, "You were saying?"

"You look amazing." I closed the distance and gave her a quick kiss on the cheek before whispering in her ear, "absolutely breathtaking."

"Thank you." She glanced at the table and the aforementioned hat. "Now put on your hat, so we can go."

"Not going to make me wear the chaps?" I asked, only half joking. I didn't want to wear them, but I wouldn't hesitate to put them on if she asked me to.

"Maybe another time." The mischievous glint in her eye gave me an instant hard on.

Damn it. I used the table as a shield and adjusted myself while trying to ignore her giggling. I had half a mind to drop Chase off with Mary or Meg then drag Beth back here so I could rip her costume off with my teeth and kiss every inch of her bare skin.

Instead, I picked up my hat and placed it on my head. When I turned back around to face her I pulled it low over my eyes, hoping to God I looked sexy not silly. In the huskiest voice I could muster, I said, "Yes, Ma'am, you can count on it."

That put an end to her giggles. Watching the blush spread up her neck and cover her cheeks felt like sweet victory. And made me hard again.

Worth it.

She coughed to cover her reaction.

"Come on, let's go," she said.

The only other people at Grannie's when we arrived were John and Mary, Jack and Meg, AJ, and the mayor, a woman I hadn't met but had seen on the news.

Jamie and Emily had been suspiciously absent all day. We'd joked about Jamie trying to get out of pack mule duties, since it was our job to lug all the boxes of decorations, beverages, and raffle prizes into the shop. It was Jack who started calling us pack mules last year, and it'd stuck. Mary thought it was hilarious and started threatening to crack a whip whenever we lollygagged. Her word, not mine.

"The place looks great, Mary." I said as I looked around. The lights seemed brighter, the ghost and skeleton decorations seemed more cheerful, and the music more festive. I didn't know if it was because I was new and hadn't known anyone last year, or if it was because I was hopelessly in love this year.

Probably a little of both.

Unwilling to sound like I'd lost my mind, I didn't say any of that to Mary. Instead, I asked her if there was anything I could do to help out.

She looked around. "I think we're good. Have you met the mayor?" Mary asked.

"No, not yet."

"Beth, you've met her, right?"

Beth nodded. Her eyes never leaving Chase as he walked over to Meg, who was talking to Amber at the raffle table.

Beth didn't want to admit how nervous she was about letting Chase out of her sight tonight, despite the place being filled with cops, but I could see it in her eyes and the tension in her shoulders.

I pulled her close and kissed her forehead before leaning close to her ear and whispering, "Would it help if I asked the guys to keep an eye on him?"

"Maybe a little." She hugged me and said, "Thank you," into my chest.

I didn't tell her we'd already talked about it, or that I was paying Eric and Dean to take turns watching the front door for the night. Their only job—make sure Chase doesn't leave unless he's with his mom, me, or a Sheppard.

Chapter 51

Beth

Doug looked sexy as sin in his costume and I'd pretty much been drooling since walking down the stairs and seeing him. At first, I'd been disappointed he'd forgone the chaps, but I got over it when he hinted he'd wear them for me and me alone.

After all the subtle verbal foreplay, I couldn't stop thinking about how much I wanted to see him in them. *And nothing else.* I held a cold bottle of water to my neck. *It's going to be a long night if I don't get my horny thoughts under control.*

We'd arrived early enough to help with any last-minute things needing to be done, and had a chance to talk to the mayor for a few minutes. She was a good person; not your typical sleazy politician. Her husband was a military guy, still serving as a Naval Officer, and her kids were in college. She genuinely cared about the people of Weatherford, and it showed. This was her first term in office, and it meant a lot to me she'd taken time out of her busy schedule to attend.

Doug talked to the mayor for a few minutes, then excused himself and joined John who was talking to the mayor's husband.

"Beth, so good to see you. How are you and Chase holding up?" She knew all about the ordeal and had called me to check in a couple of days after Chase got home. When I mentioned it to Mary, she said the Mayor had called John and asked about us. Weatherford was lucky; it was rare to have a politician be so caring and hands on in any community.

We talked for a few minutes, mostly about our kids. I glanced at the clock and said, "It was good to see you madam mayor." I shook her hand. "Be sure to stop by the raffle table later." I tilted my head towards the raffle tables along the far wall; the raffle items changing colors as the orange and purple twinkle lights flashed off and on.

You'd think I'd want to mingle with the guests, given the fundraiser was in my late husband's name, but I didn't. I did at the first one, but preferred working at the table where I could talk to people without the pressure. The fundraiser wasn't about me anymore, so I didn't want to be the center of attention.

"I'll stop by in a little bit and get my tickets. A little birdie told me there's a full-service spa day available this year and I want to win it."

Chase had stayed at the raffle table with Meg while I talked to the mayor, but scooted next to me after I sat down. I was relieved he seemed hesitant to wander off, but also a little sad because I wanted him to feel safe to walk around and have fun. There wouldn't be a safer place in all of Weatherford tonight.

Meg looked adorable in her costume. She wore the shirt and hat from last year, but had replaced the skirt with khaki-colored jeans. When I asked why she wasn't wearing the skirt, she said, "This way I'm a little Grannie's and a little SSI." She laughed. "But I refuse to wear chaps."

Leave it up to Meg to find a way to represent both.

I was reminding Chase he couldn't play with the raffle items on display when Jamie and Emily walked in. They'd been suspiciously absent all day. When I'd asked Doug about it, he'd shrugged and said Jamie had mentioned them having plans and they'd be here later. I'd assumed he meant later while we were setting up, but obviously not.

It took all of five seconds after they walked in for Mary to shriek with joy. I watched as she lifted Emily's left hand, then pulled her into a hug.

Jamie proposed! Meg and I shared a look before jumping up and running to join the group surrounding the happy couple. Chase was close on my heels.

Emily practically glowed, and Jamie's smile was so big it looked like it might actually hurt.

Jamie was wearing his cowboy costume and had surprised Emily with a matching cowgirl one. They looked like they could be models in a magazine, with their big smiles, bright eyes, and athletic bodies.

"Well, I guess this is a good reason for skipping pack mule duties," Mary said before hugging Jamie. When she playfully punched him, he rubbed his shoulder, feigning pain, as he asked, "What was that for?"

"For not telling me." Her smile was far too big for anyone to believe she was upset.

"Dad knew." Jamie didn't hesitate to throw John under the bus so his mom wouldn't give him any more shit.

John stepped back so he was out of Mary's reach and grinned. Mary would give him hell later, not caring that she loved the surprise. From the corner of my eye, I saw Jack step out of Meg's reach.

She saw it too. "You knew, didn't you?" She pointed at him, closing the distance.

"I, uh, Jamie swore us to secrecy." He shrugged.

It turns out the male half of our tight-knit group knew and had somehow managed to keep Jamie's secret.

"Does this mean you're moving in with us?" Meg asked. After a lifetime of feeling alone and unloved, Meg was thrilled to have a family and couldn't wait to officially call Emily her sister.

When Mary asked Jamie how he proposed, he looked at Doug and said, "I didn't yell it out while waiting in line for a banana split, but I think it was still a surprise."

Everyone laughed. Jokes about Doug's accidental proposal wouldn't be going away anytime soon. He didn't let it get to him, instead he said, "Good one, Sheppard."

Emily swatted Jamie in the rib cage with the back of her hand.

"He took me to The Carriage House. There was a chilled bottle of champagne on a table at the foot of the rose petal decorated bed." She looked at Jamie and smiled. "When I turned around, he was on one knee holding the ring box."

She showed off her 2-carat oval diamond ring, set on a thin gold band. The oval shape was perfect for her long fingers.

"You did good, son." John shook Jamie's hand and clapped him on the back.

"Very good." Mary's eyes glossed over. Her smile was almost as big as Emily's. Almost.

"After I said yes, we ordered room service and…" She trailed off.

"Relaxed in our room." Jamie finished, with a grin.

Guests started to arrive, breaking up our celebration. Before long, Grannie's was filled with locals. Some came in costume, some in uniform, while others wore their normal attire. Amber and I were busy at the raffle table, with Meg giving us occasional breaks. Doug shared bar duties with Jamie, Jack, and AJ. Two of them manning the bar, while the other two re-stocked as needed, or mingled when they could.

Emily's best friend Ashley arrived a little while later, wearing a skin-tight red she-devil costume, which was borderline not family friendly. *Oh, to be young again.* I happened to be looking at the bar and laughed when AJ's eyes almost popped out of his head once he saw her.

Ashley was too busy squealing and hugging Emily and Jamie to notice AJ drooling over her. She and Emily ducked into a corner and spent the next ten minutes in animated conversation. I could only assume Emily was giving Ashley all the details of her proposal.

As the evening wore on, Chase built up his courage to walk around. The temptation to join his favorite men, and talk to the uniformed police officers, overpowered his nervousness.

The fundraiser was in full swing with people dancing, chatting, and filling the raffle jars with blue tickets. Chase danced with Meg, or at least he tried to. He was having trouble keeping up with the steps to the line dance, but it wasn't stopping him from having fun.

I looked over at the bar to see Doug watching Chase. He had a soft smile on his ruggedly handsome face, and his steel blue eyes were filled with love. *If things work out, he'll be Chase's stepdad.*

Not if, when. Because I didn't see a way we wouldn't work out for the long haul.

After the song ended, Doug and Jamie were relieved of bar duty. Doug scooped Chase up in his arms and brought my giggling, squirming child to the raffle table. "Chase thinks we should dance."

"Does he now?" I couldn't hold back my huge, goofy smile.

"I do." Chase piped up.

"Maybe later," I said. "I can't leave Amber alone at the raffle table."

"Break time." Meg walked around Doug laughing as she said, "Go. I'll help Amber."

"Thanks."

"Hey Chase, want to help me sell tickets?" Meg asked.

"Yes!"

Doug put him down, narrowly avoided getting kicked in the family jewels as Chase wiggled in his excitement. *The world would be a better place if every kid had the love and support Chase does.*

Doug held out his hand for me as I walked around the table.

"Have fun." Meg waved, and told Chase to do the same.

"We will." Doug led me to the dance floor. The timing was perfect, since the DJ was playing a slow song. *Did he plan this?* I stepped in and wrapped my arms around Doug's neck as he wrapped his arms around my back.

I barely heard the music as we swayed back and forth. My head on his chest, listening to the steady *thump thump* of his heart. His cheek rested on my head.

I fought off the intrusive voices telling me I shouldn't be dancing with another man at the fundraiser held in honor of my late husband. Would people judge me? Would they not want to give to the cause because I'd moved on?

The fundraiser isn't for me. It hadn't been since the first year. Even then, they'd raised so much money there was enough left over, after Phil's funeral expenses were paid, to help a widower in Fort Worth.

No one was judging me. Everyone I'd talked to had expressed nothing but happiness at hearing I'd found love again.

Get out of your head! I forced my shoulders to relax.

"Everything okay?" Doug asked, his tone curious rather than worried.

He must have felt me relax after I kicked out all the negative thoughts. I pulled back a little, looked into his eyes and said, "Perfect."

I glanced around as we danced and saw AJ and Ashley dancing. *He didn't waste any time.* Good for them. According to Emily and Meg, they'd hooked up a few times but weren't dating. I wondered if that'd ever change for them; stranger things had been known to happen.

The rest of the night was a blur of ticket sales, mingling, and dancing. By the time the last guest left, I was ready to take off my boots and put my feet up. But it'd have to wait. We had to pack up the raffle items and ticket jars, clear out the liquor, and get the dining room cleaned up and put back to normal. At least we could leave the decorations up since they wouldn't interfere with business.

Mary and John would announce the raffle winners on Sunday. It usually meant a busy day for Grannie's since a lot of the prizes could be picked up and people always grabbed a coffee and snack while they were here.

Chase offered to help clean up but fell asleep in a booth when he sat down to rest after telling me, "I'm sleepy, Mommy."

Poor kid. It was way past his bedtime. He'd sleep in late tomorrow, and probably be a little crabby, but he would've been miserable if he'd missed out on the fun.

Doug carrying a half-asleep Chase as we said our goodbyes felt like the most natural thing in the world.

After we got home, Doug carried Chase upstairs to his room. I didn't bother with making him change or brush his teeth before putting him to bed. One night wouldn't kill him.

Then Doug swept me off my feet, literally, and carried me to my room.

He waited while I got changed and washed my face in my en suite, then massaged my feet for a few minutes before kissing me goodbye. Those five minutes were a little slice of happy feet heaven.

"Want me to walk you out?" I asked as I snuggled further into my blankets.

He chuckled. "No, I think I can manage."

"Lock up when," I covered a yawn, "you leave." I'd given him a key to the front door the day before. It was a big step, but it felt right.

"Of course." He leaned down and kissed my forehead before kissing my lips. "See you tomorrow, Beautiful."

I opened my mouth to say goodbye but yawned, so I waved instead.

Chapter 52

Doug

It had been two weeks since the Wyatt Foundation Fundraiser, and Beth and I were doing great. Chase was no longer having nightmares and enjoyed spending extra time with his Uncle John or Auntie Meg, who frequently volunteered to babysit for us.

Beth and I took advantage of their generosity as often as we could. Especially when Meg offered to host a sleepover. Emily had officially moved in with Jamie, so as an added bonus, Chase got to know his Auntie Emily better.

We spent most of our time at her place, except for our intimate dates. Those we spent at my apartment because she still wasn't ready to have me in her bed or let me stay the night. I reminded myself things had progressed rapidly, so it was natural for her to need time.

I was being patient, for now. At some point, she'd have to let me stay. And when I proposed for real, she'd have to let me move in because I had no intention of waiting until we got married to live together.

I'm patient, not a saint.

The meeting alert on my phone buzzed, so I grabbed my laptop and headed to the conference room. We were reviewing applicants for full and part-time positions. SSI was growing fast, and we needed to hire more people to meet the demand and expand our services.

"Let's get started." John's authority came through even when he used his normal speaking voice. "Jamie, Jack, and I have narrowed down the list of candidates, based on experience and skill sets."

I was about to ask why I was there, when Jamie answered my question.

"Because we pride ourselves on being a family business, we'd like everyone's input."

"Even mine?" Meg asked.

"Even yours. You're an integral part of SSI."

Apparently, they'd met like this before interviewing me, agreeing I brought unique skills they wanted.

"We posted for two full-time and two part-time positions, but we'll only need to hire one full timer because Jaden moved up his start date."

Jaden was the youngest Sheppard and he was supposed to start next fall, after taking a year off to backpack across the country after his enlistment ended.

I didn't know much about Jaden, having only met him once at Jack's wedding. And then he'd been too busy catching up with his family to talk to me beyond introductions. When

Jack and Jamie talked about him, they usually referred to him as the pain-in-the-ass little brother and called him the wild child. AJ couldn't wait to get to know him, thinking they'd be easy friends.

If he was anything like his father and brothers, he'd be a good addition to SSI.

"When does he start?" AJ asked.

"Early spring," John answered. "He'll be doing security work until he earns his degree. It'd be better for SSI if the other person we hire has, or is qualified to get, their PI license."

Meg took a folder off a stack then handed the stack to Jack. "Take one, pass it down."

After we all had folders, John spoke. "You'll recognize the first applicant in your folders."

For a brief second, the only sound was the rustling of folders opening. Then there was a collective murmur of acknowledgement as we all nodded. Agent Catelyn Maxwell had applied.

I'd already started reading when John said, "I know we all worked with her, but take a minute to review her resume."

AJ whistled out a long breath before turning the page over to read the back. I had to agree; her resume was impressive.

"Impressive," Meg said after finishing, "her profiling skills would come in handy."

There was no doubt about that. She earned a criminal justice degree while serving in the Marines, four years as enlisted and four as an officer. Attached to her resume was a glowing recommendation from Agent Jones.

"Did she say why she wants to leave the FBI?" I asked.

"No, but I'll ask during her interview," John answered.

"The fact Jones wrote her a referral suggests she's leaving on good terms," Jack added.

More consenting murmurs.

"Any reason I shouldn't bring her in for an interview?" John asked.

We all chuckled when AJ said, "She seemed a bit uptight when she helped us find Chase, but that might be the suit the feds make her wear." Every one of us had worn a suit for executive protection duty assignments, and every one of us joked about not liking how stiff and formal it felt.

AJ had a point, if she was uptight all the time she might not be a good fit? We were a small private company and didn't do things like the FBI. I finished my thought out loud, "Maybe that's why she's looking to join the private sector."

"If there's no objections, I'll call her and set up an interview." John picked up the next resume. "Let's review the rest of the candidates."

By the time John dismissed us from the meeting, we'd narrowed it down to seven candidates for John to interview; two for the full-time position, the rest for the part-time positions.

I looked at my watch, five-thirty, and smiled. *I'm done for the day.* I packed up my gear then raced home to clean up.

I didn't want to be late for my dinner date with Beth and Chase.

Chapter 53

Beth

Doug spent Thanksgiving with me, my mom, and Chase. He'd come over early to help me prep and to watch Chase. When I said goodbye to pick up my mom, he told me not to worry; he and Chase wouldn't let anything happen to the turkey. Chase had giggled, because it didn't make any sense to him, but it was Doug's way of telling me he had everything under control.

I loved him for it.

Chase was so excited about helping Doug, he barely said goodbye. They were in charge of making the mashed potatoes and mac and cheese while I was gone.

This might be our first holiday together, but him being here feels natural.

I stopped by the cemetery, before going to my mom's to wish Phil a happy Thanksgiving in heaven and let him know Chase and I would be okay. I'd told him about Doug on a previous visit, and knew in my heart he'd approve of him, not just for me but for Chase, too.

Luckily, my mom was having a good day and had the energy and strength to walk to my car with only her cane for help. I helped her into the car and put her cane in the back seat before getting behind the wheel.

"Doug's a little nervous about meeting you." I told her as I pulled out of her driveway.

"As he should be."

I was happy to hear the hint of mischief in her voice. As her health continued to decline, she had more bad days than good. Thankfully, her mind was still sharp.

"Now Mom, be nice." I playfully chastised her. I had no doubt she would be. She wanted me to be happy, and she could tell I was from the way my eyes lit up whenever I talked about Doug. Mary said the same thing.

"I will be, but I'm meeting the man courting my daughter for the first time, so I have to make sure he's good enough for her." I glanced over in time to see her smirk. She was enjoying this, playing the protective mother.

There was no logical reason for me to be nervous; I knew my mom would like him, and he'd like her. Any doubts I might have had before were removed when I overheard Chase telling her how much he liked Mr. Doug during our last visit.

She'd said, "I have a feeling I'll like him too because he makes your mom happy."

Stupid happy tears.

Doug and Chase were setting the table when we walked in. Doug took the orange and brown cloth napkins from Chase so he could greet his grandmother with empty hands. Then walked over after setting down the utensils he'd been setting out.

I loved how Doug found fun ways to include Chase in different chores. *They make a great team.* It not only strengthened their bond, but it helped teach Chase to be a self-sufficient man. Something I'd sworn I'd do early on and had been working towards since he was old enough to swish a play broom. I refused to raise Chase into be the kind of man women complained about.

Thankfully, Phil hadn't been that kind of man. *Neither is Doug.*

"Chase, why don't you introduce Grandma to Mr. Doug?" I encouraged after he started listing off all the things he'd done to help us today.

"Okay." He took my mom's hand and led her to Doug. I watched to make sure he remembered what I'd told him about being careful. So did Doug.

"Grandma, this is Mr. Doug."

Doug held out his hand for a handshake, but Chase hadn't let go of her free hand.

"Chase, I need my hand sweetie." My mom pulled her hand free and shook Doug's. "It's nice to finally meet you."

"The pleasure is all mine, Mrs. Burnell."

"None of that Mrs. Burnell nonsense, you can call me Dolly, or Mom."

I knew she'd approve of him but hadn't expected it to happen before she took off her coat.

Doug nodded, his smile as he made eye contact with me radiating pure joy. Despite my reassurances, he'd been nervous about meeting her. "Can I help you with your coat?"

"Thank you, Mr. Doug," she answered, causing Chase to giggle. He knew adults didn't use the Mr. or Mrs. like he did.

"None of that, you can call me Doug." He winked at Chase before helping my mom wiggle out of her coat. "Can you hang up your Grandma's coat?"

"Yes, sir," Chase answered the same way he'd heard the guys answer John countless times.

Even if I hadn't found a good man to love me and help me raise Chase, he still would have grown into a damn fine man.

My mother laughed before asking, "When did he start saying that?"

"He picked it up at Sheppard & Sons," I answered, knowing I didn't need to say anymore. She'd met John, and understood the dynamic in the family.

When the food was done, Doug and I made plates for my mom and Chase, then for ourselves. Because my mom couldn't drink alcohol, I served her and Chase sparkling grape juice. Doug and I enjoyed a sweet white wine.

Dinner was filled with lots of love, laughter, and delicious food.

Mom was feeling a little weak after dinner, so Doug helped her walk her to the couch.

"You're a true gentleman, Mr. Doug," she patted him on the arm, "and a perfect role model for my grandson."

Color rose in Doug's cheeks as he thanked her.

"Come sit with me Chase. I want to hear all about school," my mom said.

"Okay." Chase ran to the living room and hopped up onto the couch. "Yesterday we couldn't have recess…"

I tuned him out as Doug and I finished cleaning up. Doug put the food away before carving the rest of the meat from the turkey and setting the bones aside so I could use them to make broth later. While he did that, I rinsed the dishes and loaded the dishwasher.

"Have you always made your own bone broth?" Doug asked as he watched me shove the turkey skeleton into my crockpot.

"Yup. Mom always made her own and she taught me how."

"That's cool. My mom wasn't much of a cook, not that she couldn't," he paused, "she just preferred not to."

I didn't like the sad expression that crossed his face so I explained how to make it.

"It's easy. You fill the crockpot with the bones, add water, and cook for thirty-six to forty-eight hours."

"That's it?"

"I add celery, carrots, onion, and garlic for the last twelve to eighteen hours. It doesn't change the flavor much, but it adds extra nutrients."

I could see his mind working. He was a guy who liked to eat T-Bone steaks, BBQ ribs, and chicken wings. "Can you use any bones?"

"You can, and you can mix them." I secured the lid and turned the pot on low. "I keep a bone bag in my freezer. When I have enough to fill the pot, I make broth."

"I'll have to try it." He wrapped his arm around me and kissed the top of my head. "But first I need to buy a crockpot."

"You can always borrow mine." I hugged him back.

I could get used to this. We'd only been together for two months, but it felt natural to have him in my kitchen, helping me with a holiday meal. Even if I wasn't comfortable having him spend the night, yet.

I'd gotten over my concerns about Chase waking up with Doug here, but was still nervous about Chase coming into my room and seeing us together. It might not seem like a big deal to most parents, but I'd slept alone Chase's entire life.

I was also weirded out at the thought of having another man in the bed I'd shared with Phil, but I was working on it.

Doug will only be patient for so long. And I wanted him here with me.

Chapter 54

Doug

After attending the SSI family holiday party, Beth and I brought an exhausted Chase home. He insisted on leaving milk and cookies out for Santa, so he and I got everything ready while Beth was upstairs changing. While we waited, he tried to convince me it was okay for him to have some too.

"Let's ask your mom first."

He sighed as his shoulders sagged. *How does someone so small sigh so big?* His reaction made it clear he expected his mom to say no.

I put my hand on his shoulder. "Come on Little Man, help me pour the milk."

Before we finished filling the coffee mug Chase had picked out, Beth came back downstairs in red and green plaid leggings and a tee shirt with a cat tangled up in Christmas lights. Her curly hair was pulled back in a messy bun.

God, she looks gorgeous.

"Mommy, can Mr. Doug and I have some milk and cookies too?" The little bugger included me in his request, knowing it'd be harder for his mom to say no.

When Beth looked at me, I shrugged and gave her my most innocent impression. If it made Chase happy, I'd have milk and cookies, with Beth's permission of course.

"One each, and only half a glass of milk," she answered with a smile, "after you change into your pajamas."

While we were eating our one cookie each, Chase asked if I'd be sleeping over.

I'd love to kid.

"I want you to keep watch and wake me up when Santa gets here."

We had drastically different reasons for wanting me to spend the night.

Beth and I shared a look, we'd agreed I'd go home tonight and come back in the morning.

"Chase, I-" Beth started.

"Please Mommy, can Mr. Doug sleep over with us?"

Beth closed her eyes and inhaled sharply.

I waited patiently while she made up her mind.

"Okay, but you have to be a good boy and go to sleep right away."

I could see the nervousness in her eyes when she made eye contact with me. I smiled, hoping to ease her concerns. I'd stay on the couch, if it made her more comfortable.

Beth read Chase his favorite Christmas story before bed. When she came back downstairs, she was laughing.

"He wanted to stay awake, but fell asleep three pages in." She shook her head back and forth as she sat on the couch and curled up in my arms.

After relaxing quietly for a few minutes, I offered to sleep on the couch. I considered offering to go home and come back early, before Chase woke up, but I wanted to stay.

"Doug, I know I've been hesitant to have you stay the night, but I don't want you to sleep on the couch."

Does she mean what I think she means?

"Would you prefer it if I went home?"

Please God, let her say no.

She turned and stared into my eyes, then took my hands in hers before answering, "No. I'd like you to stay. Here with me."

I couldn't have held back the smile splitting my face in half if my life had depended on it. I squeezed her hands before pulling her into my chest and wrapping my arms around her.

"I'd like that too." I whispered in her ear before kissing her neck. I could smell her signature floral scent and couldn't resist nibbling on her ear.

"But only to sleep," she said, laughing as she pulled away. "Chase won't sleep through the night."

"I promise to behave." I said as I stood up. "I should run home to grab some clothes." And my toothbrush. "Do you need me to grab anything while I'm out?"

"No," she answered.

Thanks to Chase, Christmas Eve would be the first night I spent in Beth's bed.

I understood her fear about Chase walking in, and hoped she'd get over it sooner rather than later. Married couples dealt with it, so could we. It was the last hurdle to conquer before our relationship could progress to the next natural phase.

Whenever I got frustrated at how slow things seemed to be going, I'd remind myself we'd only been dating three months and things were progressing at a normal pace, if not faster.

It just feels slow because I'm all in. But Beth wasn't there yet. She loved me, there was no doubt in my mind, but she was being cautious and working through her fears about replacing Phil, both in her life and in Chase's.

We'd talked about it a few times, and I reminded her every time I wasn't going anywhere. I also made sure to tell her that while I wanted to be a stepdad to Chase, I had no intentions of trying to replace Phil.

By the time I got back, Beth had put Chase's gifts under the tree.

"Want to eat another cookie?" She asked me as she dumped out Santa's milk.

"Sure, do you usually eat them all?"

"No, I leave one or two whole ones, and a half-eaten one." She laughed. "Chase likes to find them in the morning."

"Cute." I picked up two cookies and fed one to Beth before popping one in my mouth.

I don't regret my choice to stay here for Christmas, I thought as I got ready for bed in the en suite. There was no doubt I'd made the right decision. When my mom called to ask when, not if, I was coming home for the holiday, I'd almost changed my mind. Almost. I'd told them about Beth and Chase, but were still surprised I wanted to spend my holiday here.

My relationship with my parents wasn't great and the idea of spending a holiday with them, instead of with the woman I loved and the amazing, energetic child I wanted to adopt, was unappealing. Ignoring the disappointment in her voice when I told her I wasn't coming home, I invited them to visit me in Weatherford after Christmas. She said maybe, but I wouldn't hold my breath.

I brushed them from my mind and focused on Beth.

"Should I shut the door?" I asked as I walked towards the bed.

"Yeah, thanks."

I sat next to her, on top of the comforter, and asked, "You're sure you're okay with this?"

Beth reached over, took my hand. "Come here."

She didn't need to tell me twice. I closed the distance, making the center of the bed sag with my weight as I leaned over and kissed her. She reached up, wrapped her hands around my neck, deepening the kiss.

My brain knew it couldn't happen, but my body didn't get the memo. "Beth, we should stop before I lose my self-control."

Not that I want to stop.

Beth's face was flushed when she looked at the wall separating her room from Chase's, then at her door. "You're right, we should." She didn't look like she wanted to stop either.

"You know, Chase is getting bigger and might want to move into the bigger bedroom."

One of her fears was Chase hearing us, but if Chase moved down the hall the thin walls wouldn't be a problem. Her soft laugh was all the encouragement I needed.

"You know, in case maybe you want me to spend the night when you aren't expecting Chase to get up to look for Santa." I was only half joking.

"I'll have to teach Chase to knock." The sparkle in her eyes made my heart swell and my dick hard. It didn't care that we couldn't do anything tonight; it was reacting on pure animal instinct to the promise of future nights.

"That'd be helpful." The thought of putting a lock on her bedroom door crossed my mind, but it wasn't safe. Teaching Chase to knock was a better, and safer, option.

We woke up early and were drinking our coffee when Chase came running down the stairs.

"Santa was here." He jumped for joy when he saw the gifts under the tree, then ran over to the tray and noticed the milk and cookies were mostly gone. "He ate the cookies."

I understood what the Grinch felt like when his heart grew three sizes as mine filled with joy while watching Chase tear into his gifts. I bought him a few gifts, including a remote-control dinosaur. Beth wasn't sure about it at first, but I'd finally worn her down. She got him a new bike and a helmet, along with other things moms bought for their sons, but their sons didn't care about, like books and socks.

Chase gave me a baseball glove, so I could help him practice tee ball. From the outside it looked like the simplest of gifts, but to me it was a life changing moment. He wanted me to do dad things with him, which was the best present he could have given me.

When he told me he'd still practice with his Uncle John, "so he doesn't feel sad," I nodded and suggested we all practice together.

Beth gave me a new watch, to replace the one I'd broken at work. It was black with a slim band and waterproof to two hundred meters. It was much nicer than the cheap replacement I'd bought.

Beth gasped when she opened the heart-shaped diamond necklace and matching earring set I'd picked out for her. Having discovered her love of jewelry, I'd decided to spoil her. I was clasping the necklace when Chase got off the floor and bounced over.

"I'm hungry," Chase said.

"Want some of Doug's special pancakes?" Beth asked.

I'd promised to make her crepes, but she wasn't sure Chase would eat them unless we called them pancakes.

"With chocolate chips?" he asked.

"I can add chocolate chips if your mom says it's okay."

"It's okay." She turned to me as Chase ran to the kitchen and whispered, "But not too many."

After breakfast, I showered while Beth and Chase cleaned up. I tried to help them, but she insisted I didn't have to since I'd cooked.

"Who wants to come with me to pick up Grandma?" Beth asked.

"I do. I do."

"You have to get dressed first."

We spent the rest of the day celebrating, eating, and relaxing. I taught Chase how to use the remote to his dinosaur on the back patio while Beth and her mom had some quiet time in the house.

Later that evening, Chase curled up on the couch between me and Beth and fell asleep.

Best Christmas ever.

Four Months Later

Beth

Chase was antsy as we waited for Doug. He was taking us out for my birthday, and had surprised me by convincing Chase to wear a suit and tie.

"Chase, please stop fidgeting."

"Will Mr. Doug be here soon?" He sighed with impatience and boredom.

I looked at the clock and answered, "He should be here any minute now."

Before Chase could say anything else, the doorbell rang.

"I'll get it!" Chase jumped off his chair and ran to the front door.

"What do we do before we open the door?"

He pulled his hand away from the deadbolt and yelled, "Who is it?"

"Mr. Doug."

Chase unlocked the door and opened it. "We've been waiting for you." He made it sound like we'd been waiting for hours instead of minutes.

"You look grown-up in your suit." Doug's wink to Chase had conspiracy written all over it.

Chase grabbed Doug's free hand, the one not holding a breathtaking bouquet of yellow and pink roses, and dragged him to the kitchen where I was waiting.

I took the opportunity to ogle Doug, who looked exceptionally handsome in his dark gray suit, while Chase was occupying his attention. His suit was clearly tailored to show off his strong muscles and accent his best features. The color brought out the gray in his steel blue eyes and made his short red hair pop.

"Look Mommy, Mr. Doug brought you flowers."

The smile on Doug's face as he looked down at Chase announcing the obvious could've lit the blackest night.

"Thank you, Chase," I said.

When Doug handed me the bouquet, I held it up to my nose and inhaled. I loved the smell of fresh roses; it was intoxicating. This bunch was even more so, because it was from Doug, on my birthday.

Doug loved giving me flowers. I thought back to the bouquet he'd sent me on Valentine's Day. It was borderline ridiculous. It looked like he'd combined two huge bouquets to make a gigantic one.

Mary took a picture and sent it to John, who'd sent a perfectly reasonable, normal sized, bouquet to Mary. She meant to tease him, but in the end, it was John who ended up teasing Doug.

Then, because they didn't want to look cheap, John, Jamie, and Jack ordered more flowers for the women they loved.

Doug then surprised me with a single red rose when he picked me up for dinner that night. It was far more romantic than the bouquet occupying half of my dining room table. He'd blushed when he apologized for the size, explaining it hadn't looked nearly that big in the picture.

Doug's voice brought me back to the present.

"Happy Birthday, Beautiful," Doug said as he kissed me in greeting. His pupils dilated as he looked me up and down. "I love your new dress."

Thank you, Meg and Emily. They'd helped me pick it out last week. I wanted to look special, they insisted on saying sexy, for tonight and they hadn't failed me. The dress was a pale yellow halter that hung just above my knees. The white leather belt matched the large daisies embroidered on the skirt and where the ties met the bodice. I had a darker yellow cardigan on to keep the early spring chill at bay.

"Thank you." I blushed at the hungry look in his eyes.

I felt Doug's gaze on my back, as I put the roses in a vase, and it was sexy as hell. It was moments like this when I wished I had the freedom to take him upstairs and have my way with him. Thoughts like that were always accompanied by a pang of guilt, even though I knew better. I loved Chase and wouldn't change a thing, even during my horniest moments.

When we got back from our Valentine's Day dinner, I'd asked him to stay, grateful John and Mary had offered to keep Chase overnight. Doug hadn't hesitated and practically dragged me upstairs. *But that can't happen tonight.* I grabbed my purse and keys while Doug adjusted Chase's tie, then we left.

We were only in the car a few minutes when Chase asked, "Where are we going?"

"It's a surprise."

Another wink. I wasn't sure Chase saw it, but I did.

What are they up to?

"Will they have chicken nuggets?"

His new favorite food was chicken nuggets. He still liked mac & cheese, but now asked for chicken nuggets just as often.

"I don't know, Kiddo. We'll find out when we get there."

"I'm not a kiddo anymore."

Chase had turned six in March and was always looking for ways to prove he wasn't a kid anymore. He was ready to be an adult.

"I guess you're right, you're not a little kid anymore," Doug agreed. "Can I still call you Little Man?"

After agreeing, Chase monopolized the conversation, telling Doug all about his day, and what he'd given me for my birthday: a card and clay ring holder he'd made at school. He complained about wearing a tie, but stopped when Doug explained how men sometimes wore ties to look good on special occasions.

"Like Mommy's birthday and Auntie Meg's wedding?"

"Exactly. And for dates." Doug glanced over at me and winked.

I'd been nervous he'd be impatient with Chase's frequent interruptions and having to revolve our schedule around Chase, *especially our sex life,* but he'd taken it all in stride. Whenever I tried to apologize, he'd remind me he knew he was signing on for a package deal, and then he'd tell me he loved us both and wouldn't have it any other way.

Doug had made reservations at Chuck's Steak and Lobster, an upscale seafood restaurant. To my surprise, Chase was on his best behavior as we walked in and followed the hostess to our table. Doug must have made a special request because our booth was in the back corner, offering us a modicum of privacy.

I slid into the booth next to Chase who was already playing with the salt and pepper shakers.

"Chase, stop playing with those."

"Okay." He obeyed and picked up his menu.

What had Doug promised Chase to get him to be so well-behaved?

The server brought over a bottle of champagne and filled our glasses before setting the bottle on the table. He fished a can of Sprite out of his apron and poured some in a plastic flute for Chase.

Okay, what's going on? Sure, it was my birthday, but I hadn't expected Doug to go to such lengths for it. It wasn't even a banner year.

Doug thanked the server, who said he'd be back to take our orders in a few minutes, then raised his flute and nodded for Chase to do the same.

"Happy Birthday, Beth."

"Happy Birthday, Mommy." Chase mimicked Doug.

I lifted my glass and we all clinked. The champagne bubbles tickled my nose as I sipped it.

Doug handed me a small box, wrapped in red foil paper. The kind of red foil paper jewelers used.

"Happy Birthday, from me and Chase," Doug said as I accepted the gift.

Was he proposing? It'd explain the champagne. My fingers trembled as I opened it. There was no way he'd propose by having me unwrap the ring. *Right?*

Right. It was a jewelry box, but instead of a ring there was a gorgeous heart-shaped aquamarine, Chase's birthstone, pendant inlaid in a gold bezel on a delicate gold chain.

"I helped pick it out," Chase said proudly as I wiped my eyes.

"Thank you," I kissed the top of Chase's head. "Both of you."

"You're welcome," Doug said, smiling as I put on the necklace.

"Shall we look at the menus?" Doug asked as he handed me one before picking up his own. He must have gone straight to the kid's menu because he said, "You're in luck Little Man; they have chicken fingers."

Doug ordered their signature dish, filet and lobster, with a baked potato on the side. It sounded so good, I ordered it too, only I asked for the small filet.

After we finished eating our mouth-watering dinners, our server cleared our dishes, including our wine glasses. When he reached for our flutes, Doug asked him to hold off.

After the server left, Doug refilled our flutes with the last of the champagne, giving Chase a half an inch in his plastic one.

What's he thinking Chase won't-

Doug stood, moved to the edge of my bench, and took a knee. "Beth, I'm going to do it right this time. I love you, and if you'll have me, I'd be honored to be your husband." He reached in his pocket and took out a red jewelry box.

Chase was now standing on the bench. "And my daddy?" he asked, using his outside voice while he bounced on the bench and clapped.

Tears filled my eyes as I searched for words and came up empty. I wanted to tell Chase to stop bouncing on the bench, making me bounce too, but I couldn't find those words either.

Doug gave Chase a look that made him stop bouncing as he said, "Inside voice." He looked back at me. "Yes, if your mom says yes, it'd be my honor to be your dad."

He opened the box, revealing a large sparkling round diamond with a smaller diamond on each side.

Yes, that's the word I'm looking for. I was so excited I finally remembered the word, I shouted, "Yes!"

"Inside voice, Mommy," Chase said, disrupting the moment.

Most women wouldn't think getting engaged with a six-year-old present was romantic, but I wouldn't have changed a thing.

Doug stayed on his knee as he placed the ring on my finger.

"I promise to love you, protect you, and spoil you every day of our lives. I promise to be the kind of man Chase can look up to, and be the best stepdad a boy can have."

"Yes." I repeated with a squeak. I should have said more, but my love for the man in front of me robbed me of my words.

Ready for the next adventure in the Sheppard & Sons Investigations series? Click here to pre-order BETRAYEDand read all about AJ's adventures as he protects an heiress who can't stand violence.

Acknowledgements

Thank you, Reader, for choosing to spend some time in my world. I hope you enjoyed it.

I want to thank my Proof Readers: Nina, Paige and Jocelyn. And my editor: Nina. Your feedback was invaluable in helping me polish my story. A big thanks to Maria Secoy, and the mentor team at All Write Well–this book wouldn't be in your hands if I hadn't found them!

I also want to thank my friends, who have surrounded me with love and support while listening to me chatter on endlessly about my characters and plot lines over many glasses of wine.

Thank you all!

Also by

Sheppard & Sons Investigations:

TAKEN: Jack and Meg's story
BEATEN: Jamie and Emily's story
MISSING: Doug and Beth's story
BETRAYED : AJ and Blake's story
CAGED: Jaden and Catelyn's story

WebPage

About the Author

Eveline Rose fell in love with storytelling in a high school creative writing class. Eveline currently lives in the Chicago area with her cat, Prince, where she pours her heart and soul into her characters for your reading pleasure. She's a theatre geek who can swing a sword, and a self-defense instructor who can shoot the bullseye. Eveline spends her free time volunteering in her community, hanging out with her friends, and of course reading. One topic she can chat about for hours: Tudor history. Eveline's promise to you: every romantic suspense novel will include a strong protective male hero who will save the woman he loves, and every heroine will get her Happily Ever After. Eveline is a member of Chicago North Romance Writers Group.